Maybe, PROBABLY

To the Tiktok that started it all when it said,
"don't date his friends, date his new girls brother"

Author's Note

This story is about heartbreak and healing. While dealing with these there are also other topics that may be triggering or unfavorable to others. Your mental health is important, so please proceed with caution.
Some Content and Triggers include:

- Cheating (alluded to, not of the main characters, off page)

- Grief and trauma

- Death (recounted on-page)

- Body shaming

- Pregnancy and childbirth (not graphic)

- Bodily harm via sporting accident

- Profanity

- Graphic sexual acts, not limited to:
  masturbation, fingering, squirting, oral sex, use of toys, public sex, penetrative sex.

- Anxiety and PTSD (on-page)

Chapter One

Harper

"**H**ARPS, COME ON. WAKE up..."

I grumble as I throw the blanket over my head, turning the comforter into a cocoon of warmth and sleep. There is no way that it is morning. I swear I literally just put my Kindle down and closed my eyes. The "one more chapter" mantra repeated until the next thing I knew, it was three a.m, and I had finished the whole book. I slowly peek my head out of my blanket burrito to see the handsome face of my boyfriend, Dalton, looking down at me. His dirty blond hair is nothing more than a wet mop on the top of his head, his piercing blue eyes framed by those Clark Kent glasses he wears so well. When he first got them, I would tease him. That was before I realized how sexy he looked with those glasses on. Taking my time to appreciate the way his six foot two inch frame towers over me, I run my gaze along his bared broad chest. His stomach is toned, but not like rock hard abs, and don't get me started on that defined V making its way down to the pajama pants hanging low on his hips.

I don't understand how someone can look this good in the morning.

He leans down, using his thumb to wipe the corner of my lip. "Sorry you just got a little bit of drool right ... here. Got it," he says, pulling back. I gasp as I run my hand across my mouth. He tilts his head and barks a laugh.

"Ugh, you're such an ass!" I whine, flinging the covers off myself and rolling out of bed.

He offers his hand and pulls me into his chest. I wrap my arms around his waist, burying my face into his chest. The smell of pine needles and cinnamon flood my senses, and my body goes slack as I relax. I swear, nothing smells better than Dalton.

We've been together since we were sixteen. High school sweethearts get too much of a bad rap; we were told our relationship wouldn't last. I had a moment where I believed that too. Even though we attended different colleges, we came out stronger, proving everyone wrong. Now, we rent this cute little house just outside of town, and it's like our own personal little getaway from the big city. The house sits in a quaint neighborhood where you know your neighbors. We look out for one another, and the block parties are legendary. Not to toot my own horn, but my potato salad has been a crowd favorite for three years now. Every year I have to make sure I make a bigger batch than the year before.

We have our rhythm here.

I sigh happily as Dalton plants a kiss at the top of my head. His hands run over mine, unclasping my grip from around his neck as he steps back. I make a disgruntled noise at the loss of contact, pouting. Scrubbing my face, I try to rub the exhaustion away as I mentally prepare to start my day. "What time is it?" I ask from behind my hands. A light chuckle rumbles from him as he responds. "It's nine-thirty. I was going to let you sleep a bit longer, but I got called into work." I reach my arms above my head, stretching my body while I pin Dalton with a look he knows well.

He gives me an exasperated look. "Please don't, Harps."

But what does he expect? We had plans today and he's canceling them because he got called into work. *Again.*

"I don't know what to tell you, Harper. We have a huge project, and it needs to be perfect."

"I'm sorry," I sigh. "You're right." I step toward him, plastering my apology smile on my face. I press up on my toes to give him a kiss, but before I can, his hands grip my sides and he eases me backward. I stumble back slightly from the momentum. *What the hell?*

"It's fine," he huffs. "Why don't you go take a bath or something. We can go out when I get back from work." He takes a step forward and kisses me quickly on the forehead. Before I can respond, Dalton has walked out, leaving me alone in our bedroom. *Weird.*

He's been acting strange lately, but I can't put my finger on why. As soon as I try to talk about things, he'll come home from work in a fantastic mood. Bringing me flowers. Coming home with take out. And when I ask him what brought the unusual behavior on? Dalton just replies with a simple, "I thought I could save you from having to do the dishes after cooking supper tonight."

Sighing, I look around. Our bedroom is simple. A king size canopy bed, the walk-in closet, and the various touches across the room that make it ours. The best part of this room? The master bathroom that is connected to the room, making escaping the world that much easier. His and hers sinks lay along one side of the room, accented by grey and agate tiles that adds to the vibe. But my favorite part of the bathroom is the beautiful clawfoot tub. It's so deep, the water covers my breasts and stomach while I lounge surrounded by warmth and lavender scented bubbles. A tub like this was literally on my checklist of must haves when we were looking at places. I love my baths. My body instantly relaxes when I submerge myself, and I slowly feel myself sink into bliss each time.

***

I'm in the kitchen with my "Dance Jamz" playlist in the background as I clean up after eating lunch. I was feeling the music so much that I moved onto the fridge. I don't do a deep clean as often as I should, so I decided to do it now while the momentum is there.

Once all the contents of the fridge are on the kitchen island, I take a quick break to shoot off a random fact of the day to my best friend, Evie. I can't remember when I started this. I think it was a joke to get out of telling her something. Whatever it was, it stuck, and I have an app I go on daily to get a new fact. Satisfied, I grab the rest of the cleaning products from under the sink.

Harper: Did you know crocodiles can't stick out their tongues?

I don't have to wait long until my phone vibrates on the counter, telling me she's responded.

Evie: Have I ever told you that you're weird?

Harper: Multiple times, but I like the fun facts.

Evie: Can they seriously not stick out their tongues?

Harper: They can't! Apparently it's a membrane that holds their tongue down!

Evie: That's so strange lol I miss your face bestie, when can I see you!?

Harper: Maybe after supper? Dalton and I are supposed to do something this afternoon to make up for him ditching me this morning. Said we'd do something just the two of us.

Evie: Ugh fine, I'll be over at seven.

Chuckling, I place the bucket in the sink, filling it with vinegar and hot water– I hate using chemicals when I don't have to– I get to work cleaning my fridge. I don't even know how much time has passed, but just as I finish, I hear the front door open and close.

"Hey babe!" I shout over my shoulder. I head to the sink to empty out the bucket and begin rinsing it out. "Where did you want to go this afternoon? You know you didn't really give me any details on what you wanted to do. I know the apple farm is starting their harvest... maybe we can go over there and collect apples and I'll make apple crisp with fresh apples. I know it's your fav– "

But when I turn around, he isn't there. I could have sworn I heard him walk this way, but he must have gone to the bedroom. I shrug and begin to put all the food back in the fridge. It takes me a bit longer to get everything put away but I get it done, dancing while I do it. I'm so into the music I must have missed Dalton coming back into the room. I'm admiring my organizational skills in my fridge, when I hear a thud behind me, followed by my name.

"Harper."

My back straightens and I stop what I'm doing. Dalton doesn't use my full name. Like ever.

Unless he's mad.

I turn and my eyes connect with soulless orbs. There is no trace of any emotion coming from his demeanor. It's like he's shut every emotion off, detaching himself completely. Usually, I can anticipate this, but this moment has taken me by surprise. Warning bells begin to ring in my head. "What's...uh... Is everything okay?"

This sardonic chuckle escapes from his lips before he shakes his head.

"No, everything is not *okay*, Harper."

It's then that I notice the bag by the front door. My heart rate instantly begins to race and my throat begins to tighten. What in *hell* is going on?!

"What do you mean? Did something with your work project go wrong?" My brain is spinning as I'm trying to figure out where this coldness is coming from. Maybe he's just tired from all the overtime he's put in lately and wants to get out of town for the night? Maybe this is just my brain playing tricks on me and he's surprising me with a night away.

He mumbles something, but it sounds awfully close to *Jesus Christ*. Looking down at his feet, he shakes his head before he runs his hand through his hair and says, "I can't do this anymore, Harper. I'm not happy. I'm done."

I feel like I've been slapped across the face as the air whooshes out of my lungs. Am I hallucinating? Because surely I didn't hear what I think I heard. My mouth is agape before I close it and open it again to try and say something. Anything.

But I think my brain is short circuiting.

"I... uh... What?" I finally get out.

"You can't really be that dense, Harper. I haven't been hiding my unhappiness here."

Okay, *ouch*.

"I- I mean I noticed there was some tension but I didn't think you were *unhappy...*" I say quietly. I begin to fidget with my hands, something I do often when I'm overwhelmed and holding in my emotions. Then I get the telltale feeling of tears stinging the back of my eyes. I look up and quickly blink them away.

"I haven't been happy for *months*!" He booms. I flinch back at the volume of his confession. "I thought it was just a little moment, that things were too ... I don't know, comfortable or something." He roughly runs his hand through his hair, his shoulders stiff. If we were in a cartoon you could see the frustration pluming off of him. "But I can't do this anymore. Last night kind of solidified it for me."

I stand there, my mouth agape in shock. It takes my brain a minute to register something Dalton said. "... last night solidified it?"

"Yes!" His tone becomes more agitated with each word. "The way you always poke fun at how my parents are. How I was raised. Like they're some stuck up snobs who would never give anyone below them the time of day!" He starts to pace, and I just stand there. I mean sure, I poke fun. But come on, his parents *are* a little stuck up... okay, at least his mom is. "And then there's whatever is going on between you and my mom." A*aand there it is.* "I don't understand why you two can't just get along. She is just looking out for me."

A laugh bursts out of my mouth. "You have got to be kidding me. Why can't we just get along? Where do you want me to start?" I scoff, waiving a hand through the air. "The backhanded compliments I get about my body? The constant criticism she gives me, or how about the fact that half the time I don't know whether she sees me as a human being or another person to do her bidding?" I run my fingers through my hair in frustration. "We've been together for eight years. Since we were sixteen, she has *never* liked me. Not ever. I've taken years of her negativity and poor treatment of me. I've acted like it doesn't affect me, it does Dalton.

It doesn't just slide off my back. It cracks my armor, and she makes me feel like I'm never going to be good enough for you!"

I begin to think about the dinner last night with his parents. Just after they arrived, she threw her coat at me as she walked past, barely giving me a hello before heading into the kitchen.

Dalton comes through the patio door with the steaks and chicken on a platter. His smile widens as he sees his parents. "Mom, Dad, hey! Just give me a second to put this meat down, and I'll grab you both a drink." He makes his way over to our farmhouse style dining table and places the cooked meat in the center of the set table.

"Oh, don't be silly, my sweet boy. Harper can get us drinks. I mean, she isn't doing anything," Judith croons to her son, while side eyeing me with disdain. Jesus Christ this woman gets on my nerves. Forcing a smile on my face I say, "Of course! A red wine for you, Judith? And bourbon for Keith, right?" I turn toward the bar cart, grabbing the wine glass and filling it with red before she answers. I found this cute little antique shop last month, and when I saw the bar cart, I couldn't say no. It was the perfect accent to our home.

"Oh Harper... you can't have red wine with chicken breast. That's a dreadful pairing... I'll take a Chardonnay... you do have white wine, don't you?"

My movements falter as I pour Keith's bourbon. My hand moves just enough to tap the full glass of red wine. With my hands full, I can't do anything more but watch it shatter, liquid splashing across the floor. "Oh shit," I mutter as I quickly grab the paper towels and begin cleaning the red wine that is now everywhere on the kitchen floor. I manage to clean up all the liquid and all that's left is glass. I should probably give it a quick mop with the Swiffer after using the broom, just to catch any small pieces and we're good. As I walk through the kitchen, I feel the heat on my face creeping up my neck, and onto my face. Of course my clumsy ass would manage to make a huge mess at dinner with Dalton's parents. I grab the broom and the Swiffer and head back into the kitchen.

"I am so sorry, I'm such a klutz, just give me two seconds and it'll all be cleaned up and I'll get you your Chardonnay," I say with as much bravado as I can muster.

Judith responds with a tsk noise. She might be the only person who would scold me over a flipping accident. "Don't worry about it. Dalton has finished what you couldn't complete."

I'm brought back to the present as I notice my cheeks are damp. I quickly use the back of my hand to wipe away the tears that have so rudely escaped, while scolding myself for letting the tears fall.

"That right there." His fingers point directly at me in accusation, "What you just said. That is one of the reasons I'm unhappy. I just wish you guys could get along. How can I be with someone who can't get along with my family? They're my family, Harper. They aren't perfect, but they love me and want to see me happy." He sighs, walking toward me placing one hand on my cheek. I back away utterly shocked. I don't want him to touch me right now. How can he touch me so affectionately while simultaneously smashing my heart to pieces with a sledgehammer? "I really wanted this to work. I've been trying, but I just can't do it anymore."

Heavy silence wraps around us, and it feels like we're in a standoff. But in all reality? The fight is leaving my body, and a numbness is taking over. I can see in his body language where this is going to go. "Say it then."

"It's over. I'm going to stay with my parents until we work out the details of the house and getting my name off the lease. I'll schedule a time next week for me to come and get the rest of my things."

There isn't anything I can do in this moment to change his mind.

"Okay."

I'm standing in the kitchen with a bottle of wine and my largest wine glass sitting next to it. My glass is full as I bring it to my lips, but the smell hits me and I scrunch my nose up in distaste. This isn't what I want. Staring off into oblivion, wondering when my life took this turn, and how the fuck

I'm going to be single. I haven't been fucking single since I was sixteen. Jesus Christ, what is dating life like? Ew, no. I can't even think about that. Fuck relationships. I'm just gonna do me.

I lose track of time as I sit in the quiet, flipping through every emotion. When I snap out of it, I grumble a "fuck it." I tip the glass back and chug the wine that I previously turned my nose up at. My body recoils reactively to the drink. The wine was definitely not what I wanted. I go to the fridge, looking for the blackberry cider that I prefer. Seeing that I still have a full six pack, I do an internal happy dance before grabbing it and storming for the patio. Slamming the door behind me, I head toward the porch swing but stall. Nope. I can't sit there. Spinning on my heel, I walk down the stairs to sit by the fire pit.

The sky is starting to fade from day to early night; the blues turning into a mix of pinks, oranges and yellows as the sun begins its descent into the horizon. The crisp wind blows around me, reminding me that fall is approaching. I inhale the signature musty earth scent marking fall's approach, and it starts to settle something deep inside me. Things might be shit right now, but a fire in the crisp autumn night might be enough to fix it. Quickly I set up the fire pit, layering the wood in a cabin like pattern before adding the kindling to the center. Sticking my hand into my pocket I remove the lighter I grabbed earlier from the kitchen, bringing the open flame to the center. I watch as the fire catches and the kindling begins to ignite. The heat slowly washes over my body as it begins to build.

The wood crackles under the blaze of orange and white. The pungent odor of new fire bleeds into my senses as it stokes higher. I crack open my can of cider. The crisp flavor settles into my tastes buds as I sit back and try to enjoy the fire.

⁂

A couple hours have passed and I'm staring into the smoldering flames, going over tonight in my head for the billionth time. "This is such bullshit," I mutter to myself before bringing the can up to my lips. I tip my head back to finish off what's left of the cider. Reaching down to grab another can, I realize that was the last one. "Fuck... even more bullshit!" I mutter as I toss the empty onto the soft grass. I'll pick that up later. I can't be bothered to do it now. I'm comfy and warm from the fire.

"Okay, what is bullshit? And I guess it's a good thing I have these with me?" I startle at the noise and turn around to see my best friend in the entire world coming down the deck stairs, holding up two six packs of cider. I drunkenly smile at her.

"You're my hero!" I slur. As I reach out for one of the pack, Evie stops and gives me a skeptical look while holding the cases back out of my reach. "Okay, what's going on? Why are you drunk at." she looks at her watch, "seven thirty p.m... and where is Dalton?"

I stare at her for a minute, wondering why my best friend is standing in front of me right now. I snort, "Honestly, I forgot you were coming over." Then, I make grabby hands at one of the cases of cider she is currently holding hostage from me. I don't drink like this. I like cider every once in a while, and the occasional glass of wine. I never drink to get drunk. I've never really liked the lack of control that comes with being drunk. "Tonight is bullshit. Running out of cider was bullshit. Dalton's mother is bullshit. And most importantly... *Dalton* is fucking bullshit." I finish with a drunken sneer as I make another pathetic attempt to get a can of cider from my best friend's iron grip. I know I'm going to feel like complete shit in the morning. But it's not like I work tomorrow. And even if I did, I work from home, so I can look like a trash panda, and as long as I don't have any video conferences, I'm golden. Perks of being a freelance book editor.

Fingers are snapped in front of my face, bringing me back to reality. Evie takes one good look at me and opens one of the cases. She proceeds to sit next to me. Looking over at me, she surveys me with caution. "Babes, are you okay? Why is Dalton bullshit?"

I look at her as tears begin to fill my eyes. "He left." I choke the words out, my mouth going dry.

Evie's eyes go wide, and she takes another big swig of the cider before replying. "Well, *fuck*." She falls back into her seat and exhales slowly. I can tell by the look on her face that definitely wasn't the response she was expecting. She was expecting me to tell her we had a stupid fight and now he's out at the gym working out his frustrations.

"You're going to have to start at the beginning and run it back to me. Because what the *fuck*, man." Evie sits up and bends her leg, allowing her body to face me. She reaches out, offering me her hand for comfort, which I immediately take. I lace our fingers together. Evie has been my rock since fourth grade. Betty Rogers pushed me down during recess because I was taking too long to go up the ladder of the slide. Evie went up to her and decked her right in the face. From then on, we were inseparable. She's heard about all my ups and downs. All the fights I've had with Dalton over the last eight years. She was there for me when my dad left my mom, and then when I didn't hear from him until I was twenty and he needed money. She is my ride or die, the person I'd call if I needed to hide a body. I would take a bullet for her, as she would for me. So it didn't take me long at all to decide whether or not I'd tell her. I look at our hands twined together before I take a deep breath and start from the beginning.

Chapter Two

Harper

"W HAT IN THE EVER loving *fuck* is wrong with that guy? This doesn't add up. There *has* to be more to this story. He is holding back on some shit. There's no way the shitty relationship you have with the witch has anything to do with this. If that was the case, you guys would have ended things a long time ago." Evie's walking around the fireplace now, and she's pissed. I don't think I've seen her this mad since Betty Rogers, and that's saying something.

"I don't know, Evie. You might be right, but honestly, I'm just exhausted. My brain hurts from overthinking. I've gone over the last couple months in my mind, and I don't remember anything out of the ordinary. This morning when I went in for a kiss, he redirected me, but it didn't really stand out that much...I don't know," I sigh and rub my eyes. I'm ready to crawl into my bed, turn on some Netflix and pass out with background noise so my mind doesn't wander, even asleep. As if reading my mind, Evie gets up, puts the fire out, and stands in front of me.

"Come on. Up. Let's go to bed. We will put on trashy TV until we pass out. In the morning we will go get the greasiest breakfast ever and then have a besties day." She smiles softly at me as I stand and wrap my arms around her, hiding my face in her neck.

"What would I do without you?" I sigh.

She wraps her arms around me and laughs. "Crash and burn, bitch." I smile to myself before I pull away from her and stumble into the house.

I don't know when or how I make it to my bed, but I do. I decide to stay curled up on my side as Evie and I yell at the TV.

"I can't believe how realistic that toy elephant cake was!" I say in disbelief.

This is exactly what I needed. Laying in bed, with my best friend, watching a show about cake. My eyelids start to get heavy, and I snuggle down into my comforter. Today was an absolute shit show, and it was definitely in the top five worst days of my life. I don't know what I'm going to do, and I know for sure I haven't even begun to process this shit inside my brain. I most definitely haven't even acknowledged the bludgeoned organ that is currently sitting beaten and bruised in my chest where my heart once was. I just. I can't. My heartbeat starts to pick up, fixating on everything that I need to get sorted out. I need to figure out my finances to make sure I can still afford to live here on my own, and go through literally everything in this house and purge everything that is Dalton from this house. What am I going to tell my mom? She *loved* Dalton. I know exactly how that conversation will go. I'll tell her we broke up, and then I'll be the one consoling her about it. And then.

"Whoa now. I'm going to need you to take a breath, babes." Evie chimes in, effectively shutting out my brewing panic attack. I snap my eyes to her, before I nod my head then take a deep breath as she continues. "Whatever is going on in that beautiful brain of yours needs to cut it out. We got this. I'm here, and I will be here through it all. You're not alone. You hear me? You. Are. Not. Alone." Reaching over Evie's fingers lace with mine and she brings it to her chest, holding it close. Her eyes don't leave mine, the intensity of her hazel eyes tells me all I need to know.

"You are my person Harps. I got you, okay?" Tears brim my eyes as I quickly nod my head. I wipe away the tear that escaped and give a soft laugh.

"Gods, when did I become such a cry baby?" I sniffle and look my friend in the eye. "I seriously don't know what I would do without you. I love you to bits." She smiles at me then wipes her own eyes. And it's then that I realize that her eyes are glossy too.

"I love you too, Harps. Now sleep. We have some greasy food calling our name when we wake up." I give her one last laugh and then I roll onto my stomach and get comfy. It only takes a minute before sleep envelopes me and takes me away.

Chapter Three

Harper

WAKING UP TO THE intensity of all mother fucking hangovers hits me like Harry and Ron trying to run through the portal to Platform 9 3/4 in *The Chamber of Secrets*; fast and hard. A long groan escapes me as I stretch and turn over. I'm instantly assaulted by the sun. Fumbling out of bed, I catch myself as I start to lose my balance from the sheets wrapped around my legs. Slamming the black out curtains close, I sigh with relief as the darkness consumes the room again.

Sweet relief. I love those curtains.

I flop back into bed, reaching out and grabbing my phone to check the time. 9 a. M. Today's going to suck.

"Dont let the mushrooms talk to you like that," Evie grumbles beside me as she repositions herself, throwing her leg over me. I throw my hand over my mouth to stifle my giggle, Evie has always talked in her sleep. She ranges from having a normal sleep conversation, to absolute nonsense. This morning seems to be the latter.

"You're majestic." Evie continues, mumbling into her pillow. I can't breathe, my body shaking with laughter as I weasel my way out of bed and rush to the bathroom. A snort escapes my lips as the door clicks closed. I quickly go to the washroom and brush my teeth. There is a moment I attempt battling with my jet black hair, trying to untangle the mess that the night has made. I sigh in defeat before putting it up in a messy bun. That's a future me problem. I don't have the energy to tackle that disaster right now. First coffee, then grease.

Just as I'm rinsing out my mouth, I notice Evie is walking like a zombie to the other sink. She grabs the toothbrush that is designated for her at my place. Dalton used to get all grumbly about Evie sleeping over, but in the end it was actually him who bought her a toothbrush to leave here. She sleeps over often enough it just made sense to have her own things.

I thought it was a sweet gesture of him showing his support in my need for my best friend sometimes. "Morning," I grumble to her as I put my toothbrush away. I face her, leaning my hip on the bathroom counter as Evie starts brushing. I get nothing more than a grunt from her in response. She's the worst morning person ever. I snort and say, "I'm going to get changed then I'll make us the good stuff."

I make my way out of the bathroom and toward my walk in closet. Rubbing my eyes with one hand, I swing the other to the light switch to turn it on. After my eyes adjust to the room, I freeze. And just like that, everything from last night comes rushing back to the forefront of my mind.

The heartache comes barreling at full force as I remember him leaving with his bags.

His half of the closet is completely empty. There are a few stray hangers on the ground from him clearly rushing to pack his things while I was in the kitchen. The empty space gives that painful reminder that it's real. It's a real fucking punch straight to my gut. A garbled sound escapes from my throat as the tears begin streaming down my face.

He's gone.

Last night actually happened.

"*What the fuck,*" I manage to choke out.

"Harps? Are you okay?" I hear Evie shuffling out of the bathroom. Wiping my face quickly, I sniffle as I begin stripping out of my pajamas. I take the moment to do some deep breathing to calm myself.

"Yeah! I'm fine, just caught a glimpse of myself in the mirror," I laugh loud enough for her to hear. It's the truth. I did look like death, and if I was more awake when I first looked at myself, it wouldn't have been an attempt to hide my emotions. I just want to grab my clothes and get dressed, but when I turn, I find Evie staring me down. Her brows furrow with concern, knowing that my comment was a load of crap. My eyes begin to tear up again, one escaping and rolling down my cheek. I shake my head hastily. "Don't." I say to her as I point my finger in her direction. "Don't come in here with that concerned look on your face. Because I can't do it. I can't have you come in here with that face, because I know what comes next. You'll come over here and you will hug me. And if you hug me I will break. The dams will break and I will cry, and I don't know if I'll be able to stop after that." I beg her, lifting both hands up in a stay back movement. "So just... don't. Please."

She looks at me for a moment before she nods. "Okay. I'll go make us some coffee." She slowly backs up and then heads out of the room toward the kitchen. I quickly swipe away the remnants of tears that were about to fall before taking another deep breath. I exit the closet and make my way to the kitchen. From halfway down the hall, I smell the sweet, sweet aroma of coffee brewing. I am a coffee snob, so I only drink Starbucks. I will spend the extra money for that siren's call, I don't even care. It's the only coffee that has never given me any sort of heartburn. I hum with satisfaction as I make my way over to the coffee pot. Evie has already set aside all the fixings to make my coffee on the counter. The first sip is always the best, except for today. It feels off today. This whole day feels off. I know the reason why I'm just not going to think about that right now. I'll deal with that when I'm alone. Yeah, bottle it all up Harper. You're good at keeping things beneath the surface. You know from experience nothing bad happens from doing that. Ha, if that was only the truth...

"Alright, this coffee isn't doing it. I need sopping greasy goodness from Ruthie's Diner. You know that place has the best hangover cure meals ever." Turning my body toward Evie, I raise my eyebrow in question seeing if she has a better option. She is currently sitting there with her palms on her forehead like she's personally studying each tiny detail of my countertop. My best friend is just as hungover as I am.

"Yes *please*, I *need* all the greasy food in my body right now." Evie's voice is low and intentional. "With a milkshake... the most chocolatey of all chocolate fudge milkshakes that they have ever made. I swear one sip and it touches your soul."

I laugh as I go to the front entrance and grab my purse and keys. Looking around, I realize I forgot my phone, but honestly the only person I want to talk to right now is with me. So screw it, it stays here. "Come on cranky! Let's get our grease on!" Evie shuffles behind me as she grabs her things. After locking the house, we head toward Evie's red SUV and make our way to Ruthie's. It's about a ten minute drive from my house, so I tip my head back and rest my eyes, hoping for the drive to be quick.

"So, I was thinking after Ruthie's we can walk to the boardwalk? It has everything we need to be distracted. Junk food, carnie games... bars." Evie laughs as I groan at the mention of more alcohol.

"Ugh, no. No more alcohol, I will literally do anything other than get more to drink. Do you think we could go to the apple orchard? I really wanted to go yesterday and get apples for all the fall baking... but you know..." I trail off. Baking is my absolute favorite thing to do. Apple pie, apple crisp, and not to mention, my famous apple coffee cake muffins. It's my own personal recipe, and I keep it close to my heart. Literally no one knows about the recipe except Evie. I didn't even tell Dalton. I falter a bit when I think about him and how he loved my fall baking. "Actually...nevermind, I don't think I really want to bake anymore."

My best friend's sympathetic eyes come to rest on me. I turn my body to look out the window and ignore her for the final stretch of the drive.

❦

Sunday mornings are one of the busiest times at Ruthie's, but I don't even care at this point. I just need food. Thankfully, we don't have to wait long before a table is ready for us. We already know what we're ordering. This isn't our first hangover tour at Ruthie's. We've done this routine since high school.

I always get the cheesy meat lovers omelet, with hash browns, bacon AND sausage, paired with a huge glass of chocolate milk and water. Evie takes greasy hangover food to the next level and gets a double bacon cheeseburger with a large poutine and a large chocolate fudge milkshake.

We order as soon as the waitress arrives with a pot of coffee in hand and two mugs. I take a sip of the coffee and grimace.

"Ugh I don't know why I always order the coffee here. Ruthie's has a bunch of great things but their coffee is NOT one of them."

Smacking my lips in distaste, I push it away with a sigh. Dalton was a more relaxed coffee drinker, and he never liked the coffee here either. Just thinking about him brings a pang in my chest. I glance out the window hoping to avoid Evie's gaze.

"Eight years of building a life with someone," I huff a frustrated sigh, "Eight years, Evie. And just like that." I snap my fingers, "it's over. Now, there's so much to do and I don't even know where to start"

"I know babes... but I'm here. I'll help you with it all." I hear her take a sip of the coffee, followed by her disgust. "Ick, yeah... I don't know why we always start out with the coffee either." I feel her hand cover mine, pulling my eyes to meet hers. "Is there something you wanted to get over with today? If not, I'll come by after work every day this week and we can do it together."

Staring at her, I think about how thankful I am for her. "I can't even fathom doing anything today. Let's just wander until something catches our eyes."

"Sounds like a plan," Evie replies, squeezing my hand. I give her a thankful smile. The food comes out surprisingly quick, and we dig in. Wasting no time stuffing our faces, I savor the grease now settling in my stomach.

Leaning back after effectively destroying all the food on my plate, I let out the most satisfied groan. "God, I swear this food is better than sex. I might start coming here more often."

Evie shoves a huge bite into her mouth, chewing a few times, "This food is better than sex," the words barely audible over her chewing.

I wipe my face with my napkin, piling all my dishes on top of each other so the waitress can grab it in one swoop. "Okay let's go walk this off. I'm feeling a lot better after all this."

After paying, we leave Ruthies, turning right and head toward the boardwalk. The weather is perfect and the sun feels so nice on my face. We check out all the little shops, spending hours going up and down the boardwalk. I buy a beautiful antique glass bowl to put in the middle of my kitchen table. It's going to look so gorgeous there. Smiling at my purchase and listening to Evie ramble on about some swoon date that went horribly wrong, I begin to slow my steps as we approach our local animal shelter.

"... And then this dude had the audacity to ask me if I was sure I wanted to get the chicken parmesan because of the calor— Harper? Are you even listening to me?" she asks. I was until my attention was snagged by the sign on the shop window, which reads ADOPTION FAIR. I look at her, my smile spreading.

"Harper, no. You literally just ended a relationship. You shouldn't be making such a huge decision like this after a life changing event." I purposely ignore her as I open the door to the shelter and walk in. I know she's probably right, and she's trying to rationalize with me. But the moment I saw that sign, my mind was made up. I keep moving, internally smirking at Evie following me.

The receptionist greets us with a smile. She's an older lady with short curled hair and glasses. She has a kind smile and warm brown eyes. "Hi there! Welcome to Barks and Recreation! What brings you lovely ladies in here today?"

Evie elbows me in the ribs, her voice barely more than a whisper. "We really shouldn't be here. You're not thinking straight."

I give her a pointed look before I turn back to the receptionist. "I'd like to meet the dogs please!"

Chapter Four

Harper

THE REST OF THE week flies by, and there hasn't been much time to spiral over recent events. Evie may have thought I was crazy when we walked into the animal shelter but . I fell in love with the most adorable American Bulldog named Winston. I've quickly started to call him Winnie. Having him here has made it a bit easier with Dalton being gone. Winnie quickly took over Dalton's side of the bed, firmly cementing himself as my leading man. I wasn't planning on having it happen, until a particularly hard night came. I was sobbing in bed because I thought watching the movie UP! was a fantastic idea. News flash, it was not. Having the couple walk through life, growing old together, just for her to fucking die? At the beginning of the movie!? Who does that! Winnie had jumped on the bed sensing the mood shift, quickly circling the bed before laying back down resting his head on my leg. The dog bed I purchased is useless. He's my partner in crime, and we've quickly fallen into a comfortable routine.

We get up in the morning, have breakfast, and go for a nice walk to start off our day. Winnie hangs out in my office, napping while I work. We spend my lunch break walking some more, and I eat lunch while working when we return. After supper, I sit outside at the fire while playing fetch with Winnie, letting him get his final zoomies out before we crawl into bed. It's Friday night, and I'm in the backyard, barbecuing supper. I love the taste of seasoned chicken breast with asparagus on the grill. My mouth waters at the thought of dinner. A nudge at my side brings my attention to Winnie, who gives his best puppy dog eyes trying to get a taste. Dalton is supposed to be over shortly to collect the rest of his things. I decide to do some reading while I wait, making my way into the living room to grab my tablet. I don't remember the last time I touched it as I've been reading manuscripts for the last week trying to meet my deadlines. I don't see it, so I head to the bedroom. I look through my nightstand, but it's not there. *Hmm, when was the last time I had it?* It takes me a couple minutes, but then I remember that Dalton was using it the day we had supper with his parents.

I spin in the room. I know he had it before running into the bedroom to grab his phone. I spot it hanging above the mahogany shelf that I requested Dalton hang to help with cord management. When I reach the tablet and unplug it, I notice a message notification on the main lock screen. Which is weird because I don't remember connecting my phone to the tablet. Not thinking anything of it, I unlock the screen, and it opens up to what was last on the tablet. I see messages that are connected to a phone, and it doesn't take me long at all to realize that these are from Dalton's phone; all from some girl named Chloe.

A memory unlocks of a coworker named Chloe that Dalton told me about. I even met her a few times, too. She was this petite brunette, working reception at his office. She kind of gave off this stuck up, entitled vibe whenever I came in to have lunch with Dalton. The fake smile always rubbed me the wrong way, and the way she shamelessly flirted with him in front of me had always irked me, but I'd never seen it reciprocated. She was never outright rude, but I saw the looks she'd give me.

I was used to them. After all, I usually get that response when people see me with Dalton. He is your typical good looking guy, while I am the *big* girl.

He never let anyone question it though. Dalton was always into PDA, and he had to be touching me in some way. A hand on my lower back, or quick kisses on my neck or cheek. At least, that's how it used to be. Our lunch dates slowly became few and farther between, and I eventually just stopped going. If it wasn't me being busy with work, he was canceling, stating something important came up.

I don't mean to start reading the conversation that's loaded up on the screen, but it's hard not to. I must be hallucinating because these messages aren't friendly coworker messages. The further up I scroll in this text string, the louder the deafening silence becomes. These messages are romantic ... and not just romantic. They're fucking sexual too.

What in the actual fuck!

I look at the dates. There are months upon *months* of messages. Growing lightheaded, I head to the bed to sit for a minute. Placing the tablet next to me, I close my eyes and take deep, slow breaths. The tightness in my chest begins to loosen a smidge, and then I sit with the realization of what has been going on behind my back for fucking months. I couldn't stomach reading further than that. I'm honestly a little too nervous to try and see when this all started.

Something snaps in me, because the next thing I know, I am gathering his shit up and bringing it to the front door.

It doesn't seem good enough to just leave it at the front door.

No, I need all his things *out of here*. I need them out of here *now*. My chest tightens again as everything I read continues going through my head on repeat.

I feel like all I've known is a lie.

Next thing I know the front door is open, and I'm not so carefully taking all of Dalton's stuff and chucking it out onto the front lawn. The feeling is so fucking freeing, I huff out a laugh as I grab the next handful of things and follow suit. I'm in some sort of trance as I continue to throw out every single thing Dalton left behind in this house, decorating my front lawn with it.

Is this making a scene for all the neighbors to see? Oh absolutely.

Do I care? Fuck no.

I'm on my way back into the house to get another arm full of things when I hear a voice from the front lawn. "What the fuck?! Harper what are you doing!?" My head whips around as I see Dalton climb out of his dark blue Nissan Altima. He quickly scrambles to grab his things, checking them for damage. His head snaps up and he makes eye contact with me. I glare at him and make my way through the door, out to the front lawn. He begins to walk toward me.

"Harper...don—"

He doesn't get to finish his sentence before I launch my arm full of crap, sending it sailing through the air, before landing across the yard. It's then that I hear a satisfying crunch as whatever it was breaks. I should feel bad, right? I am throwing his belongings on the front lawn like the crazy person you see in movies. But in light of what I've just learned, I get it.

I totally fucking get how someone could be so livid, they just wanted to get rid of every single thing that belongs to the person.

It almost feels cathartic doing this. I knew something was off with the relationship, but I always debunked it to comfortability. We were both more irritable, but we always made up in the end. I thought nothing of it.

On the other end of the spectrum, I feel so unbelievably stupid. How could I have missed something like this? How could I have missed that this person, who I have spent so much of my life with, was fucking the receptionist at his job? I scoff and shake my head, silently berating myself for my stupidity in not noticing sooner.

"—Harper! I'm fucking talking to you!" Dalton bites, snapping me out of my own thoughts.

I glare at him as I respond angrily. "What?" He stares at me in disbelief, throwing his hands up in the air as he begins collecting some of his things and muttering to himself while he brings them to the trunk of his car. Tears prickle at the back of my eyes, and I look up in an effort to blink them away.

I will not cry.

Nope, I will not cry in front of him right now. I will keep it together, and the moment he finally leaves, I will go to my kitchen and make the strongest fucking drink there is. And only once I have that drink will I allow myself to cry.

He stomps back up the front lawn, throwing his hands in an exasperated movement. "Well? Are you going to tell me why the fuck you're throwing my things on the front lawn right now?" He bends down to grab another armful of things, and then a disgruntled noise comes from Dalton's mouth.

"My snow globes! They're shattered!"

A snort laugh escapes before I can school my emotions. I quickly slap my hand over my mouth as he turns, shooting daggers my way. Let me tell you, if looks could kill someone…

"I'll get a garbage bag." I quickly turn on my heel and rush back into the house, snickering to myself. I fucking hated those stupid snow globes. They were the tackiest things ever, but he insisted he needed them every time we traveled somewhere. When I heard the crack, I was hoping that it would be those things. My little moment of triumph was interrupted when I could hear the stomping footsteps coming up behind me. I continued to the sink and opened the cupboard underneath grabbing a garbage bag, when he started berating me again.

"Harper, what the fuck! Why is all my shit over the front lawn?!"

I stand up quickly, back tense. I turn around slowly and lean up against the counter. Looking him in the eye, I cross my arms and raise one eyebrow when I reply, "Are you really that dense, Dalton?"

He looks blankly at me and waits.

The silence is deafening before I straighten myself and finally speak. "Ask Chloe."

His face pales, before he tries to hide his reaction. But he isn't quick enough. I see it. There's rage in his eyes before he huffs. "I don't know what the fuck you're talking about."

"Oh, really?" I scoff, pushing off the counter. I brush past him, leading into the living room, passing down the hallway into my bedroom. Snatching the tablet from the bed, I make my way back to find Dalton standing awkwardly in the living room as Winnie is standing by him, sniffing around. Dalton's nose scrunches up as he regards Winnie. As I enter, he notices me. His eyes see the tablet in my hand, and I see his jaw tighten.

"Yeah, you forgot to disconnect your messages from my tablet." I explain, unlocking the screen. The conversation is still where I left it, my eyes scanning over the conversation quickly before continuing. "Do you talk to everyone you work with like you do with your receptionist?" I toss the tablet down onto the couch before heading to the patio door to let Winnie out. "You know, it all sort of makes sense now. The late nights, the cold attitude Chloe always gave me when I was at the office when we used to go out to lunch. The distance."

"You're sounding crazy. Chloe was just a friend from the office nothing more—" He goes to continue, but I cut him off before he even has a chance to spout off whatever bullshit he was about to say. I walk back to the couch and pick the tablet up, scrolling until I get to the part I want to share.

"Chloe: When do you think you'll be able to get away from that leech? I got something from your favorite store today and I want to show you." I cock my head and rest a hand on my hip. "And don't get me started on the pictures of her modeling said things from your *favorite* store."

A look of panic quickly washes over his face when he finally realizes he's been caught. Dalton sputters, and I can see the wheels turning in his head as he tries to come up with something to cover his tracks. I literally have the proof in my hands. One of the perks of being together with someone for so long is that you can read them like a book. Granted, maybe I don't know him as well as I thought I did.

I know *this* though. He always gets angry when things don't go his way.

"Well, what the fuck were you thinking snooping through my messages? It's not my fault you found something you didn't like."

My head snaps back at the *audacity* of this man. You've got to be kidding me.

"You know what Dalton? I…" I sigh. "I just don't care anymore. It's over. You clearly moved on well before that was even decided. I just … just get the rest of your shit, and go." I plop myself on the couch and rest my head on the back of the couch, closing my eyes. So much has happened in the last week, I honestly don't think I could take any more bad news.

I hear barking coming from the patio door, so I get up and let Winnie in. He is instantly at my side, nudging my hand. When I look down at him, I smile. I'm so glad I found him, he's exactly what I needed in my life.

If Dalton could do one thing right, it would be to shut up and leave.

But this isn't a perfect world, so really I shouldn't be surprised when he ruins the moment.

"It's outbursts like this that are the reason I pulled away. You always blow everything out of proportion." He laughs. "You know what? I'm glad it's over. It honestly should have happened sooner. But I found some satisfaction in doing this behind your back and you had no idea."

My head snaps in his direction at his confession. I stand in utter disbelief of the words that came out of his mouth. This isn't the Dalton I fell in love with. Hell, this isn't even the Dalton I have shared a life with over all these years.

The man standing in front of me is a complete stranger.

Taking a deep breath, I look back up to him, and it's like a weight has been lifted. As much as what he said hurts, it was exactly what I needed to hear. "Just get out."

"Gladly." He turns and stomps out the door, slamming it so hard, it rattles.

I sit back down on the couch and take a minute to just breathe. Staring across the living room, I take a moment to let everything sink in that's just happened over the last hour. The break-up sucked initially, but I like to think I was making the steps to move forward. I should have known there was another shoe to drop. Because why wouldn't there be? A sardonic laugh bubbles past my mouth as I think about everything. Then I feel a nudge at my hand and I look down at Winnie who had jumped up on the couch and laid down next to me, with a concerned, but love-filled, look on his face.

"It's okay Winnie boy. We won't be seeing that man again, I promise." I lean down and kiss the top of his head. Clearly, that was noted as an invitation to also receive kisses too, because he bounced up quickly and began licking my face. I laugh, and lightly push him away so I can breathe. "Okay buddy that's enough. Let's get some supper."

IT'S BEEN A COUPLE weeks since the whole cheating debacle happened. After Dalton left, I texted Evie the cliffnotes of what went down. She called immediately to check-in and see if I was okay. We talked on the phone for hours, which ended with Evie falling asleep on me at around two in the morning. Whenever Evie is just about to drift off into a heavy sleep, she lets out this weird moaning noise. Once that happens, she is dead to the world, and there is no waking her up. Trust me, I've tried many times. She came over the next morning and has been making a point to come over in the evenings. Most nights, we eat and play board games to pass the time.

I know she's doing this intentionally. She wants to make sure I don't turn inside myself and become a recluse. Which, honestly sounds tempting, but my last minute decision to adopt a dog in the throes of a new break-up worked in my favor.

Winnie forces me to be present. I wake early during the week to make sure he's able to have his walk, and I carve time at the end of the day for another trek. On the weekend, we go for a hike at some of the nearby trails. I want to let him off leash when we do these hikes, so I've been slowly training him in the yard. I think he's ready, and I've been mentally planning our first off-leash excursion this weekend.

The only time I've allowed myself to cry was the day Dalton took the remainder of his things. I took a hot shower and let the tears flow down with the warm spray of the water. I don't know *who* that man is anymore, and I think that's what hurts the most of all. He wasn't always like this. As soon as he started at his firm, he began to change. I could see the stress starting to consume him as he tried to impress the partners, and work his way up there. I did what I could to try and help him de-stress at home, but he just brushed it off, claiming he was fine. As it turns out, he may have been fine, but **we** weren't.

In the kitchen, I'm staring into my fridge, debating on whether to cook or order delivery. I'm craving pad thai, and it's been awhile since I had some. Collecting the take out menus from the side of my fridge, I find the restaurant and begin perusing appetizers when I hear Winnie race to the front door. Seconds later, I hear the front door open, then close. Winnie comes barging in the room with excitement and alerts me of our guest arriving. Not like I couldn't hear her. Even if the dog didn't bark, Evie is so loud when she comes into the house. Without even looking, I can tell you her jacket is thrown on the bench, her keys tossed into my key bowl.

And there she is, coming into my view like the queen she is.

"My saviour. I was just about to order something." I meet her at the table and begin to unpack the bag, realizing that she hit up the exact place I was about to order. "You really are my best friend. This is *exactly* what I was craving."

Evie gives me a small smile. "Well duh, I'm your person. Of course I know what you want." She heads to the kitchen to get drinks and comes back quickly. We eat, and I groan in response to my first couple bites of pad thai. I'm halfway through my food when I realize that Evie has barely touched hers.

"Evie, what is it?"

She snaps out of whatever turmoil was going on in her mind and smiles. Maybe someone else would buy that smile and think she's okay. But I know better.

"Evie Rose Parker, I know your bullshit happy smile." I point my fork toward her face. "Tell me what's going on right now."

The fake smile instantly drops, and she grimaces. "Okay...I may have come here with an ulterior motive of sorts."

I raise my eyebrow at her and give her a go on motion with my hands.

"So…" She clears her throat, "I found out something. Something that is big. I mean I think it's big? I think it is. It definitely changes a lot. Or I think it would…"

"Evie," I huff. "Just rip the bandaid off already, jeez." But the more she rambles, the more my anxiety starts to climb. I hate beating around the bush when it comes to information. I grab my drink as I wait. "Dalton got Chloe pregnant."

My shock makes me spit my drink across the table, covering all of our food. After I cough a couple times, I take my hand and wipe it across my mouth.

"I'm sorry, I must be having a fever dream.I thought I heard you say Chloe. *Dalton's* Chloe. The girl he cheated on me with… is pregnant."

"Correct."

"With Dalton's child? *Dalton*? You're sure?"

Evie winces. "Well, I mean, yes? At least, that's what it looks like."

We sit in silence while I process this new information. This has to be some sick sort of joke, right? Turning, I look my best friend in the eyes. They're full of concern as she takes in my reaction.

"How did you find out?" I'm not sure if I want to know the answer, but I can't help myself.

"You know when you first found out that Dalton cheated with her and you told me? Well, one of the nights I stalked her socials. I didn't follow her or anything, but you know how the algorithm works. Ever since, sometimes her stuff shows up on my feed." She takes a quick drink before continuing. "I was on break at work, and I was doom scrolling before I finished the last stint. And there it was, right there on my news feed. Chloe got professional announcement photos of their *bun in the oven*," she emphasizes with finger quotes. Evie pushes from the chair, heading toward the couch to get more comfortable with me a few steps behind.

"Show me." I demand as I grab a throw blanket and toss it over myself, before grabbing a pillow and position it over my stomach. It's a habit that I do when I'm not feeling completely secure.

Evie grabs her phone and searches up the post. She pauses, placing her phone screen down on her chest. "Are you sure you want to see this?"

"Yes, now let me see!" I say, as my hands open and close in rapid movements. They're grabby hands to the max. Sighing, she hands it over, and my eyes lock on the page.

My stomach drops.

I thought I knew what I was going to see, but I wasn't prepared for the jab in my chest. Seeing it is surreal. Painful.

They stand together, in a kitchen that I fantasize about.

The cupboards are stark white, with black matte handles. An industrial steel hood range is in the background above the gas stove. My gaze drifts to the people in the photo.

Dalton is standing behind Chloe, with his arms wrapped around her midsection. He's looking down at her with a look of adoration on his face. Chloe's golden locks are perfectly done in a fishtail braid, swooped off over one shoulder. An apron is on her, the tie pulling in her slim, hourglass figure. There's flour all over her, and Dalton's hands form a heart over her abdomen. *Her* belly.

The one growing a child.

They're having a baby together.

I'm suddenly numb by the loss of something I thought would be mine.

Dalton and I had talked about having kids together, but we put it on hold while he was getting situated at work. I didn't mind waiting as I just started up my private editing service and was working to get my name out in the book community. I close my eyes to reign in my emotions before I take another look.

Baby Stanford arriving spring 2025!

"Hold on," I abruptly say.

"Hold. The. Fuck. On." I quickly toss Evie back her phone and grab my own. Opening my calendar, I begin doing math. We're just at the beginning of November, which means Chloe is approximately four months...

This mother fucker got her pregnant *in the summer*. Which means *he knew*. He knew she was pregnant for at least the last two months.

"What is it?" Evie asks, "you just got pale there, like someone told you that Santa isn't real. Or that you were adopted…"

"Did you look at the due date?" I ask her.

"Well, no. I saw that it was 2025 and just assumed it was the summer." She pauses to unlock her phone. I see her doing the mental math, too. "That piece of shit. He got her pregnant while he was still with you!"

"Yuuup," is all I can say as I sit there, staring. I'm not fully focusing on the details.

I look up Chloe's profile. Scrolling through her pictures, from the first glance of her profile, it's clear she's someone who posts on social media all the time.

I don't know what comes over me but I end up looking at every single one of her posts. The perfect candid shots, her perfect blonde hair, and her perfect body.

There's one of her laying on a boat, soaking in the sun in her tiny little two piece bathing suit. It is a moment I wouldn't be caught dead in because it would make me look like a beached whale. Scrolling back to the top of her page, I find myself analyzing their pregnancy announcement again. They both seem overjoyed announcing they're starting a family. Dalton looks down at Chloe so tenderly as she smiles up to him in pure bliss. For a brief moment, I imagine myself in Chloe's position. We had talked about kids over the last two years. Dalton always said it wasn't the right time, and now I'm questioning the entire thing. Apparently, it wasn't timing that was off. It was me who wasn't right.

Insecurities appear in my mind. They begin prickling up my body, pinpointing every part of my body that I love to hate. Without being aware, I'm covering my stomach with the pillow even more as I continue to look through her feed.

No matter how hard I try to work out I just can't get rid of it. I've struggled with my size from a young age. I was bullied, and dealt with boys making fun of me. In middle school, I was the center of dares because *wouldn't it be hilarious* to take me to the dance. I was just a fat girl. My mom did her best, she showed me that every size is beautiful.

When I started to really struggle, she got me into therapy. That honestly helped, and I got more confident in myself and my body. I met Dalton and he didn't care how I looked.

Then, I met his mom.

And we all know how that went. So, seeing him cheat on me and get her pregnant, instantly starting a relationship—a family with her...

Her and her petite figure.

It just stings.

The next thing I know, my phone is being ripped out of my hand. My eyes snap across the couch connecting with Evie, who has moved my phone out of reach. She's glaring at me."You need to stop torturing yourself over this picture or looking at anything on her page, for that matter. We don't like her. Full stop." I see her fingers moving over my screen, as she looks through Chloe's page herself, before continuing.

"You need to... HOLD ON." She sits up and her eyes go wide. "She has a brother. And ... oh my god, look at this delicious specimen of a human being." She quickly turns the phone around, showing me his photo.

I gape at the image.

He is the most beautiful man I've seen in my life.

His dark brown hair is cut short on the sides, but left longer on top. Long enough to style it nicely, and he definitely pulls off the most sexy bed head look. I can't see the color of his eyes because they're covered by a pair of Ray-Bans, but his face is framed with a strong jawline. Leading to a broad chest, painted with the most detailed tattoo I've ever seen.

In the dead centre of his chest is a skull wearing a crown, surrounded by flowers shaded with a smokey essence around it. With a closer look, I can see something written on the crown, but I can't get a good enough look to make out what it says. He doesn't have a six pack and his torso is not sculpted. Don't even get me STARTED on the tree trunks he has for thighs.

A thumb swipes across the corner of my lip, and my eyes snap up to Evie as she smirks. "Sorry, you just had a little drool right there, so I thought I'd help you out by wiping it off."

"Oh, fuck off." I mumble to her, as I look back to the post. It's a series of photos that Chloe had posted of a family vacation they took in the summer. I notice his profile is tagged and go to click on it. "His profile is private. That's unfortunate."

Evie chimes in."You should request to follow him."

"What?! No way."

"I mean why not? He doesn't know who you are. It's not like Chloe is going to brag about taking Dalton from you or anything. Or I hope she wouldn't or else she and I are gonna have some words."

This is why I love my best friend.

She continuously has my back. I smile at her, then launch at her to give her a bear hug. I hear a *umph* come from her as I land on top of her, followed by a chuckle.

"Yeah, yeah. I love you too. Now get off me." She sits up after I'm off and grabs her phone. "Oh crap! My phone died, I'll have to go plug it in. Can I use your phone real quick? I just need to call my mom. I forgot to tell her I can't make it up this weekend to see her."

"Yeah, go for it." I say, tossing the phone over to her. I take that moment to let Winnie outside to do his business. Flicking on the porch light, I throw on a cardigan to ward off the chill hanging in the evening air. Taking in a deep breath, I watch Winnie as he runs around with his nose to the ground. He circles the yard three times before picking a spot. He comes barreling back up the stairs, to the door, looking back at me like *hey, hurry up so we can go back inside.*

Making my way back to the living room, I stop in my tracks when I see Evie with the biggest grin on her face. Her eyes gleaming with mischievousness, and I instantly glare at her.

"Evie Rose Parker! What did you do?"

"Okay, don't kill me but..."

I lift my hand up to stop her from continuing. "Nope! I already know I don't want to hear it." I plop back onto the couch next to her and pinning her with a glare. She gives me a pleading look, one she knows I always give into. I stare at her for a few more seconds before rolling my eyes with a smirk.

"Okay, what did you do? But know that I reserve the right to hit you with this pillow if I don't like it." I raise the pillow in preparation, because I already know I'm going to want to hit her.

"Okay so..." She starts. "I didn't *actually* need to call my mom. It was a ruse."

"Evie... What did you do?" I demand.

"Well... Your Capture was still open and it was still on his page... So, because I know you won't do it yourself, I did it for you. I sent him a follow req—" her sentence is cut off as I whip her with the pillow, landing it upside her head.

"HEY! You didn't let me finish!"

I gasp, "I don't need you to finish! I know exactly what you did. Take it back. Undo it! That's so creepy!" I bury my face in my hands, groaning as I contemplate doing it myself.

"Honestly, it's just a Capture follow, Harps. What's the worst thing that could happen?"

I could think of a million things that could go wrong.

But I guess she has a point.

What *is* the worst thing that could happen?

Chapter Six
xavier

W HY DID I AGREE to this again?

Every time my parents invite me to dinner, it's the same old song and dance. Same demands and questions.

Are you seeing anyone?

You're thirty two years old, you should be settling down.

I know this lovely woman whose mother comes to my society's meeting that would be just perfect for you.

It's never: How work is going? How's the vet clinic? Hell, I'd even settle for them asking if I've had any interesting stories about any of my clients. Working and owning a vet clinic had been a dream of mine for as long as I could remember. I always loved animals. They are a lot easier to connect with than humans, in my opinion.

I exhale something between a sigh and a groan as I get out of my vehicle and make my way up my parents driveway. It's our weekly family dinner that I normally try to get out of with some sort of emergency that I say happens at the clinic. Despite my constant absences, my mom still makes it a point to invite me weekly.

However, I was told tonight was non-negotiable and that there was some "big news" being announced.

And when Penelope Hawthorne demands it, it happens.

I had given up years ago trying to defy her. She means well, but she still always gets what she wants.

I don't even make it to the door before I hear the sound of another car pulling up. I turn around and internally groan as I recognize my sister's Porsche as it pulls up into the spot next to my SUV.

I would be lying if I said it was her I was mostly trying to avoid when I come to these sorts of things. She's such a stuck up bitch and thinks because she landed a job as a receptionist, she's hot shit. She didn't have to work too hard to get that job. All she had to do was bat her eyes to daddy dearest, and *he* made it happen. She's had that man wrapped around her finger our entire lives, and it annoys the shit out of me because she didn't have to work for a goddamn thing.

I worked for everything I have achieved.

My parents may have helped by paying for my education, but I still worked while I was going through school. I had a goal to save up to open up a clinic on my own.

I wanted as little help from my parents as possible.

"Big brother!" she squeals. I cringe as I turn around to accept the tackle hug coming for me. "I'm so glad you could make it for family dinner tonight! It's going to be one for the books!" She backs up, pulling out a compact mirror to check her makeup. I'm about to say something before I see movement behind her. There is some guy with shaggy blonde hair and glasses. He's tall, but honestly average if I had to say so myself. He makes eye contact with me, giving me an awkward smile.

"Uh, hey... I'm Dalton. You must be Xavier. Chloe's told me about you." He reaches out his hand to shake mine, but I just look at it. I lift my eyes back to him, raising my eyebrow as I assess him. He isn't the usual type that Chloe goes for. She usually goes after the gym jocks with money. He may be on the taller side, but definitely not a gym type. Must be the money that got her this time.

"Hi." I reply, turning around to open the door. "We should go in. Don't wanna keep them waiting."

I help myself inside and kick off my shoes. Taking a moment to shuck off my jacket, I hang it up on the coat hook by the front door. I don't bother asking any of the staff my parents hired because I can do these things myself. I understand it's their job, but I don't let them stress about me. Especially because I know my sister will take up more than enough energy due to her *demands*.

Right on cue, the staff rushes in to get everyone else settled in. My parents' house is like something you'd see in a magazine. The front doors give way to the main foyer, and to the left of that rests a giant staircase.

I head the opposite direction to the sitting room. This room is where all the gatherings happen, memories flow through my mind as I think of the movie nights and Sunday Night Football gatherings. Looking over I see how my mom has changed out the flower on the coffee table. The warm colors perfectly blend together, but I couldn't tell you the name of the flowers. Walking up to the large bay windows I canvas the yard, taking in every detail of the meticulous care my parents have put forward to upkeep.

"There you are!" I hear the familiar voice of my mother as she enters the room. I turn away from the bay window and smile at her. She walks toward me and embraces me with a hug followed by a brief kiss on both cheeks.

"Hi, Mom," I say, "How are you doing?"

"Oh, just fantastic! Please come! We're all in the dining room, and dinner is just about to be served!" My mother turns to meet Chloe. "Chloe, my dear! You look absolutely stunning in red!" She embraces my sister then steps back still holding her by the biceps. She beams at her, before her eyes dart to that guy Derek she brought with her. "Oh! And you must be Dalton! It's a pleasure to finally meet you! Chloe has told me so much!"

She beckons us to follow with a wave of her hand.

Who the fuck has a name like Dalton? I roll my eyes and make my way to the dining room. Totally over my mother fussing over Chloe's latest flavor of the month. When I enter, I spot my father sitting at the head of the table, sipping on a drink. Looking at the brown liquid in his glass, it's his usual-whiskey.

Making my way further into the dining room, I drift toward the bar located at the far end of the room. "Good evening, Dad. Can I top you off?"

He looks up at me with a small smile. "Please."

He takes a moment, finishing off what's left of his glass before handing it to me. I empty his old ice in the sink. Filling up his glass and one for myself with ice, I grab the whiskey and fill them both up two fingers worth. Coming around the bar I place his drink beside him as I take the seat beside him.

"How is the clinic coming along, son?" He inquires.

I brighten up at the question. "It's going great! I'm working on a new project to help spay and neuter stray animals to try and help with the growing population problem we've been having with—"

"Yes, great, great" He says as he stands and walks toward everyone who is now entering the room. "Sugar plum!" He beams as he makes his way over to my sister. *Of course.*

It's hard not to be a little bitter when you've spent most of your life being pushed aside. The distance that I've tried to get from my family isn't inspired by one singular blow up. It was something that happened slowly over time.

Little by little, my parents stripped away my confidence. I don't even know if they realised they've done it.

I wear my mask well.

I can't even truly pinpoint exactly when I started to put it on. I've worn it for so long, it's just second nature now. With the almost nine year age difference between Chloe and I, there was a big adjustment when she came home. As she got older, she was treated like the little princess she still thinks she is. I grew more irritated because the older she got, the brattier she became. Then, she started blaming me for shit she did. Like when she'd break shit after sneaking home trashed? It was always my fault. I was blamed for not looking after her. I had my own shit I had to deal with. I didn't need to deal with a bratty teenager either.

I see both my parents beaming at Chloe and talking to that Dimitri guy she brought with her. I don't get what the big deal about this dude is. This isn't the first guy that she's brought to a family dinner.

Everyone finally sits down, and a minute later, the staff appear, bringing in the first course. The meal goes by smoothly. The conversation is easy, and I finally get to finish talking about my plans for the spay/neuter clinic I want to attach to my vet office. My mother goes into excited party planner mode, offering to host a charity event to help get donations for the expansion. I try to turn her down, explaining that I have a plan on how to get the funds already.

"Oh, nonsense sweetheart. It would be my absolute pleasure to put this together." She says as she pulls out her phone and begins texting people to get the ball rolling.

I should clarify that my parents aren't the worst.

They try, they do. It's just sometimes they miss the mark a smidge. I'm grateful for her offering it, but I wasn't asking for money. I just wanted to share the news of my accomplished vet clinic. It's something I've built from the ground up, on my own. I'm very proud of how I turned things around for myself.

The dessert is just being served when Chloe clears her throat. I look over at her, and she's looking a bit nervous, which is odd. She's normally very lively during family dinner. The ones I've made it to, at least.

"I wanted to take a moment to say something before we dig into dessert." She starts, "I thought we could wait until after everything is done, but I just am so excited to share this news." She's smiling now, and glances over at Donald, taking his hand.

"Mom, Daddy… we're going to be having a baby!" She says with the biggest smile on her face. My jaw drops. That wasn't what I was expecting to hear. I quickly glance over to my parents to gauge their reactions. My dad's face is pale, and my mom has this open-mouthed stare going on, like a fish. I smirk, expecting a negative reaction from them.

Their perfect princess, knocked up. I'm sure that wasn't part of their plans for her.

My mom shakes the shock off her face then matches the expression on Chloe's face.

"I'm going to be a Grandma!" She screeches, before getting up and circling the table to hug my sister and Dennis. Dad clears his throat and gets up, following. Shaking Dale's hand. Everyone exchanges pleasantries and congratulations. My mom begins going on about what they need to do to prepare for the baby. Then Chloe turns and makes eye contact with me.

"Well big brother, what do you think? You're going to be an uncle!"

I know she's excited, and I try to act like I'm happy for her. I do. But she can see through my fake smile. "Congrats to you and Dane, brat."

She scoffs, placing her hands on her hips. Here we go.

"His name is Dalton! You know this, and you're just playing rude by not using the correct name! Don't think I can't see your fake enthusiasm as anything but jealousy!" A little stomping motion follows the outburst. I said congratulations and she turned it around to me being jealous? Far from it.

I laugh, "Jealousy? Okay Chlo, whatever you need to think to make you feel better about yourself. We all know you're thriving on being the centre of attention with this news." I shake my head and toss back the rest of my drink. Standing, I place my napkin on the table and make my way to my parents. I kiss my mom on the cheek and shake my dads hand. "I'm just going to get going, I have surgery early in the morning. It was a great dinner. I'll see everyone here next week."

I turn to my sister and sigh, "Really. Congratulations." She glares at me before grumbling a thank you. I put on my fake smile and then turn to the father-to-be and say "Deke." Giving him a nod, I continue. "Good luck with everything but especially dealing with my sister."

I turn on my heels and make my way out of the room as I hear the screech of my sister telling me Dean's real name. I couldn't care less, but all the power to him for not only putting up with my sister, but with the added pregnancy hormones as well. I know as I'm walking out of the house my mother will be blowing up my phone tomorrow. She will defuse the situation here, and then in the morning, scold me for how I "handled the wonderful news."

The drive home is quick, and I pass the time by blasting mind numbing music. I pull up to my house. It's a small property, but I've put a lot of work into it. I turned the old barn into my clinic, and with the spay/neuter clinic I have planned to build, it'll make a great attachment.

The little farm style house isn't much but growing up with an extravagant home taught me that I am content with something smaller. The outside still needs a bit of TLC, but after having to replace the shingles this summer, everything else is going to be on the back burner a bit until I can finalise the plans for the clinic expansion.

I walk through the front door and toss my keys and wallet in the bowl I keep on my entry table. Making sure the door is locked, I head upstairs to my bedroom. The master bedroom is located at the back of the hall. It's a decent size, but I'm pretty minimalist when it comes to my room. I have my king sized bed and a dresser that holds all my clothes, and off to the right is my en-suite. I make my way in there, turn on the shower and strip out of my clothes while the water warms.

Placing my hands on the sink, I look at myself in the mirror. The dark circles under my eyes that are permanent fixtures at this point. I slept like shit last night, just like every other night since I was eighteen. The night terrors come and go, but with the stress of the work, they've been coming more frequently. Taking a deep breath, I step into the shower. I release a deep groan as the steaming water rolls down my body. My tense muscles instantly relax, and I reach over, grabbing the body wash and lathering up. I quickly wash my hair and exfoliate my face-guys can take care of their skin properly too. Turning off the shower I drag myself out and dry off quickly. I don't bother with putting on clothing as I crawl in between the sheets, laying on my back and staring at the ceiling. I turn my head to the side to check what time it is. Eleven thirty. Ugh, six a.m. is going to come quickly. I throw my hand over my face.

Easing my body into the mattress, I finally start to relax a bit when I hear my phone ring on the end table. *Shit*, I forgot to put it on silent. I reach over and turn the ringer off, but just before I put it down, I look at the notification that kept me from passing out...

Capture: You have one new follower request.

Chapter Seven

Harper

THE NEXT WEEK PASSES faster than I expect. I thought it would drag. Thankfully, work has been busy. I had a few author meetings, which took up a good chunk of my time. I didn't realise how many books I took on until I sat down and looked at my planner.

Normally I'm organised, and even in the throes of chaos, I thrive. But I am not thriving right now. Trying to figure out who you are single, and working your full time job can make for some complications. I promise myself that I will take some time off after this. I didn't originally make plans to take time off over the holidays since I always use the Christmas holidays as my catch up time. Christmas is slow in publishing; not many authors want to release a book that close to the holiday.

I've decided.

I'm going to take some time off.

I'll give myself two weeks off for Christmas and New Years Eve. After that, I can focus on getting my groove back and spending time with people I care about.

Confident in my decision, I finish off my work day shooting off an email to my clients informing them of my impromptu vacation. I double checked that there were no deadlines during that time. This may be last minute, but I would never screw anyone over. I have a week to get everything in order for my clients before I take my time off.

With the emails sent out, and a game plan for what I'm going to do for the next week, I decide to celebrate choosing myself. I go out back with Winnie, get the fire started and curl up on the outdoor furniture as I play fetch with him. I pull up my phone and order some take out for supper. *Treat yourself, girlfriend.*

I sent off my order for my favorite Chinese joint. I haven't had Chinese food in forever, and I'm already salivating with the thought of wontons. My phone vibrates in my hand, snapping me out of my daydream of all the MSG I'm about to inhale.

Unlocking my phone, I see that I have a Capture notification.

You have one new like.

I open the app to see which picture got attention. I see it was one I recently posted of Winnie, curled up beside me on the couch with my Kindle in my lap. Flipping back to see *who* liked my post, I nearly fall out of my seat when I see the username.

X.Hawthorne

Xavier. Chloe's hot brother.

He just liked *my* photo.

I flashback to the day I foolishly let my so-called best friend "borrow" my phone to call her mom. That day she earned a spot on my shit list and when she requested to follow his *private* Capture account. She said it's not a big deal, and the worst thing that would happen is he wouldn't approve it.

Sure. A woman could dream. But then he accepted the request. And not only did he accept it, but he followed me back.

Now?

He's liking my stuff. I mean it's Winnie, so it's hard *not* to. I understand the appeal of that cute fuzzball. I never looked at his profile after he accepted my request. I couldn't, although it was tempting.

Tonight though, I give in to the temptation, and I click on his username. His profile pops up but it is nothing like I expected it to be.

It's full of animals. Farm animals.

Huh, I did *not* see that coming, especially after seeing his sister's extravagant lifestyle on her profile. I didn't plan on going through his entire profile, I swear, but my fingers couldn't help themselves. I scroll past a photo of an old tin tub in the yard, filled with water. It's not far from the ground, and splashing inside are two Mallard ducks. I have no idea what kind of duck that is, but it's adorable. One duck stretches, flapping its wings wide. In the background there are more animals—chickens, goats and—a donkey named Clyde. The little girl in me who always dreamed of a hobby farm squeals at this discovery.

After I finish scrolling as far down as I'm willing without it being creepy, I look at his bio.

He's a vet.

Just when I thought he couldn't get any hotter; not only is he an animal lover with his own little farm, but he cares for them too. Be still my beating heart.

The notification that my Chinese has been delivered comes across the top of my phone, so I reluctantly shut my screen off, making my way to the front door.

The rest of the night consists of food and reading, followed by an early bedtime. It is the most normal Friday night I've had in awhile, and I truly need that. My drama meter is *full*, so I pray to whoever is listening to let that be the last of it.

The next morning I'm awakened by what feels like a ton of bricks being tossed onto my chest. It's just Winnie on top of me.

"What in the ever loving– Winnie, off!" I groan. Winnie leaps off the bed and starts running toward the kitchen. Scrubbing a hand down my face, it takes me a moment to realize I slept in. I look at the clock, and it's just before ten. I'm refreshed, and I don't think I've slept that good in a while.

I get out of bed and make my way down to the kitchen to let Winnie out back. Throwing my hair up into a messy bun, I start the coffee. I don't care how cold it gets outside, I will drink iced coffee all year round. I decide it's the perfect day to take Winnie out to Sailor's Point, and it's secluded enough that I don't have to keep him on a leash.

I spend the rest of the morning cleaning house so that when I come home exhausted later I can relax. After eating lunch, we head out. It's about a twenty-five minute drive before we're climbing out of my Honda Pilot in this beautiful countryside.

I hook Winnie up to his harness to start, with the intention of taking him off of it when we start the hiking trail. I make sure I have enough water for both of us, and of course a snack for when we reach the top.

Winnie excitedly paces on the leash while I'm getting all geared up. A little whimper comes out as he nudges my hand. I smile. "Hold on, big guy, let me get this backpack on, and we can head out." I scratch his ear before slipping the straps on.

Locking the car, we head off in the direction of the hiking trails. It's the best this time of year when the tree leaves are beautiful hues of orange, red, yellow and green. I take a deep inhale of fresh air, and a calmness washes over me. I didn't know how much I needed this until I got here. A little bit of exercise on one of my favorite trails will put me into the perfect mindset.

The trail starts out on a semi flat. During the summer, the trail is more defined from the constant stream of hikers. But now? It seems to be a bit overgrown, like it's been awhile since the last hiker was here. A little overgrowth is perfect for what I have planned.

"Come here, Winnie boy!" He comes to me and immediately joins me at my side. I give him a treat I have stashed in my pocket. "Good boy. Okay, I'm going to let you stretch your legs a little bit." As soon as I unhook him from the leash, he stands at my side as I keep my hand on his harness. I shake my head as he shimmies in both excitement and anticipation for what's to come.

The moment I let go, his nose hits the ground and he starts running around. He's in his element. A smile blooms on my face as I watch him explore, following closely behind him.

Forty-five minutes later, I'm huffing and puffing as we reach the top of the trail.

❧❧❧❧ ❦❦❦❦

We take a break at the top so we can both drink some water. Winnie sniffs and runs around some more. God, I'm out of shape, and I know my body is going to be sore tomorrow. I love the pain of a good workout the day after, but it's *building* the habit of working out that's hard for me. I have my shit together when it comes to work, my fitness goals doesn't always match. Winnie has been a great reason to keep to my routine. I promise myself that we are going to walk the trails every weekend.

The sight around us is absolutely beautiful. The trail ends at the top of a high mountain, overlooking a breathtaking expanse of autumn colors. Reds, yellows, and browns scatter across the horizon. The breeze is starting to chill as the warmth disappears with the sun behind the mountain off in the distance. I take in my surroundings, enjoying the silence of nature. A few minutes later, I decide we should head back before the sun fully sets.

I whistle Winnie over, and because he responds instantly, I reinforce his behavior with a treat and affirmation. "Well, what do you say, my boy? Should we head back down now?" I scratch his head and then laugh at myself. "Look at me, talking to you like you're going to answer." Shaking my head, I gesture to Winnie that we're leaving . He's a quick learner, picking up everything I've been working on with him.

We make our way back down the trail to the car. It's always easier when you're going downhill. We've almost reached the bottom when Winnie darts to the right, a growl exploding from his throat.

"What the– Winnie, here!" I yell. Hoping he heard me and will come back to the command. Instead, all I hear is the rustle of the bushes. My heart stops when I hear Winnie yelp.

I panic.

"Winnie, where are you? Winnie, here!" I start to move off the trail in the direction of where he darted. I don't make it too far when I start to hear the rustle of bushes again. Winnie runs out, his pace panicked.

I instantly know something is wrong.

There's something on his snout. He's moving too fast for me to get a good look, but when he circles around behind me, he angles his head down and uses his front paw to scrub at his face. Crouching down to try and get a better look at his face, I softly say his name. I manage to get his head up and see half his snout covered in porcupine quills.

"Oh my God, Winnie! Look at your face!" He makes a smacking noise and it's then I notice porcupine quills in his mouth too. "Oh Jesus, okay. Come on my boy, let's get you out of here. Oh my God, we need to get you to a vet."

I hook him back up to his leash and begin to race back to the car but that seems futile, as Winnie continues to stop and paw at his face. Without thinking it through, I pick him up and make my way back to the car as fast as I can. I haven't even figured out a vet for Winnie yet. Why didn't I do this sooner? God I'm such an idiot. There has to be something close by.

As soon as Winnie is into the back of the car and situated, I jump into the driver's seat, pulling out my phone. I search "vets near me" in Google, and get a couple options. I choose the first one I see and press call.

It rings three times before someone on the other side answers. "Hawthorne Creature Clinic, my name is Todd. How can I help you today?"

"Hi there, I'm sorry to bother you. My dog just got attacked by a porcupine. We aren't a client, but you're the closest vet clinic from where we are. Do you offer emergency services? Or is there any way we could see someone today?" I rush out. I'm not even confident that I have taken a breath since Todd picked up.

"Oh my! The poor thing! Let me just look to see if we can squeeze you!" He puts me on hold, and my knee bounces while I wait. After what feels like forever, the receptionist returns. "Good news! We can fit you in today, why don't you make your way over, and we will get you all situated with everything once you get here! I just need your name and your dog's name."

Sighing with relief, I reply. "Yes of course! My name's Harper Beckett and my dog is Winnie! I should be there in about twenty minutes! Thank you so much!" I end the call then turn the car on. I put the location into my GPS and make my way over to the vet clinic. I can hear Winnie pacing in the back seat, with the occasional whimper coming from him. Poor guy must be in so much pain with all those needles in his snout.

"It's okay buddy, we're going to get you some help right now."

Fifteen minutes later we're pulling up to a little farmhouse. It's gorgeous. Though, it could use a little TLC. As cute as the house is, I'm assuming that this isn't the clinic. Following around the driveway to the other side of the house, I see what looks to be a barn. As I get closer though, I spot the sign *Hawthorne Creature Clinic*. Thank God I'm at the right place and didn't just drive into someone's property. That would have been embarrassing.

I park quickly and get Winnie out. Cold air rushes over my face as Winnie and I push inside. The barn's interior is a drastic change from the rustic exterior. The muted colors of the office interior is just like any other– rows of chairs, a line of doors down one side, and people waiting. Along the walls are cute black and white photos accompanied by a row of doors. I assume those are the examination rooms, and across from the doors is the seating area.

Walking up to the front desk I'm greeted with a friendly smile. "Hi there! Welcome to *Hawthorne Creature Clinic*, do you have an appointment?" I look down at their name tag and see the name Todd labeled on there, in slightly smaller font underneath it says *they/them*.

"Uh hey, yes. I called about twenty minutes ago regarding my dog Winnie."

"Oh yes!" They reply and stand up to look over the desk and pouts when they see the condition of Winnie. "Oh you poor baby! Okay, I just need you to walk him over to the scale behind you so we can get his weight and then I'll show you to the room." They point to the scale and I walk him over. "Okay, looks like he is forty kilos. I have this form I need you to fill out, but you can do that while you're waiting for Dr. Hawthorne." They motion their arm toward the second door and I follow behind them into the examination room. After thanking them, they hand me the clipboard and shut the door.

The exam room is orderly with its metal table and a chair off to the side. The room has a sterile feel and smell, but that's a good thing for a vet's office. I sit down in the chair and start to fill out the information form. I am so thankful I decided to keep the pet insurance the shelter offered, because it will help with some of this bill. Winnie is laying in between my legs. He's nervous, which is understandable. He's in pain, I took him to this strange building and I'm sure everything smells funny to him.

I give him a few pats on his head, avoiding any quills, and then continue filling out the form. I'm so consumed with all the questions, I don't even realise the door opens until I hear the most soothingly, deep voice.

"I heard that we lost a fight with a porcupine today." The vet walks in looking at his tablet, which I'm assuming has Winnie's basic information on it. He looks up at me, and I freeze.

No.

There is no way.

Because the man standing in front of me is no other than Xavier. Dalton's new girlfriend's *hot* brother. *He's* the man who is going to be taking care of my dog.

I'm sure I look like a fool sitting here staring at him with wide eyes. He raises an eyebrow, expectantly.

Shit. I should introduce myself.

"Hi!" I say as I stand up, "Yes, he most certai—" My sentence is interrupted as I topple forward. I was so flustered, I forgot that Winnie was resting between my legs, and as I stood up to shake his hand I completely tripped over my dog.

Everything happens in slow motion, and there's absolutely nothing I could do to avoid what's about to happen. Horror and panic wash over me as the hand that I intended to use to shake his drops to the front of his pants. I basically grab his crotch as I fall to the ground.

I let Jesus take the wheel and accept my fate of face planting on the floor. The floor never comes though, because suddenly I am suspended above the ground. My foot flies forward to balance myself better as strong hands grip my shoulders.

"Oh my God, I am so sorry," I stammer, as I struggle to straighten myself out. Heat rushes to my face, and with my complexion, I probably look like a summer strawberry right now.

I hear a curt voice above me. "It's fine. Really. So, tell me what happened."

My eyes flick up to his face, and I'm met with a hard look. Deep midnight blue eyes piercing me paired with a sort of scowl on his face. Great. I've pissed him off. This is going so well. I start to wring my hands together, before sitting back down in my chair.

"So, we were out at the Sailors Point trail, I've been working on his off leash training. On our way back, he just took off into the bush. I tried to call him back then I just heard him yelp. By the time I found him he was like this. You guys were the closest place. Thank goodness you guys had an opening. He's the first dog I've gotten on my own." I continue to look at my hands, knowing that the next words out of my mouth are just going to be pure word vomit. "To be honest, I don't know what I'm doing. I adopted Winnie on a whim when I walked by the shelter and saw that they were having an adoption fair. Not that I randomly decided that I was going to get a dog, I've been thinking about getting a dog for awhile. My ex and I were talking about getting one. Then *that* ended, but I still wanted to follow through and get a dog. It was like fate when I came across this adoption fair. When I saw Winnie, I just instantly connected with him. He's probably one of the best things to happen to me." I let out a big gush of air.

I'm met with silence. I haven't looked up at him since I started rambling. Giving myself the courage, I glance up, and what I see was not what I was expecting. Winnie is on his back, getting tummy scratches. If he didn't have the obvious quills coming out of his face, you wouldn't have guessed anything was going on with this dog. *What a big baby.*

But that isn't what made me pause. What stopped me was the small smile that was on Xavier's face when he was focusing on Winnie. I'm amazed at how he was able to keep him calm and look at his face at the same time. I didn't even realize that he was checking him out. I thought we were sitting in awkward silence at my accidental crotch grab.

"So, these don't look too deep." He says, snapping me out of my thought bubble. "I'm still going to have to take him back and put him under anesthesia to get these quills out though. It'll allow him to be still and for me be able to take them out without possibility of any quills breaking and staying embedded. Plus, this way he won't react when I do it, which can cause him to tear things open more. We don't want that."

A million scenarios and questions run through my head.

"How long will it take?"

"It shouldn't take too long, no longer than two hours. Like I said before these quills don't seem to be too embedded so I don't think it will take me too long to remove them all successfully. I'll send you home with some antibiotics and something for the pain." His eyes focused on his tablet, his finger moving along the screen. "My assistant will go over all of this with you before you take him home for the day. I'm just going to go back and get everything sorted out. Someone will be back to come and get Winnie. Do you have any other questions?"

I shake my head. I look down at Winnie, and feel the prickle of tears starting at the back of my eyes. I look up at the ceiling, blinking rapidly trying to clear it away.

Clearing my throat, "No. Uh, actually. Is there additional paperwork or anything I need to fill out?"

"Yes, there will be a consent form for you to sign. One of my techs will come with the forms for you to sign, then they'll take the big guy back to get him prepped. You can stay in the waiting room while we're working on him."

I nod my head, while carefully scratching Winnie's ear.

"Than—" I'm cut off by the click of the door. I realize that he just left the room without a word.

"Well, okay then." I take a few deep breaths and continue to give Winnie attention until he inevitably gets taken back for surgery. I signed the forms that were given to me and was redirected to the waiting area. I couldn't imagine myself leaving the vet while Winne was being worked on. Plus, we live out of town, so it doesn't really make sense.

An hour later, I start to get stir-crazy. I was able to pass some time answering work emails, but now, the silence is uncomfortable. I pull up Evie's number and hit the call button.

"Hey babes! I was actually just thinking about you! I was going to see if you wanted to go out for drinks tonight!" The happy-go-lucky chimes of my favorite human instantly calm my nerves.

"Honestly? After the day that I've had, that sounds fantastic." I huff as I run my fingers through my hair.

"What's wrong?"

"Oh God, where do I even begin? First, I went out to Sailors Point. I've been working with Winnie on his off leash training, and it's the first time we've done it outside of the backyard. I can only do it so many times in the backyard before we have to actually try it out in public, you know? He's been doing so well, and we were on our way back down. But out of nowhere, he takes off, and then I hear him yelp. So I race over to find him, and his poor face is covered in porcupine quills."

I hear a gasp come from Evie before I continue.

"So, I got him in the car, and looked up the closest vet. Thankfully, they could see him right away. I'm sitting there in the exam room and you would *not* even fathom a guess on who comes through the staff door to check out Winnie's face."

She's silent for a minute. "Okay, spill, bitch! Don't keep me waiting."

I huff a laugh, "No one other than the hot brother of Dalton's new boo."

"Shut. The. Fuck. Up."

"Oh, but it gets better. Me being in the absolute shocked state that I was, stood up to shake his hand and introduce myself. Well, I flipping trip over Winnie and go down. Not only do I fall into him, but he catches me before I face plant onto the ground. And as I was falling down, I threw my hands forward at an attempt to catch myself but ended up copping a feel of the guy's junk. Evie, it was so embarrassing and he was so short with me. I think I totally offended him." At this point I'm leaning forward with my elbows resting on my knees. One hand holding my phone, the other holding up my head as I look at my feet.

There is silence, and I check my phone to see if it's still connected. Then all of a sudden I hear a snort, followed by a roar of laughter. "You... yo—." There's a brief pause for more snorts to escape then she continues, "Shut the fuck up." More laughter follows.

I give her a minute before I finally say something. "Yeah, yeah. I know. I don't even think I could ever look him in the face again. I'm hoping that his assistant comes to let me know how everything goes."

I stay on the phone with Evie, and she does her best to keep me distracted. She's actually doing a great job too. She even got me laughing a few times too.

"Miss Beckett?"

"Evie, I gotta go. I'll text you." I don't give her a chance to reply, and hang up so I can focus my attention on the lady in scrubs in front of me.

"Hi, yes that's me! Sorry about that. How is he?" I start to wring my fingers nervously.

She gives me a small smile, "We were able to successfully get all the quills out. He is having a little trouble coming out of anesthesia. It's nothing to worry about, but he's a bit more sluggish than we would like. So, we would like to keep him overnight."

"What does that mean? Is he going to be ok?" I feel my chest starting to tighten, anxiety starting to claw at me.

"Oh yes, we have no concerns that he won't come out of this! It's just precautionary, we have a staff who stays overnight and keeps an eye on them. And Dr. Hawthorne lives on the property if there are any emergencies. I want to assure you, I don't have the slightest concern that we're going to need to call him."

The tightness starts to ease in my chest a bit; the fact that they have a staff who stays overnight is comforting. I know he won't be left alone all night. The assistant works with me to sort everything out, and we go over the bill before I pay for everything. I say a silent goodbye to the chunk of money leaving my bank account. They let me go back to say goodnight to Winnie, assuring me that he will be fine for the night. He was asleep when I went in there, surely sleeping off the remainder of the drugs in his system, but he looked good.

I feel comfortable enough to leave and head home. I text Evie giving her the update, and finalising our plans to meet at O'Shays, one of the local bars we have. It's one that Evie and I always go to when we need a girls night. It has karaoke on Fridays, and the drinks are amazing. It's like a hidden gem in the city and I absolutely love it because it doesn't get crazy busy.

And after the day that I've had, I totally need a drink... or three.

Chapter Eight

xavier

I FORGOT TONIGHT WAS *Karaoke night...*

I grimace as I hear the intro of *The Bad Touch* by the Bloodhound Gang start. I understand wanting to blow off some steam while belting out some good music, but there are certain songs that are tacky. This is one of those songs.

Don't get me wrong, all I want to do is let off a bit of steam too. Today was absolutely ridiculous. We were completely booked to the brim today, but I still took on that extra emergency appointment. As soon as I heard that the dog had a run in with a porcupine, I couldn't let the poor thing wait.

So, I ended up working through my lunch break instead to make sure that we didn't fall behind. To say that was a terrible idea is an understatement. I may have gotten a little grumbly and short, and wasn't my usual self. When I'm at work, I'm my happiest. I love being able to help animals and make sure they're healthy. I get so committed that I skip meals when I shouldn't.

Which leads me here.

I'm sitting at O'Shays, waiting on my double bacon cheeseburger and fries, and sipping on a whiskey on the rocks. As chaotic as the day was, I kept going back to the same moment of my day. The woman from the emergency appointment. She looks so familiar but I can't place my finger on where.

Her emerald eyes captivated me and held me hostage like I was caught in a snare. I wanted to continue to be trapped in them, but was interrupted when she hastily got up and proceeded to trip over her dog. I watched as the movement tumbled her forward and I acted on instinct, catching her. I wasn't fast enough to prevent the graze of her hand over my cock, which twitched at the contact.

I helped her upright and immediately took my hands off her. A feeling washed through me that I haven't felt in so long, and it made my head spin. I could blame the lack of food as my reasoning for being so short with her, but it was more than that. The zing I felt from a mere touch put me on edge, and it sent me back to the last time I felt like that. And that threw me off more than the lack of lunch. As soon as I got everything sorted out with her dog, I ran out of that room, letting my assistant take over.

I needed fresh air, I felt like my lungs were constricting. Busting through the back door I walked toward the picnic table. I put it out here for the staff, so they have a place to sit outside on the nice days we have so they aren't cooped up in the staff room to eat their meals or take their breaks.

Thankfully nobody is out here while I deal with my inner turmoil. I don't have the time for this today, so I sit down at the picnic table, putting my head between my legs as I take a deep breath. In for four, out for four. It's the only calming tactic that has ever worked for me, and I take solace in that as my heart rate begins to calm down.

I'm brought back to the now as my plate of food is placed in front of me. I nod my thanks to the server and dig in. I try to hold in the groan of approval with that first bite of the delicious cheesy goodness that is this burger. This is exactly what I needed. There is something so comforting about greasy food after a long day. Especially when having zero desire to cook my own meal. I'm no stranger to the kitchen, in fact, I actually like cooking. I find it relaxing. Being able to follow a recipe, mixing in all the ingredients and creating something that's so good.

Once I was old enough, I started paying attention more to cooking. Edith, my parents cook, took me under her wing when I was ten years old. She used to catch me often peeking through the doors watching the kitchen. I thought that was where all the magic happens. The food was always good at home. Edith cooked the best meals, and she made something new once a month, just to spice things up. After the thousandth time that she caught me watching, she finally told me to come in. Grabbing a stool she placed it beside her, she waved me over. "Come here boy, if you're going to be peeking through that door while I'm cooking you might as well learn something."

It was probably one of my favorite memories from my childhood. And probably why I find cooking and food so comforting.

I wouldn't necessarily say my parents were uninvolved in our lives. My parents did support me through all my endeavors when it came to sports and school events. They were always there, but there was an appearance to uphold when it came to these social events. My mother being the social elitist that she is, she always made sure she was involved in *everything*. Spearheading everything that had to do with the PTA, taking the lead in organizing any social gatherings, fundraisers, you name it and she was running it. She was the president of the PTA, after all.

But just because your parents appear to be involved in your life, it doesn't necessarily mean they are there for you. I had to face many demons without them. Hell I'm still facing demons that they know absolutely nothing about because I stopped trying to confide in them a long time ago.

I feel my phone buzzing in my pocket, and I pull it out to see who it is. With a smile on my face, I accept the call.

"Monty, my guy. How are you doing?"

"Oh, I'm not bad, just looking at this sad brute at the bar stuffing his face full of meat."

I burst out laughing and turn around just in time to see my friend, Ben Montgomery, or Monty, making his way to my side. With a slap on my shoulders, he takes the stool next to me.

"What brings your ugly mug to a grungy old place like this?" I ask him, taking a sip of my drink.

Monty signals for the bartender, who comes up seconds later. He orders his drink, then looks at me. "Well, I haven't talked with you in a bit. I just happened to be driving by when I saw your Ford in the parking lot, so I figured that I would pop in and surprise you. Make sure you haven't been body snatched or some shit."

I lift my hands at his statement. "Okay, okay, I get it. The clinic has just been super busy with the upcoming renovations for the spay and neuter clinic, and I've done nothing but eat, sleep and work." I run my hand through my hair, like I've been doing a lot lately. It's getting a bit long. I've been debating whether I should cut it or grow it out again.

I huff a sigh, dipping my gaze from his, briefly. I really haven't been keeping in touch lately, now I feel like a dick. "I'm sorry I haven't been reaching out in a bit. How are you doing? How about Josie and the rugrat?"

Monty smirks. "Oh, they're the same as usual. Josie is about six months pregnant now, and she's starting to feel a bit uncomfortable. Cries at the drop of a hat. The other night I came to bed and she was bawling. I asked her what was the matter. She was crying because she couldn't find her glasses. And when I pointed that they were sitting on the top of her head, she cried even harder. I tell you man, pregnancy hormones are wild." Shaking his head, "Shiloh isn't much better. Giving us both a run for our money."

I chuckle, "Is Shiloh still crawling in your bed at night?"

"Nah man, he's finally sleeping in his own bed. But now, he wakes up purely just to wake us up. He isn't even completely awake either. He wakes up, wakes Josie up, who then wakes me up. I walk him back to bed and he crawls in, rolls over, and goes back to sleep." He shakes his head with a huff of disbelief, "Like what the fuck?"

He scratches his chin and then takes a drink of his beer. "I mean I'm thankful for the kid to be in his own bed, especially before the new baby is here. I can't even imagine how it would be trying to get him in his own bed with a newborn."

"Hopefully he doesn't regress and wants back in once the baby is −" I don't even get to finish my sentence before there is pain radiating in my shoulder from the punch Monty just gave me.

"Don't jinx that shit man. Or I swear to fuck whenever you have kids I'm going to buy them the noisiest toys."

Rubbing my shoulder, I grumble, "okay, man, shit." We look at each other then start laughing.

We spend the next hour catching up on everything. I make a promise that we will try to get together once a week to shoot the shit, even if it means he helps me with some maintenance around the farm. If I have to chase Clyde out of my back porch one more time I'm going to lose it.

I forget what time it is, but I don't forget that it's still karaoke night. The horrible singers have been making background noise as we have our conversation. I think I'm about to call it a night when I hear a familiar tune come up on the machine. While waiting for the person to start singing, I send a silent prayer that whoever it is doesn't butcher one of my favorite songs. My back straightens as I hear the first line of the song come out of the speakers. I know that voice. It's the voice I've been thinking about on repeat all day.

I quickly turn myself around on my stool, facing toward the stage and there she is. Her jet black hair is curled and laying placed off to the one side of her shoulder. She's wearing this romper outfit that hugs her luscious curves. The material stretches over her thick thighs, over the curve of her hips. They look perfect enough to have a good grip on them. My eyes move up to her breasts that are pushed nicely together, accentuated by the low cut of her romper. She looks so relaxed and carefree as she sings. She's pointing at someone in the crowd, and I immediately follow her pointed finger to see who it's pointed at.

I find myself relieved when I see that she's just pointing to another girl who is singing back to her. The relief doesn't last long. Just because she's singing to another woman doesn't mean they can't be together. I should understand that the most, not judging someone based on their looks. You never know who someone is attracted to. I find myself looking for the connection first, and if there is no connection, it doesn't matter how attractive the person can be. If that spark isn't there then that's it.

The song starts to end, and I haven't taken my eyes off her this entire time. I have no idea if Monty has continued talking to me because I'm not even remotely trying to pay attention, and I'm not even sorry about it. Just as she's belting out the next words, deep emerald eyes connect with mine. I see her eyes widen in surprise, and I'm sure mine match. I wasn't expecting her to be able to spot me in the busy pub. But when our eyes are connected, there was no way I would look away. I see her eyes trail down as much as my body as I'm sure she can see. And when her eyes make their way back up, meeting with mine, I give her a small smirk. Her eyes widen slightly more before she finishes her song, puts the mic back in place and runs off the stage looking at her feet.

I hear a chuckle off to my right, and I look over to see my oldest friend staring at me with a knowing smirk.

"What?" I level him with a look. He laughs and holds up his hands.

"It's nothing." He scrubs his hand across his jaw before continuing, "I just haven't seen that look on your face in a long time. Not since..." Monty trails off, a knowing look crossing his face.

"Don't. It's nothing like that. She's just a girl who came into the clinic today. I helped her dog by getting some porcupine quills out of his face."

I hear the hiss come from his voice. "Shit, that poor dog. That must have hurt." He shakes his head and takes a swig of his beer.

"Yeah, the whole appointment was different. I mean I've dealt with quills before. This isn't my first rodeo, you know? But I took it on as an extra, so I skipped lunch to make sure I didn't fall behind."

"Ah yes, a hangry Xavier isn't something you want to mess with. I feel sorry for any poor fucker who had to deal with you." Monty chuckles, and he reaches over to try and grab one of my fries.

"Fuck off these are mine!" I move my plate away from his grabby hands before he can get to it. I proceed to grab a fry and put it in my mouth. What can I say? Sometimes I can be a little feral when I haven't eaten, and I don't like to share my food.

I hear a guffaw from my friend before he says, "Right right. *Joey doesn't share food.* How could I forget." He gets a smirk from me from quoting one of my favorite TV shows, before I dig back into my food, finishing off the remainder that's left.

"So was this girl a poor victim of the dreaded hangry bear?"

I grumble, "maybe. A little bit. But I was also an autopilot just trying to survive. Although it was kind of funny. When I came into the room, I was looking at his charts, just trying to familiarise myself a bit more with the dog. Just as I lifted my head I had to toss my tablet onto the counter to catch this woman who was toppling over her dog and heading toward the ground. I was able to catch her but not before she got a handful of my cock on her way down."

Monty tilts his head back and bellows a laugh as he takes in the story. "You're joking," with a serious look given to him he laughs even more. He's keeled over, wiping his eyes from the tears that are falling from his eyes. I roll my eyes, I go to take a drink and realise that it's gone. Signalling to the bartender that we'll both have another, the bartender is quick to give me a refill. I turn to face Monty and pin him with a look.

"Why don't you ask her out?"

I half spit, half choke on my drink. I begin coughing to get the burn of whiskey out of my throat before I look at him. "Excuse me?"

"You heard me. Ask her out."

"No, thanks."

"Mhmm, and why not?"

"Because I don't need a girlfriend. I can't sacrifice the time I have to allot to someone else. I have the clinic that I pour my blood, sweat, and tears into. We're so close to the renovations starting, I can taste it. Once those start then I really won't have time for anyone else." I feel like a goddamn broken record. What is it with everyone trying to set me up lately? I huff and shake my head before downing the rest of my drink and slamming it on the bar top. "I mean, between you and my mother, I swear."

Monty examines me for a moment before humming and saying, "Well I mean. You ask her out, take her on a date or two. And your mom will get off your back for a bit at least."

I sit there for a minute contemplating what he's saying. I mean, he's got a point. If I ask her out and take her out once or twice it will give me enough leverage to shut my mother up. Then when it inevitably ends, which it will, I can chalk it up to just not working out and she'll back off for a while longer. It would give me enough time to potentially get through the renovations at the clinic before she starts bugging me again.

I tilt my head to the side, then point at my friend thoughtfully. "You do have a good point there, Monty." Just as I finish that sentence, I hear the sweet as honey voice behind me ordering a drink at the bar. Monty pats my shoulder before signalling to the bartender that he wants to square up his tab. With that, I know he's going to quietly sneak out and let me do what I need to do. What I *want* to do. Do I want to do this? No. Yes. Maybe.

Fuck, just get it together and ask her out for Christ's sakes.

I swivel myself around in the direction of the voice that may very well haunt me. I take a moment to get a closer look at her, I was in such a haze at the clinic that I barely paid attention. Getting closer, I can see her luscious lips. They're just waiting to be bit. *Woah, where did that come from?* Before I think anymore into it, I clear my throat to hopefully catch her attention.

"So, have you fallen into any other guys' laps recently? Or was it just me?" I see her back straighten before she turns her head toward me and glares. *Shit. That sounded dickish.*

"Shit, sorry. I didn't mean it like that. I just said the first thing that came to my brain. It's been a long day." I rub my hand at the back of my neck and give her a sheepish smile.

She stares at me for a minute, before her eyes begin to sparkle with mischief and she smirks. "I think that's very daring to ask a lady before even offering her a drink to lessen the blow of her embarrassment today."

I chuckle, "Well we couldn't have that. What are you drinking?"

She hums, pressing her pointer finger to her chin and taps it in thought, "Vodka, soda and lime please!" I signal the bartender, who comes up and I order our drinks. When we both have fresh drinks in front of us, I wave my hand at the open bar seat beside me. "Sit."

Her eyes widen slightly and she quickly sits. I notice the tint of pink on her cheeks as she focuses on her drink instead of making eye contact. Well that won't do. I take my forefinger and place it under her chin, bringing her gaze up to mine. I notice the breathless gasp that comes from her mouth before my eyes bounce back and forth between her own. She's got the most hypnotising emerald eyes. "I wanted to start off by saying sorry." I start.

Her nose wrinkled with confusion. "What do you mean you're sorry? If anything, I should be apologising to you. I mean, I copped a feel before I even had a chance to introduce myself. It's Harper, by the way. In case you forgot, which I understand if you did. I'm only one measly pet owner in your busy day of work." Her hand flies to my bicep, eliciting sparks along my skin. "Oh my God, which reminds me again, I'm so sorry about that. I don't even know what I was thinking. I totally forgot Winnie was at my feet when I stood up to shake your hand. God, I still can't believe I did that. I mean you're YOU Mr. Gorgeous Vet." she says, waving her hands between us. "Saving all the animals, then there's little ol' me. Well, not little. Far from that, I mean, I try and –" I chuckle, and decide at that point to put her out of her misery.

"It's fine. I could tell you were a first time pet owner." I grab my drink and take a sip. She follows suit quickly, and the pink tint on her cheeks has deepened to a rosy shade. "And I wanted to apologize if I came off as short today. I had skipped my lunch to make sure appointments wouldn't run behind. I've been told I can be a little abrasive when I skip a meal." Now I'm avoiding looking at her, and I'm not entirely sure why.

I feel her hand cover mine. My eyes shoot to hers, and the zing that goes through my body immediately makes me uncomfortable.

I pull my hand from hers. Harper pulls hers back to her lap and begins playing with them. "It's okay, no need to apologize," she says softly. "I know I become almost feral when I miss a meal, especially when I'm so caught up in work. I don't even realize it until my stomach started screaming at me." She tilts her head up to look at me with a gentle smile playing on her face.

"Well, I feel like I should make it up to you somehow. Could I buy you another drink?"

She looks at me for a moment, then down at her drink. She nods. "Yes, I'd like that. Thank you."

We spend the next hour just talking. I find it surprisingly easy to talk to her. The silence is filled with Harper rambling but I don't find it annoying. When she does ask me about myself, she listens and doesn't interrupt. She follows up with questions, and it's like a breath of fresh air. My only social interactions lately have been with my parents, staff or animals.

She's laughing at her own joke when a snort comes out of her. Her eyes widen in horror. "Oh my god, I cannot believe that I actually just did that." She covers her face with her hands, placing her head on the bar top.

I chuckle. "Don't worry, it's endearing."

"Ugh, of course you would say that." She says in disbelief. Her head swings up, gaze meeting mine. I raise my eyebrow in question. "I just mean, you're just so," She waves her hands up and down my body like I'm supposed to understand what that means.

She sees the look on my face and huffs before continuing. "I just mean, you're this gorgeous guy, and don't give me some egotistical smirk or baffle like you don't already know this. Clearly, you do. But you care for animals, and you have your own shelter. You're funny, and surprisingly easy to talk to. Never in a million years would I have ever thought that I would bump into you in a bar and strike up a conversation with you, and then you ask to buy me another drink. It's almost too good to be true, and it just makes me think something is fishy. Like that Chloe put you up to this or something–"

"Hold on." I interrupt, while putting both my hands up in a slow down motion.

Her eyes are the size of saucers, and I can see panic flaring in her eyes. "Oh my God, this isn't something like that. Oh my God. I'm so sorry. How stupid of me. I'm sure you don't even want to continue this. I'll go." She pushes from her seat, but I grab her hand and spin her back around.

"Don't go," I say. I can't let her go under the impression that I think anything bad.

"So, you mentioned my sister. How do you know her?"

She looks away from me, her hands go to her hair as she begins to play with it.

I make sure I keep my tone neutral. "I'm not going to judge. I'm just trying to understand what just happened, If you don't want to talk about it, that's fine as well. You shouldn't feel like you owe me anything."

She nods her head, filling her lungs with a deep breath. "No, it's okay. I mean, I let it slip already, so I might as well get it off my chest."

And that's exactly what she does.

She explains everything that's happened over the last few months. How her ex was distant but she didn't think anything of it. Their fight before he ended things, how she found messages between him and my sister dating back months. She even said how she found my Capture during a drunken night with her best friend. Although, I don't think she meant to let that slip, but when she starts rambling I hardly want to make her stop. I love listening to her talk. The moment from the clinic clicks, the missing pieces falling into place. What gets me the most is how poorly this piece of shit treated her. My sister's actions aren't surprising and furthermore, I knew I didn't like Dwight the moment I met him. When she finally finishes I can see the red lining her eyes, evidence she was restraining a cry while telling me this.

"Well fuck Deke. You don't need him anyway," I state.

She looks me in the face for a minute, confusion etched between her brows. Then she bursts out laughing. My head tilts in confusion as I try to figure out what's so funny. She snorts, and covers her mouth while laughing more. *What the hell is going on?*

When she finally calms down, she finally lets me in on what's so funny. "I'm sorry, did you call him Deke? You know his name is Dalton right?"

I look her dead in the eyes. "Really? I thought it was Deke or Duke or something. Hmm. Good to know." I shrug before taking a sip of my drink.

"Wait...I'm sorry, but do you call him Dalton at all?"

"Uh, I don't know? I guess Chloe did correct me a few times, but I didn't think much of it," I reply, shrugging as I finish my drink.

She snorts again, "This is fucking gold. Evie will love this." She sees the question written on my face, answering, "She's my best friend, and she's always hated him. So she's going to *love* this."

I nod with understanding. We sit in silence for a few minutes, the sounds of karaoke surrounding us.

Then it hits me.

"I think I have the perfect plan."

Chapter Nine

Harper

"I THINK I HAVE the perfect plan."

I look over at him and see the mischievous glint dancing in his crystal blue eyes. A little flutter of excitement works its way through my stomach from that look.

"And what would that be?"

His lips quirk to the side, resulting in the most panty dropping smirk I've ever come to experience first hand. Flutters start to reappear, descending deep into my core. I bring my thighs together to quell the ache that has started to form. Whatever he has planned, it's either going to be crazy, or too good to pass up.

"You see, this could benefit the both of us. You can get some revenge on Dukey boy, and I can get my parents off my back for a bit."

A scoff leaves me, and I find myself raising my eyebrow in question. "Get your parents off your back about what exactly?"

Sighing, he swirls his empty glass around on the bar top. "For as long as I can remember, my mother has been fixated on the fact that I'm single. Apparently, running a successful vet clinic doesn't mean anything if I don't also have someone by my side to show off my success." He shakes his head while looking into his cup. "She's made it her life's mission to find me someone to be with. She even set me up on a blind date once. She didn't tell me it was a blind date, I found out when this woman approached me knowing my name and introduced herself to me. Don't get me wrong, it's not that I don't want to find someone, but the clinic is thriving. I want to expand it and make it *better* for everyone who has pets. So that has been my focus."

I smile because the passion in his eyes is evident in how much he loves his job.

"I can say first hand how good you are at your job. Even if your bedside manner needs a little work." My shoulder softly bumps into his.

He sighs. "I swear to you I'm not always like that, you caught me on an off day." He looks at me with some defeat in his eyes, his smile a little sad.

"It's okay," I say. " I was just bugging you." I take a hefty gulp of my drink while the conversation stalls.

His lips lift briefly before his features turn more serious. "So, I guess what I'm asking you is– will you be my fake girlfriend?"

My thoughts slam to a halt, the question held up like a billboard in my head as I try to comprehend what he just asked. Is this really something I want to do? Fake dating? I don't know if I can prevent myself from falling for this gorgeous man, even unintentionally. And when this inevitably ends? I'll be left with a broken heart, while everyone else moves on with their lives.

But to see the look on Dalton's face when I show up to his new family dinner would be priceless. So *satisfying*. I'm still battling with myself on what to do when I'm brought back to the present when Xavier grumbles something under his breath. I wait for him to repeat it so I can actually hear him.

"This was a stupid idea, I'm sorry. Forget I brought it up." He raises his hand signaling to the bartender for another.

Slightly panicked, I reach out, gently placing my hand on his forearm. "No, no. Sorry, I'm just thinking it all through. To be honest I'm probably *overthinking* this whole thing. Let's just kind of go over what exactly it is that we would be doing." I don't look at him while I'm talking. I was so transfixed on the tattoos under my finger tips. I didn't realise how many tattoos he has, I mean, I saw he was tattooed on his Capture. But seeing them up close is a whole other experience, and I am mesmerised by the intricate work of the roses that work up his forearm, as it twists and curves around.

He clears his throat, and my eyes snap up to his. Heat creeps up my cheeks at being caught ogling his ink. I take my hand away quickly and grab for my drink, embarrassment swarming me. Then I do what I do best.

Word vomit.

Again.

"I just mean, are we just doing this for family dinners? Or are there other events that you need me to join you at? I don't have many outings per say where I'll need a fake boyfriend. I'm an editor, and I work from home so I don't have much going on. I'm not really close to my family, so there are no Christmas ordeals or dinners that need to take place. Evie is my only true family, and she's been there for me for as long as I can remember. The only other person I had was Dalton, but we both know how that went." I down the remainder of my drink, taking a moment to look around the bar. The sound of off-tune music floods the space, encouragement and soft laughter filling in around it. People truly enjoy karaoke night; it's magical, and I completely get it.

I spot Evie staring intently at me, and her stare alerts me to the fact that I'm rambling and making a fool of myself. She quickly jumps up, making her way toward me. "Anyways, so you know. Just ground rules. Planning. That kind of stuff. I like to plan, I like to know exactly what is going to happen, and if we could write it down somewhere that'd be awesome. While I like to plan, I swear I'd forget my own head if it wasn't attac—"

"Hi there! I'm Evie!" She interrupts by wrapping her arm around my shoulder, sinking into my side, extending her hand for a shake. Effectively silencing my onslaught of word vomit with a single action—perfect.

Amusement shines in his eyes, as a low rumble rises from his throat, smokey and thick, before he extends his hand to shake Evie's. "Hi, Xavier." When I look up I'm startled to see that his eyes haven't drifted from me. "I was just trying to make some plans with Harper here to get coffee sometime."

Stunned. Silence. My lips fall open in an "O" shape, and I'm unsure if I heard him right. He can't possibly be talking to me right? Wait, no. Of course he is, he said *Harper*. That's me. I'm Harper. *Holy shit, what?*

"Uh yeah! I mean, yeah coffee. Sounds good. Oh look! My drink is empty! I think I have had about enough for tonight though." I push the empty glass toward the other side of the bar and run my hands down my thighs. "Evie, are you ready to head out?"

Evie eyes me skeptically, but she nods. "Uh yeah, that was why I came over here. Our ride share is just about here."

I look over at Xavier, giving him a small smile. "Well, I guess that's it, then. It was really nice talking with you." I start to get up but feel a hand on my forearm. I look at the point of contact and then my eyes move over to those stunning blue eyes that are focused on me. A small smirk rests on his lips.

"Can I get your number?" he asks, voice low and directed only to me. "You know, so I can take you out for coffee?" He winks, and I realize he's asking me out to start our secret tryst.

He wants to pretend to date to get his parents off his back. I get the benefit of revenge on Dalton, and I get the satisfaction of seeing the shock on his face. Ha, that'd be a sight to see. I'm softly chuckling to myself but feel the energy shift. I look up and see Evie with a hand over her mouth, holding in a laugh at my expense. My eyes trail over to Xavier, and he's still looking at me, one eyebrow raised when our gazes collide.

"Uh yes, you can. Here one second, let me grab my phone." I reach for my pocket, and realize that it's not in there. My brows furrow as I try to think where I put my phone. I check my other pockets, then half mindedly hold my boobs to check if I put it in my bra at some point. Nope. Not there either. I reach to grab my purse next.

"If you're looking for your bag, it's right here." Evie passes me my bag. She's clearly been holding it the whole time. I grab it from her and find my phone. Thank God. I unlock the screen and open my contacts before I pass it over to him to fill out his information.

A second later I see his phone vibrate on the bar top. "You know, to make sure I have your number, too." He passes my phone back to me, and I put it back in my bag.

Xavier gives me a wink as he says good night, and I give a little wave as Evie drags me out the bar. A small smile forms at my lips as I replay the night, but as the cool air hits my face, Evie spins around and levels me with a stare.

"What?" I ask, feeling the heat prickle across my cheeks and neck. I begin fanning my face in an effort to cool down.

Evie raises an eyebrow at me and waits, challenging me. She plays her cards well. She knows I hate silence. So she just stands there, staring at me, with her arms crossed over her chest.

I survive for one minute before I give in. "Ugh, what! We had a couple drinks and we talked okay?"

Silence. *Fuck* she's good.

"We talked and we got to know each other a bit more. Not only is he easy on the eyes Ev, but he has a hobby farm of *rescued* animals he's encountered over the years." I throw my hands up in exasperation. "RESCUES ANIMALS!" I raise my voice for emphasis. "And then... *and then* I do what I do best. I word vomit. I got so anxious and nervous that this man is talking with me—not just through a screen— but is talking to *me. In person.* So, what do I do? I spew everything that could possibly come to my mind." I'm now pacing back and forth in front of Evie, who is trying to contain her giggles.

I point in her direction. "Stop it. This isn't funny!"

"It's kind of funny though, Harps." Evie shrugs, unbothered by the amount of words I've just said. "When you get drunk off a hot guy, the word vomit is uncontrollable."

"Yeah well, during my spewing, I let it slip about how Dalton cheated on me with his sister."

A gasped laugh comes from Evie, as her eyes widen. "Oh Harps. You didn't."

"Oh." I sarcastically laugh, "I sure as fuck did. I let it slip and tried to take the words back. At that point though, he encouraged me to share more."

"And you went ahead, didn't you?" Evie is holding back tears from laughter at this point. I'm glad someone is enjoying my misfortunes.

"You know damn well I did!" I exclaim, my hands raking through my hair. "And then you know what he said after all that?" I stop and turn my body to face my best friend, who just rotates her hand in a go on motion. "He says he has a great plan! That we should *date*! DATE! Not the," I raise my hands to form air quotes. "Romantic-I'm-interested-in-you way," I sigh. "He wants to fake-date so his parents get off his back and I can stick it to Dalton." I snort, remembering how Xavier refused to call Dalton by his actual name.

"This is ridiculous, right? I should text him right now and tell him no." I reach for my bag and begin searching for my phone. Before I can make any progress there are two palms on each of my shoulders.

"First. Take a breath. You're panicking. Follow my breathing." She takes a deep inhale. Lifting my head, I take a deep inhale. Then she slowly blows it out, and I follow suit. We do that a couple more times before she loosens the grip on my shoulders and lets go, taking a step back. "Better?"

I nod.

She returns my nod. "Good. Okay, now secondly. You should do it."

My mouth drops open. I didn't hear her correctly. I couldn't have, because if I did... She just suggested I go through with this whole thing.

"I'm sorry. What?"

Evie huffs out a sigh, rolling her eyes. "Oh please, you heard me babes. You should do it. He's hot, you're hot." I snort and Evie gives me a pointed glare. "Stop it. Don't act like you aren't hot."

"I mean... Sure if you like all this." I sarcastically say as I run my hands up and down my body, leaning into all my insecurities.

"Don't talk about my best friend like that. She's smart, gorgeous and any guy should get on their knees before her. If you were into girls, I would totally make you forget all about men." She ends with a smirk on her lips.

"Oh for fuck's sake Evie," I chuckle. Playfully I shove her shoulder, shaking my head. Evie came out as bisexual just after high school. She has no shame about it and will blatantly hit on any man or woman, whether they're straight or not. She doesn't sleep around. She just likes to flirt. I've only seen Evie in one serious relationship, if you could call it that. She distanced herself from me, the longer they were together the less I saw her. Until she showed up on my door in the middle of the night telling me it was over. Part of me wonders if it impacted the way she sees herself when it comes to relationships.

"You know I'm serious, babes! But I digress. What better way to get back at that cheating fucker than to show up at Thanksgiving dinner, unannounced, with Dalton and Chloe at the same table. I would *love* to be the fly on the wall when that happens."

"That sounds like a terrible idea." I laugh.

Evie shrugs. "Eh, maybe."

I give her a look.

We both burst into laughter. I link my arm in hers and we pile into our rideshare.

We sit in silence for the little time it takes to get back to my place. I let my forehead rest on the cool window, to ease some of the heat and the oncoming headache that's sure to happen. Then next thing I know, I'm being nudged awake by Evie, telling me we're home.

I shuffle out of the vehicle and we head inside. It feels weird being home without Winnie. He's only been in my life for a short period, but that furry creature already fills my heart with so much joy. Once through the door we kick off our shoes and I lock the front door.

"I'm going to go get us some water." Evie mumbles, shuffling in the direction of the kitchen. I head the opposite way to the bedroom. Walking into the en-suite, I quickly wash off my make-up and brush my teeth. I strip out of my clothes and pull the band t-shirt and shorts from last night back on. I pass by Evie, letting her get ready while I set up the TV.

Crawling under the duvet of my bed, I groan in satisfaction at the softness of the sheets. It feels like I'm being wrapped up in the warmest hugs when I cozy under them. I grab the remote, taking a moment to pull up a streaming app on TV while I wait for Evie. Grabbing my phone off the nightstand, I begin to scroll through social media. As I'm scrolling, I land upon a photo of a rustic bar top with two drinks on it—one with hues of red and a lime on the rim, the other holds a dark amber liquid. I instantly know these are our drinks from tonight, and my suspicion is confirmed when I see that it's his account. He'd posted the photo with the caption: 'Here's to new beginnings.'

I smile to myself, but let it quickly fade because I *can't* get my hopes up. It can't mean anything. We literally just met.

But I can't help the slight flutter my heart does when I think *what if?*

What if it becomes more?

Before I even know what I'm fully doing, I open my messages and input his contact. When I finish writing the message, I hesitate for a split second before muttering "fuck it."

> Harper: I don't remember if I said yes to coffee

Ugh that was stupid. Before I can double down, telling him to ignore me, bubbles dance on my screen. Fuck. He's typing, and before I can spiral further, my phone vibrates.

> Xavier: Well, I don't recall you saying no. So that must mean…

> Harper: As long as you don't mind my awkward word vomit about how hot you are, then when do you want to go?

> Harper: Omg. Forget I said that.

> Harper: Excuse me.

> Harper: I'm just going to go change my name and skip town.

Xavier: Lol I think your rambling is adorable, and great for my ego.

Xavier: How about Thursday afternoon?

Harper: Sounds great! Should we meet at Ruthies?

Xavier: Sure, but let's take our orders to go. It's much easier to get to know someone when we're walking or driving some-where

Harper: You're not going to murder me are you?

Xavier: Lol no. I promise

Harper: That sounds like something a murderer would say.

Xavier: I'll see you Thursday, Harper. Have a good sleep.

Harper: Goodnight.

There is a heavy plop on my bed as Evie jumps into it, laying on her side facing me, with her hand holding her head.

"What was that smile about?" she asks incredulously.

"Nothing. Just making those coffee date plans."

Evie squeals before she launches herself at me, a harumph leaving my body at the sudden contact. "I'm so proud of you! This is going to be the best revenge on that sleazeball!"

"Yeah, yeah. Now get off me!" I say, shoving her off.

We get comfortable in bed and I throw on *Brooklyn 99*, one of our go to comfort shows. We spend the next hour watching the show, laughing and joking. As I fall asleep, a wave of contentment wash over me.

Chapter Ten

Harper

T HE REST OF THE week goes by in a blur. Winnie came home earlier in the week, and I was thrilled to have him back. His face looked a bit rough but he's looking much better. We won't mention the cone of shame he was required to wear since he kept scratching his face. Silly goose.

It's finally Thursday, and I'm proud of myself for not cancelling on this coffee date. Xavier and I have been talking on and off throughout the week. He tells me little stories about himself, the animals he has, and how he came to have them.

I've been working on solidifying my schedule for the next couple weeks as a distraction for my nerves. Thanksgiving is next week, then it's two and a half weeks until Christmas. I gently remind myself I will be taking those two weeks off, no matter what. I will *not* talk myself into taking on a heavier load just so I can get ahead.

Now here I am, in my closet looking at the pile of clothes I've tossed on the floor after trying them on. "Come on Harps, get it together, it's just coffee." I tell myself while I look into the mirror. I've currently got my hair in curlers, some light neutral make up with my go-to deep red matte liquid lipstick. Currently, I'm wearing a pair of boyfriend style jeans with a black tank top. Reaching for my lucky red plaid sweater, I hesitated slightly. Coffee is *casual.* I remind myself as I grab my sweater and toss it on. I'm giving myself a final look in the mirror when my alarm goes off on my phone, warning me that if I don't leave in the next ten minutes, I'll be late.

I swear, if I didn't set alarms, I'd get so wrapped up in whatever I'm doing and be late. Being late today is not part of the plan. Deciding I'm happy, I grab my favorite pair of black combat boots and quickly run to the en-suite to take the curlers out. Some hair spray and hair tossing later, I'm giving Winnie a kiss and a dental treat before racing out the door.

⸎⸎⸎⸎⸎ ⸏⸏⸏⸏⸏

I arrive at Ruthie's five minutes before our agreed upon time, and I silently pat myself on the back. I make my way into the diner. It's quiet, the silence full of anticipation for the coming dinner rush. The waitresses are restocking when the bell above the door rings, announcing my arrival.

"Hi, sweetpea!" Ruthie yells from behind the counter as she puts a fresh pie in the display. I return her greeting with a smile. "Hi Ruthie! How's the diner been today?"

She waves her hand dismissively. "Oh, you know how it gets. It wasn't too long ago since you were my top waitress here. Running circles around these old bitties."

"Nice, Ruth." Denise scoffs with a shake of her head, but I catch the little smirk on her face as she reloads the napkin dispenser.

"Now, what brings you here without your partner-in-crime?" Ruthie asks, grabbing me a coffee cup.

"Actually," I start. "I'm going to be taking my drink to-go today, Ruthie, but I'm not ready to order just yet."

Ruthie's eyes shoot up both in surprise and with questions. Before I get the chance to reply, the bell above the diner door rings again. I don't turn around because there is no way he's here yet. No one ever shows up on time. After all, Dalton had always made me wait almost fifteen minutes past the time we planned to meet.

"Hey there, Ruthie. How is Mrs. Noris doing?" A voice says from behind me, the low timber making me press my lips together in anticipation. Quickly, I spin around and find a six-foot-something man wearing jeans and a dark green hoodie. He has a black baseball cap casually tossed backwards on his head. I don't know what it is about a man who wears his baseball hat backwards that makes me drool. *But holy hell.* When my eyes stop on his face, his piercing blue eyes are staring back at me. There's a little smirk on his face, and he gives me a once over as he comes to stand at my side.

"Oh, she's doing just fine, dear," Ruthie says with an endearing look on her face, a sly smile forming on her aged lips as she sees us together. "That cat I tell you, stubborn as an ox! She hated going in that carrier to go to the clinic, so I got the cold shoulder when we got home."

Xavier chuckles. "You know Ruthie, I've told you a million times. I can come to your house if it's such a struggle for Mrs. Noris. It's just a check up."

"Bah," she says with a wave of her hands. "I can handle her, it's fine. Now enough about me, what can I get you today? Some pie?" She leans on the counter, pointing at the pie case. "I just made this one fresh out of the oven! Or do you want some of my hot apple cider, I know it's your favorite"

"You like hot apple cider too?" I say in surprise. "I don't see many people drinking it. I love it in the fall around Thanksgiving, it just makes the season so much better." I've started playing with a napkin on the front table.

"It's my favorite fall drink actually, but I'll only get it from Ruthie." When I look up, he's giving Ruthie a grin and a wink. I smile to myself, then notice he's looking at me again. "Should we get two hot apple ciders to-go then?" My smile stays as I quickly nod my head. I reach to grab my wallet and get a bill to pay for my drink. When I get it out, Ruthie is already giving Xavier some change, and I slip the bill back into my purse. He turns, handing me one of the hot drinks. "Shall we?" he asks, motioning for the front door.

A soft smile forms on my lips as I get up to follow him out of Ruthies. We stand on the sidewalk for a moment, and the silence between us is louder than the noise all around.

"Soooo," I start, peeking at him through the corner of my eye.

Xavier chuckles softly to himself. "Well, we have a few options here." He pauses briefly, facing his body toward mine. I mimic his movement before he continues. "We could go out for a hike."

I snort. "Right. Because that went so well for me last time."

"Fair enough. Well then, that brings us to option two. What are your thoughts on ducks and goats?"

My heart picks up its pace. Is he suggesting we go to his hobby farm? The answer is absolutely yes. I try to calm my emotions because I don't want to come on too strong with my eagerness.

"I mean, I haven't met any in person before, so I don't have many thoughts."

"Would you like to meet some?"

"Uh, yes please!" I squeak out with such excitement, I start to bounce with energy before I catch myself. "Sorry." I clear my throat, and quickly school myself before looking back up to him. "Should I follow you out there?"

He shakes his head. "Nah. Why don't we take my truck, and I'll drive you back to your car after?" I'm sure my eyes look as wide as saucers. He holds up a hand in surrender, the other keeping a firm grip on his apple cider. "I still promise I'm not a serial killer. Truly just wanna bring you to my farm." It's his turn for his eyes to go wide at the realisation of what he just implied. "Uh, to see my animals! You know the rescue animals I have? Oh God." His hand raises to begin rubbing the back of his neck.

A chuckle bubbles out of my mouth before I can stop it. At least I'm not the only one who can blabber like a fool sometimes. "It's okay, if it's anyone who understands saying the awkward thing?" I shrug. "It's me." Our eyes connect, and there's a pregnant pause.

Xavier takes a step closer, he offers up his free hand. "Shall we, then?"

I put my hand in his, and follow him down the sidewalk. We finish the last of our apple ciders and toss them in a garbage can as we near his black Ford F-150. He opens the passenger side and motions for me to get in. I grab the support bar as I lift myself up. He makes sure I'm settled before he shuts the door and walks around the front. I take the moment to really watch him. He takes his baseball cap off, running his fingers through his hair before placing it back on his head...backwards. My stomach does little flutters at the sight. I begin to imagine what it would be like to take the cap off and toss it on the ground as I straddle his lap. My mind wanders, imagining my fingers combing through his hair, as his lips brush a path down my throat.

Woah. I shake my head out of that train of thought, pressing my thighs together to release the building tension. The driver side door opens, and Xavier is hopping up and buckling himself in before starting the truck.

"You ready?" He asks with ease.

"Let's do it."

The ride to his farm was chill. Xavier told me a couple stories about his donkey, Clyde, that had me crying from laughing so hard.

"Stop!" I snort. "He did not break into the porch."

"I wish I was kidding, I woke up to him laying on the couch I left in there. Needless to say, I got rid of it after."

"Did you actually get rid of it?" I ask, while wiping at my eyes.

There's a beat before he answers, "Okay, no. I moved it into his stall, and he sleeps on it every night."

"That is probably the sweetest thing I've heard." My breathing slows as the onslaught of laughter ends. The truck had stopped at this point, and I didn't even realize we were here. I unbuckle myself, moving to open my door, before I'm interrupted. "Wait, let me." Xavier, quick as the wind, unbuckles himself and opens his door, taking the time to hit the lock button before jumping out. Did he seriously just lock me in the truck to stop me from opening my door? He runs around the front of the truck, unlocks the door and opens it for me, then offers his hand.

I raise my eyebrow in question, as I take his hand and slide down the truck. My feet land awkwardly on the ground, sending me flying forward.

Again.

This time I crash into a solid wall of chest, the hand not holding his landing in the center of his broad chest as I stabilize myself.

"*Ohmygod*," I rush out, "I'm so sorry, my feet landed weird and I—"

"Really it's okay, I don't mind catching you when you fall."

Heat rushes up my cheeks, and I awkwardly tap his chest, then take a step back "Well thank you...Again, for catching me." I run my hands down my front, as if dusting myself off, but I'm really just trying to stop my hands from going clammy. "So, you promised me some ducks and donkeys."

"Uh yeah, follow me." He motions to the worn path circling the right side of the house. As soon as we round the corner, you can see the fenced area. I'm startled when I hear a loud bray coming from one side of the fencing. "Oh for fuck's sake." I hear Xavier mumble as he jogs over to the left side of the fenced area. And that's when I see it. A grey shaggy haired donkey with his head and front leg sticking out of part of the fencing. The poor thing looks like he was trying to get out and realized too late that he couldn't fit. I start laughing, but it dies quickly in my throat as Xavier's ass comes into sight. His dark blue Levi's perfectly formed around his back side.

I'm so transfixed on Xavier that I don't realize that he's already got the donkey out of the fence and back in his enclosure. He turns around and catches me so clearly checking him out. Quickly averting my eyes, I feel the heat of embarrassment make its way up my face. I try to think of something to say. Anything. But nothing comes out. My mouth opens and shuts with every attempt. When my eyes finally lock onto his, they are shining with amusement.

"It's a nice ass, eh?" He comments with a smirk. I look at him dumbfounded before finally snapping out of it.

"I mean, I don't want to boost your already large ego." I retort with triumph that I finally was able to say something back.

He throws his head back with a laugh. It's so hearty and carefree. I instantly know I want to hear it again, but I don't understand why he's laughing.

"I meant Clyde, my donkey." He uses his thumb to point behind him, in the direction of said donkey who was just stuck in the fence. I throw my hands over my face with a groan. "But I do appreciate the comment."

I peek through my fingers to stare at him, where he gives me a wink. "Come on, let me show you around."

Xavier spends the next hour showing me around his small farm. It's not anything like I've ever imagined. The more he tells me about it, the more I swoon at this man. Not only does he own all of these animals, but they're all rescued. In some way shape or form, he has taken them in when no one else has wanted them.

He tells me the story of Clyde and how he came to him as a baby. A farmer came to the clinic stating that the mom rejected him. The farmer was older, and he couldn't do the care that is needed for a baby donkey but didn't know what to do. Xavier said it didn't take him long to say he would take him but to give him the day to sort something out to accommodate the young foal.

"That's how this farm started though, with that doofus over there." He points at Clyde, who is currently chasing around a soccer ball and pushing it with his nose, braying happily. We are both leaned up on the fence to Clyde's area, watching him for a few minutes before he notices Xavier and comes trotting over. Clyde nudges at Xaviers neck and chin, rubbing his snout on him. Xavier laughs before pushing him off gently, "Alright, alright. I know what you want, give me a second." He looks over at me and smiles. "He wants a snack, let me run into the house and grab some apples and carrots for him, and then you can feed him." His eyebrows jump with enthusiasm.

"Me? Uh okay!" I've never had any experience with any sort of farm animal before, but it can't be that hard, right? Clyde has now moved over to me and is trying to get my attention. He fluffs my hair up with his snout, blowing air into my face. I squeak at the feelings, but turn to pat him. I start to scratch under his chin, and he seems to like that because he slows his movements, letting me continue. Until a moment later, when Xavier is making his way back. Clyde swivels his head in his direction, braying loudly. I turn around to see Xavier has started to lightly jog his way over with two carrots and an apple cut in half in his hand. When he reaches me, he passes off the carrots and then holds his hand out with one of the apples for Clyde to take. The ornery donkey wastes no time.

When Clyde has finished the apples, Xavier looks over to me, offering his hand. I go to give him the carrot, but instead, he grabs my wrist and directs my hand over to Clyde. "Oh I don't –" I begin. The carrot reaches close to Clyde and he begins to chomp on it happily. I let out a breath of a laugh as I watch Clyde eat. When the carrot is gone, the donkey sniffs around a bit before turning around and begins to run the loop of his enclosure.

I peer up at Xavier in awe. "That was so fun! I've never fed any sort of farm animal before! Realistically, I've never even *owned* an animal until Winnie. So I guess that just makes sense that I haven't. This was fun. Thank you for taking me here."

"I'm glad you like it. Come on, I have one more spot to show you." He tilts his head in the direction he wants us to go. I begin to follow him down a trail around the fenced area as he continues. "This spot is a little out of the way. It's where I keep the ducks. They have free range of the property, but they like this area because of the pond I made back here."

We round a corner and I see the body of water that's there. It's shaped like an hourglass, with a ramp at the top part of the water. It's encased in large slabs of stone that allow for a natural look. Behind the rocks there are various plants scattered around the circumference of the pond. By the ramp, it leads up to a small building that has an open door. I can't see what's in there from this distance but I'm assuming that's where the ducks go at night. There are outside string lights hanging in the trees, giving a soft illumination of the shaded area. I can see a few of the ducks swimming in the pond–wait. There are two types of ducks. The first couple are white feathered with orange beaks. Over by the shed, there are several ducks with a mix of brown, beige and white, and some that have a gray body mixed with brown and white and its head is green. I remember when I was growing up seeing those types of ducks at a campsite. We would go and feed them every once in a while, and they were super docile. I had one eat right out of my hand!

I smile at the memory, as I stare out in awe. "This is-" My sentence is cut off as I see two ducks barrelling toward us at a speed I've never seen before, using their wings as extra momentum to get to us faster.

Oh, shit.

Chapter Eleven

xavier

F UCK.

I was so caught up with watching Harpers expression as she was taking in the ducks enclosure that I forgot to give her the warning about these fuckers. The thing is, they're food motivated. I used to have treats in my pocket when I first got them. They caught on quickly that my pockets were always full of something, like they are right now. What they don't realize? It's only *me* who has the treats in their pocket.

So, when I see the wide eyed look on Harper's face before she starts booking it to the left side of the pond, I already know that these damn ducks have seen her pockets and set their targets on her. I try to intercept them as they power forward, but trying to herd ducks is just as bad as you think it is. They easily dodge my efforts and continue their pursuit of Harper.

She screeches as she continues to run. "Wait, Harper!" I try to warn her that she shouldn't go that way. It's uneven ground, and if you don't know where the holes are, it's guaranteed you'll fall. Harper isn't the most *graceful* of humans, either. Just as I'm about to call for her again, I see it happen in slow motion. I see one foot go down to plant on the ground. Then, I watch as her foot rolls, and she careens forward toward the ground. My feet are moving before I even realize what I'm doing.

I hear the harumph as her body collides with the ground. "Oh my fuck!" She screeches as the ducks begin their descent to her jean pockets. It only takes me a short time before I'm by her side. I quickly grab into my pockets and throw the cracked corn away from Harper's body. Her hands are still covering her face when I turn to her. The ducks have officially left, happy to have accomplished their mission.

I caress her shoulder, letting her know that it's me. "Hey, you're okay. I'm so sorry I forgot to warn you about these greedy assholes." Her eyes connect with mine as she peeks between her fingers. The emerald green shines with fear.

"That was fucking terrifying. Those things must be Satan incarnate." Her voice trembles as she begins to sit up. I can't help the laugh that bubbles up from my chest as her words settle into me. I take a step back and offer my hand to her. She hesitates for a minute before she puts her hand in mine, and I pull her up.

"Yeah, they're assholes. I meant to tell you they're food motivated and think everyone's pocket's have cracked corn in there." She side-eyes me quickly before letting go of my hand to wipe off the grass and dirt now covering her. The warmth of her hand in mine quickly fades, and it sets something off in my chest. I take a step back quickly as I rub my knuckles over the crown on my chest. The tattoo is an everyday reminder of my past.

A hiss slips from Harper's lips as she tries to take a step forward on the foot she twisted. I'm immediately back at her side offering her support.

"Crap, this is just what I need." She continues mumbles to herself, the words running together

Before she can protest, my one arm slides behind her back and the other behind her knees, as I pick her up and head back to my house.

"Xavier!" She squeaks. "Put me down! You don't need to carry me. Honestly, I'm fine."

I grunt, continuing the trek back to my house. "It's fine. I don't want you to injure yourself more than you already have. Now, shush."

Her lips thin, like she's holding her tongue from saying something. Eventually she sighs. "Thanks, I guess," she mumbles.

We reach my house, and I walk straight through the screen door on the porch. Using the arm that's under her knee I lean forward, opening the door and walk through the threshold. I veer to the right and head straight to my sectional couch. The olive green suede couch has honestly seen better days, but I haven't bothered to replace it. It's comfy as shit, and I love laying on the couch watching the hockey games with Monty when he can make it out. Placing her down on the center cushion of the long side of the couch, she shuffles back and forth to get comfy. Dropping down at her feet, I grab her foot gently, unlacing her shoe.

"Oh, I can do that." She stutters, reaching down and removing the shoe I was unlacing. I don't miss the wince on her face when she takes off her left shoe. I gently grab the bottom of her left foot and bring it up to get a better look. Before I can lift up her pant leg, I can already begin to see the swelling of her ankle. I place it down lightly before I get up and head to the kitchen.

"Wait— where are you going?"

"That ankle is already swelling, I'm going to grab you some ice and ibuprofen to help with the pain and swelling." My sentence leaves no room for argument as I open my fridge and grab the ice packet from the door of my freezer, then grab a bottle of water and stick it into my sweater pocket. Grabbing a dish towel, I wrap it around the ice pack while I make my way back down the hallway, stopping quickly at my small bathroom to grab the ibuprofen and stuff it in my pocket. Continuing my trek down the hall toward the woman who has easily taken over my thoughts over the last couple days. The faded brown mixed in with the beige of my hall carpet shows the wear and tear on it. It just reminds me of the home I made for myself and the comfort that comes with it.

Harper is exactly where I left her, leaning back against the couch with her left arm across her upper stomach and her elbow resting on that left hand while she chews on the thumb of her right hand. "Hey." I say in a low voice so I don't startle her. Her eyes flick up to mine. She removes her thumb from her face and sits up straight while rubbing both hands down her thighs. The movement makes me notice the thick thighs that look like they could be the comfiest things to use as a pillow.

I quickly shake my head out of that train of thought and sit next to her. Grabbing one of my throw pillows, I toss it on the coffee table.

Bending forward, I guide her swelling ankle and rest it on the pillow before blanketing the ice pack overtop. "We'll let that sit for about twenty minutes before we take it off and see where you're at then, okay?" Harper quickly nods her head in agreement. I grab the water and ibuprofen from my pocket and pass it over to her. She takes a tablet and swallows it down with some water. I watch her throat work the water down with each gulp.

I clear my throat, bringing my right hand to the back of my neck, rubbing it, "I guess while we wait, we can discuss what I offered back at the bar."

Harper's lips twitch as she looks at me. "And what exactly was it that you were *offering* me Xavier." I realize the innuendo of my words as soon as she puts emphasis on the word offering.

I feel my cheeks heat a little bit. "Oh man, I didn't- uh." Sitting up straighter, I clear my throat. "About fake dating. The *offer* of fake dating."

Amusement shines in Harper's wide eyes as I stumble over my words. One hand coming up to her mouth, like she's trying to hide her growing smile. Her focus moves from me to a spot in front of her, and her head moves side to side as she considers my words.

"I understand how this could benefit me. It would give me the advantage of sticking it to Dalton after finding out he cheated on me with Chloe. But I don't understand what you get out of this. You said it would get your parents off your back. Why?" I go to open my mouth in answer but she immediately continues, "I mean maybe it's none of my business. But- I think if we're going to do this we need to understand *why* we're doing this. And establish some ground rules. " Pausing briefly, she looks over at me, a shade of pink tinting her cheeks. "You can tell me to stop talking whenever I get too much. I- I tend to ramble when I get a little anxious."

A smirk begins to form on my face as I take her in. She's been moving her hands the whole time she was talking. She uses her whole body to talk and I find it endearing, it shows her passion.

"My parents have been bugging me about getting into a relationship for some time. It's been a long time since I've dated. It's not something

I've taken the time to do. My schooling, and then the clinic, have been the most important thing to me. Everything else has kind of fallen to the wayside, which I'm okay with. My mother, however– well, it drives her crazy." I sit back and stare ahead of me. A sigh leaves my mouth, and I run my hand through my hair. "So I figure, if we do this. It'll make my mom happy and if I take you with me to whatever family events she has planned for the two months then –" I shrug, not thinking I need to finish my sentence.

We let the silence linger for a few minutes. Then she replies so casually. "Okay. Let's do it."

We've spent what feels like forever talking. At some point, I toss something on the TV before running back into the kitchen to make some popcorn and grab some different drinks. I tell her about Josie and Monty. I tell her all the stupid shit we used to get up to when we were younger. Harper comes back with equally stupid things she and Evie used to get up to as well.

It isn't until her phone goes off that I realize how much time has passed. It's amazing for the time to pass this way with someone I barely know, but I feel a sort of comfort I haven't felt in a very long time. It sets my stomach in a weird knot that I can't shake off.

"I'm sorry" she says as she quickly looks at her phone, "It's just Evie checking in on me. Making sure I haven't been kidnapped or murdered." She pauses a second before smirking at me. "Don't worry, I told her you're quite the host for someone who kidnapped me."

"Tell her that your ransom is going to include all the medical support I gave while you were being held captive."

She mock gasps. "I'm sorry your creatures of Satan chased me down." Before she starts laughing, she quickly types out a response on her phone, then shuts the screen off and puts it down. She takes in the living room before she comes back to me with a warm smile.

"So, when does this fake dating commence?"

I scratch the scruff that's begun to grow on my face. I think about when the next family dinner is. "I guess the next mandatory family dinner I have to go to would be Thanksgiving next weekend. So, I guess then?"

"Okay." She nods her head in agreement. "Thanksgiving dinner it is! Is there a dress code? How nice do I need to look?"

I look at her for a minute, and before I think any better of it, I let the words come out unfiltered. "You don't have to work too hard to look nice." I freeze. I didn't mean to say that, but I can't take it back. It's true. She has this natural beauty to her. I couldn't not find her breathtaking. And honestly, I don't want to take it back.

I continue, shoving the cringe from my mind. "It shouldn't be that bad, dressing up wise. The dressier event would be the Christmas Eve dinner party, but I don't think we will have to worry about it too much since our relationship is so new."

Harper shifts on the cushion before placing her weight on her hand resting on the arm of my couch. The ice pack I'd given her has been off for a while. Harper tried to walk a little while ago when she needed to use the washroom. She had a bit of a limp, but told me she was fine otherwise. As she pushes off the couch, I step toward her, grabbing her bottle of water. Harper picks up the popcorn bowl, tossing a few random items into it. "Okay, that sounds good then." Her fingers reach for the last pieces of trash scattered as she continues. "You should probably take me back to my car though. It's getting late, and I have to get home, get Winnie his dinner and let him out."

"Of course. Here, let me take those. You get your things together, and I'll run this stuff into the kitchen then I'll drop you off okay?" She nods her head, reaching down to grab her phone. I quickly drop the bowl off in the kitchen, grab my keys before heading back to the front door. Harper has her shoes back on at this point and is waiting for me.

I find myself smiling as I make my way over to her. I stop beside her, opening the door and I look back at her. Nodding in the direction of my truck, I tilt my head outside. "You ready?"

Chapter Twelve

Harper

I BARELY NOTICED THE hours of the day slip past, and before I knew it, it was Friday. Evie and I had a sleepover Sunday night. She just found out that she's going to be losing her job in a couple of weeks due to cutbacks. Since it was a temp office job, she knew it wasn't forever, but it sucks that it happened right before the holidays. If it were me, I'd be so stressed out, but Evie is very much a go with the flow person. It's why we fit so well together. With Xavier's family Thanksgiving dinner slowly approaching, Evie has taken it upon herself to ensure I'm ready...both mentally and when it comes to my outfit.

Xavier and I have been texting throughout the week. We've been discussing the story of how we met, and the most logical is to use the story of Winnie being attacked by a porcupine. I'm a terrible liar, so it's easier for me to go with something based on the truth.

When Xavier told his mom that he was bringing a date, apparently she was ecstatic. This causes nerves to fester in my stomach at the thought of meeting his parents. The people pleaser in me wants things to go well, despite it being just an arrangement between the two of us.

Tonight, I chose a more natural look. The smokey eye with the perfect mixture of browns and beige. Finished off with a little shimmer of gold in the inner corner of my eye. The black winged eyeliner is on point and probably the best I've ever done. I lean over the vanity, rollers in my hair while I finish off the matte mahogany lipstick. I love makeup and the creative freedom that comes with it. There's something so fun trying new techniques and watching as the blend of colors turn into something so stunning.

Satisfied with it all, I get to work cleaning up the scattered makeup mess on my vanity. Grabbing my lipstick I head back to the bedroom, placing it on my dresser and retreating to my closet to grab my outfit.

Evie is sitting on my bed playing on her phone. From the sounds of it, she's swiping her way through a dating app while I finish getting ready.

"Anything good there?" I yell at her while grabbing my black tights. I begin to shimmy my legs into them, the fabric hugging my curves. Setting them into place, I grab the maroon sweater dress and carefully pull it over my head, trying to avoid hitting any of the rollers. The material slides over my curves, forming to my body perfectly. I quickly grab a pair of brown knee high boots to pull the whole look together.

I walk out of the closet as Evie huffs a sigh. "Ugh I don't know. I hate these apps because they're not made for bisexuals. I can't just have a slew of men and women to look through. I have to change my preferences if I want either or."

I shake my head with a smirk forming on my lips.

"Oh, is that all?" Making my way over to my dresser that has my jewelry on it, I quickly take the rollers out of my hair as Evie continues.

"I know I shouldn't be complaining." She pauses. "But..."

"But you're still going to?" A smirk forming on my lips as I finish her sentence.

She clicks her tongue and finger guns in my direction, which I see through the mirror. I shake my head as I roll my eyes at her with a laugh. "You look hot." Evie states as she watches me put on a pair of basic gold dangle earrings.

I blush from the compliment. "Oh shut up, I look fine."

The hard stare that greets me from her is palpable. "When are you going to give yourself some credit?"

I turn around to face her, leaning my body against the dresser, and cross one foot over my ankle. Brows furrowed, I question her. "What do you mean?"

"I mean," She pauses, like she's trying to figure out how exactly to say what she needs to say. "You're beautiful Harper, and you have this lightness about you that draws people to you. You're a dependable person, and you're *my* person. I would hide a body if you asked." She gets off the bed and walks toward me, grabbing both my hands in hers and making eye contact. Her eyes portray no funny business, but they also have a caring softness to it as she delivers what she says next. "But you bring yourself down anytime anyone says anything relatively positive to you. You dismiss it, or you devalue it. I just wish you could see the person I see, because she's great. And she's worth loving. And worshiping."

I feel the prickle of tears beginning to form at the corner of my eye. I quickly squeeze Evie's hand before I let go to dab away the moisture. "Stop, you're going to make me cry and I can't have makeup smeared down my face." I sniff and look back at her. "But it's hard, okay, especially after all the shit that happened with the break up. It just...it can be hard to rebuild my confidence after finding everything out. Then when I add on that this dinner is like a confrontation of sorts—and we know I don't do the best with those—I just hope I'm going to be able to not fuck it up." I take a deep breath, and slowly release it. I need to calm my nerves, or I'm just going to back out.

Evie gives me a small smile, but she doesn't say anything. She acknowledges our conversation, but I know it won't be the last I hear from her about it. Just then, my phone chimes from my bedside table. I quickly walk over there and take it off the charging dock.

Xavier: I'm just leaving my house now, I'll be there in ten.

Harper: Okay! I'll see you soon!!

"Okay." I take another deep breath. I turn to look at Evie. "He's on his way."

"Perfect timing. Another minute and you would have probably bailed." She says, the tease in her voice apparent. I mean, she's not wrong. There is a lot at stake here.

I take a quick look in the mirror to make sure everything is good, and that there are no makeup streaks from nearly crying. When I think everything looks presentable, I head into the living room. I put my boots by the door so they're ready when I need to leave. Evie had disappeared when I told her Xavier was on his way. Unsurprisingly, she comes back into the living room with a mug that has steam rolling off of it.

Hot apple cider. My nerves were pretty much gone, but knowing she went out of her way to make me an apple cider completely obliterates the remaining nerves. She approaches me and hands it over "I know you're nervous, so I thought I'd give you something to calm you down."

"Thanks," I squeak out as I bring the cup to my mouth, the steam softly coating my face like a comforting caress. The scent of apples mingling with hints of cinnamon and cloves invade my senses. I feel my shoulders relax as I tip the cup back to take my first sip, the warmth of the drink spreading through my body. "You know me so well."

The next few moments are spent talking about Evie's plans. She's going to stay and hang out with Winnie so he isn't alone tonight, but realistically, I know she's staying behind because she wants all the details of whatever happens tonight. I don't blame her either. I would do the same if the roles were reversed. As I set my empty cup on the coffee table, I hear a knock on the door, followed by barking.

Chapter Thirteen

xavier

I'M STANDING AT THE door of Harper's house, waiting for someone to answer. I hear the echo of a dog barking through the door, and I quickly adjust the cuffs of my dress shirt. It's a nervous habit I get when I dress up. Basically, whenever I have to go have dinner with my family. The door swings open, and I'm momentarily stunned by the beauty that is Harper.

I've seen her dressed down, and casual; her natural beauty easy to be transfixed by. I think about the time we spent out at the farm. She wore no makeup except maybe some mascara on her lashes. She was stunning then.

But shit. Now?

I take in the knee-high boots that work up her calves, showing off black tights that hug her thighs effortlessly. The maroon sweater dress clings to every luscious curve on her body. I momentarily stop at her breasts, fixated on the way the V of the dress perfectly sculpts them together. I continue my journey up to her pouty lips, accented with the perfect shade of mahogany. I momentarily picture how her lips would feel against my own. Would they feel as soft as I imagine they would be?

Absolutely Stunning.

I watch her eyes trail down my own body, and slowly make their way back up. I find myself adjusting my cuffs again, noticing how her eyes are bewitched by the movement. When her eyes finally meet mine, they widen in surprise, realizing that I've been watching her this whole time. A redness blooms on her cheeks from being caught. I can't fight the smirk on my face. "Hey there," I husk out.

She awkwardly waves her hand by her hip. "Hi," she says, almost breathlessly before turning to grab her bag. She steps out of her house, closing the door behind her. She begins walking, but I pause and point back at the door.

"Do you need to lock up before we leave?"

"What?" She starts, before shaking her head at the practicality of the question. "Oh, no. Evie is staying behind with Winnie, that way I don't have to rush back."

I give her a nod before continuing to my truck. I open the door for her, and offer my hand to get her up into the seat. She places her hand in mine before she climbs in and begins buckling herself. Quickly, I shut her door. Hopping into the driver's side, I click my seatbelt into place as I begin to pull out of the driveway.

The playlist flows through the cab of the truck as we head toward my parents house. Thanks to shuffle, not a single genre is missed as we drive. When *Cruise* by Florida Georgia Line begins to play, I catch movement in the corner of my eye as Harper looks at me before turning back toward the window.

"I love this song," I tell her. "Every time it comes on, it gets stuck in my head for a minimum of a week."

She startles from my comment at first, like she was stuck in her own thoughts, before she gives a soft chuckle. "This is a good song." She begins tapping her hand on her knee to the beat. I linger on the movement for a minute before directing my head back to the road and focus on getting us there safely.

We drive for another five minutes before I flick my turn signal on, making my way to the gated driveway. I roll down my window and enter the gate code. Once we're through, I chance a glance at Harper to see her reaction to my parents' property. I never grew up without, and sometimes I forget how privileged I was, even though I don't take my parents' handouts. I took that privilege and turned it into beneficial action, donating to animal foundations regularly.

Parking my truck, I quickly round the front to meet Parker at her door. I click the lock on my fob to ensure Harper doesn't try to let herself out before I get there. I see Chloe's car is already here, so they must be inside already. I wanted to time it this way, making it so that we were the last to arrive in hopes the shock factor would be maximized while also keeping the awkwardness to a minimum. I help Harper down, and she stands there, staring at the front door. She begins to wring her hands together, shifting back and forth on her feet.

I place my hand gently on her shoulder, squeezing it softly. "We don't have to do this if you're not comfortable. All you have to do is tell me you changed your mind, and I'll take you right back home."

She looks at me in disbelief, like she wasn't expecting me to offer her an out. I don't know how shitty Deke was when he was with her, but I'm going to guess she was dragged to a couple events she didn't want to go to, based on that reaction.

"No, I'm fine. I want to do this, I'm just a little nervous. I'm not good with confrontation, and I honestly try to avoid it. So the fact that we are literally walking in there to cause one makes me a little dizzy." She stops wringing her hands as she looks up at me. I can see the need for reassurance in her eyes, and I will not deny her comfort.

"Listen to me. If at *any* moment, you feel uncomfortable? Tell me. I will be sitting beside you. Just grab my hand and squeeze twice, and I'll fake a vet emergency so we can leave, okay?"

She takes a deep breath and nods.

"Good girl. Now let's go see the look on Dwight and Chloe's faces when we walk in, yeah?" I extend out my arm, offering my elbow for her to link with. She snorts softly before taking my arm.

"His name's Dalton," she says, shaking her head while a soft smile curls at her lips. "You know this."

"Potato, tomato." I shrug before I open the doors and we head in.

I lead the way through the house. It's quiet, and my best guess is that everyone has gathered in the dining room. Perfect. Harper follows as

I push the dining room door open, the noise permeating the previous silence.

My mom is in the middle of a discussion with Chloe, both of whom are very consumed in whatever they're discussing. I look and see Darrin is at the bar with my dad. Their backs are toward us, so they don't see our entrance. I wait, letting things settle before poking the bears. Harper's hand on my elbow has started to tighten as the anticipation of them acknowledging our presence rises.

I loudly clear my throat. Heads whip in our direction and I take a moment to take in everyone's reaction as they realize, not only am I here, but I'm not alone. I only told my mom that I was bringing someone, but I had doubted she kept that to herself.

There are no emotions on my family's faces. My father has no visible reaction other than a curious brow raise. Derek's brows are furrowed in confusion, then I watch as recognition clicks in his head. His mouth opens and closes like a fish, but no words come out. It makes me smirk. I move over to my mother, who is now wide-eyed, and she has her hands softly covering her lips. There is a slight tip in her lips as she gives me a once over, before moving her focus to Harper. I can see my mother analyzing her, and I get a bit defensive, slowly moving my body to shield Harper from my mother's view. My eyes finally land on my darling sister. Ms. Do No Wrong. Her face is twisted into a sneer, disgust mixed with disbelief.

"You're kidding me right?" Chloe breaks the silence sarcastically. "You weren't joking when you said you were bringing *her*."

"Chloe!" Mom chides her. "What in the heavens are you talking about? Your brother finally brings a date to dinner, and this is how you treat her!" My mother stands up, making her way around the table to us. She has a smile on her face as she tries to peer around me again. Harper is still at my side holding on to my elbow. "I'm so sorry about my daughter. It's the hormones you see, as she's pregnant with our first grandbaby!" She claps quickly before offering her hand out to Harper.

Harper releases her hold so she can grasp my mother's hand.

"I'm Penelope Hawthorne, Xavier's mother. That's his father, Theo, over there at the bar. My daughter Chloe is here too, with her fiance Dalton!"

A squeak comes from Harper's mouth as Chloe snaps, "*Mom*! We haven't told anyone else yet!"

Harper schools her reaction with an impressive speed before she plasters a fake smile on her face. "It's so nice to meet you, Mrs. Hawthorne. I'm Harper."

Pulling Harper into my side, I watch my sister slowly boil. I can see the steam coming out of Chloe's ears and I'm just waiting for the kettle to squeal. Dane still has a flabbergasted look on his face, but at least he shut his mouth.

"Oh please, Call me Penelope, darling!" She states before the sound of a chair scratching the floor breaks the pleasantries. All eyes turn to Chloe who is now standing, with her eyes narrowed in on Harper. I tighten my hold on her as I prepare for the tantrum of the century.

"Oh, *please*" She snaps, as one foot stomps on the floor. Her arms cross over her chest, and she sneers in Harper's direction. "Are you seriously that desperate that you had to bribe my brother to bring you to *my* family dinner?" Chloe points aggressively at her baby daddy. "He left you. *Period*. He has moved on to better pastures, with someone who can keep up with what he wants...things that *you* weren't giving him. Honestly, I–" I go to take a step toward her to give her a piece of my mind as she continues.

"*Enough*!" A deep voice booms through the dining room, all eyes turning to my father who is shaking his head. "Chloe, what is the meaning of this? You don't speak to guests this way."

"But daddy!" She starts, but my father's hand raises, silently stopping her. I don't know how he does it, but he can somehow get her to shut up when she's on these fits. My body is wound tightly, coiled and ready to defend Harper. I can take the way my sister talks, but I'm beginning to seethe at the way she's speaking to the woman standing at my side.

"I don't know what you're talking about Chloe. I met Harper at work, when she brought her dog in with an emergency. We got to talking, and we hit it off. Honestly, what's pathetic is you thinking that the world revolves around you." My grip has tightened around Harper's shoulders. She ends up wrapping her one arm around my waist, slowly stroking circles on my lower back. The intentionality of her touch is one of the only things keeping me from completely losing it. I close my eyes and take a deep breath, but before I can continue, Chloe is at it again.

"Dalton! Are you just going to stand there and not say anything?!" Chloe shrieks, the last word ending on a high pitched note. Fuck, that killed my ears. All eyes turn to Deke, and his face is priceless; his eyes are round and wide, framed by black rimmed glasses.

He goes to take a drink, but it must go down the wrong tube because he begins sputtering and coughing. My father firmly pats his back trying to help him clear his airway. Chloe hasn't moved an inch, but her face is pinched with some emotion. Just when it looks like Derek is about to speak, Harper surprises everyone by speaking first.

"It's true. Dalton and I *used* to be together, but that ended. I truly didn't know that of all the people I cross every day, I'd meet someone who was connected to him in this situation. If everyone is uncomfortable, I can go. Dalton was here first, but I assure you there's no bad blood here." Even I am remotely stunned at Harper. She is calm and collected, and she continues to rub slow circles on my back as she talks. She turns to look up at me, giving a soft smile before she continues. "However. I plan to continue to see Xavier," she says as she turns her attention to the rest of the group. "I want to see where this relationship goes, because Mrs. Hawthorne—"

"Please, call me Penelope." My mother interjects, but motions for her to continue.

"Sorry, Penelope. You've raised a great man, one who treats me well."

My mom starts, approval coating her tone. "That settles it then. Darling, let the kitchen know we are ready for our meal. Xavier, get your girlfriend here a beverage and let's all sit down."

"But," Chloe begins.

"Oh hush, Chloe! They've spoken their peace. Just let it be, and let's have a nice dinner." Penelope chastises.

I have to hold back a laugh at the look on Chloe's face. I don't think my parents have ever let her not get her way. I'm honestly a little shocked that they said something, but I do what my mother asks, getting Harper's drink. I head over to the bar where Dad and Dwight were standing. Dad is still there, and I feel his eyes on me.

Turning to face him, I raise my eyebrow question. His lip twitches slightly before he raises his glass to me, and goes to take his seat next to his wife. I quickly make up a vodka soda with cranberry juice, and a whiskey for myself, before returning to the table. As I sit beside Harper, I lean over, placing a peck at the crown of her head as I set her drink in front of her. I hear her breath hitch, and I pause briefly before settling next to her. It wasn't my plan to initiate physical touch like that, but I know we are technically dating in everyone's eyes. My head briefly spins at the intimacy of it all. I haven't done small touches or kisses in, well, in a long time. Before I can fully spiral at the weight of what is an ordinary gesture, we're wrapped into a conversation with my parents, and I take pleasure in Harper's smile. Maybe these small intimacies aren't so daunting, after all.

The rest of the dinner goes relatively smoothly. I mean, other than Chloe seething, and Dane looking like someone has a vise on his balls. They quietly argue after dinner when everyone is making their way into the living room. I make my way over to the couch and take a seat. Harper hesitates for a minute, glancing at Chloe and Derek arguing. I grab her hand, pulling her down to sit next to me and place my hand on her thigh. I lean over and whisper in her ear. "You good?" My breath heats her skin as I watch her.

She turns her head to look me in the eyes, and I catch the change in her breathing when she realizes how close we are. Her cheeks begin to turn a soft shade of pink as she nods her head. "Yeah, I'm good. This is actually nice." I watch the emerald in her eyes shine with sincerity in her statement before I catch them drift to my lips and then back up to my eyes. They widen when she realizes she's been caught. A smile tugs at the corner of my lips, and I return the favor, my gaze landing on her plump lips. Once again, I find myself imagining how soft they'd feel. My heartbeat begins to race at the thought of placing my lips against hers, until that's all I can think about. I can't help the sudden need to lean forward and close the remaining distance between us. Before I can convince myself to back away, I move.

My lips lightly brush against hers. Harper is still for a moment before she melts, her resolve softening and I feel her lean into the moment. There is no urgency in this kiss. The smell of vanilla and lavender cloud my senses. I struggle to deepen the kiss as we become familiar with each other. *God, I was right.* I pull away slowly, and when I open my eyes, I see her follow me, chasing the way our kiss made her feel. Her eyes open slowly as the blush blooms a bit deeper on her cheeks.

"That was…unexpected." She says, almost breathlessly.

I clear my throat, trying to steady myself before I answer. "We have to make it believable, right?" The moment the words left my mouth, they tasted sour. That kiss was so much more than just an act to prove we're together. *That kiss* shook me to my core, a tsunami of emotions I'd sworn to never feel again crashing into me.

The moment her face drops, I instantly regret saying something.

"Right. Very convincing indeed." She pulls back, and I long to bring her back to me. She hasn't moved from the couch but she has crossed one leg over the other

, leaning slightly away from me. To others, she is just sitting comfortably as we have a group discussion about the holidays. To me? I see that I hurt her, and she's closing herself off. I let her have her space.

There is a tightness in my chest that makes me rub the spot over my crown tattoo again trying to ease the ache. I need to somehow make this right, and I have no idea how to do that. I'm so caught up in my head, I'm not listening to the conversation that's happening right now.

"You simply *must* join us Harper! It's such a dream up there." My mothers words bring me out of my trance.

"What?" I snap before wincing at how rude that sounded. "I mean, sorry. I was just thinking about work. What's going on?"

"The ski lodge, Xavier! I was just telling Harper here how we will be leaving the second week of December until after the New Year, and how you simply must bring her with you! You are coming up this year, aren't you?" My mother gives me her signature "mom eyes", the ones that allow no arguments but also remind me of a puppy dog pout. It normally doesn't work on me, but I think about going to the lodge. Having Harper there. I haven't gone to the ski lodge in years. The bad memories have always haunted me. However, the potential of new memories with Harper? The added satisfaction that Dwight is going to be there with my sister and my presence will make them miserable? It is more appealing than I want to admit.

I look at my mom and give her a genuine smile. "We'd love to come this year."

Chapter Fourteen

Harper

I LOOK OVER AT Xavier in disbelief. Did he really accept an invite for us to spend three weeks with his family at some ski lodge? I mean, I've never been anywhere like that, but that means three weeks of watching Dalton and Chloe all over each other. Three weeks of seeing her baby bump grow. The idea makes me want nothing more than to stay home with Winnie and Evie instead.

"Oh, I couldn't impose."

"Nonsense! We have more than enough room, and I would just love to have you out there with us! Oh, I must take you to the farmers market! I won't take no for an answer!" Penelope gets up with her phone in her hand, "Excuse me, I must get things ready for everyone's arrival!" After tapping a few things on her phone she brings it to her ear and begins speaking to someone about redecorating the room as she walks off.

I look over at Xavier in exasperation. "I mean–" I huff out a sigh. "I guess I need to start packing." The smile taking over his face makes my stomach flutter. His smirk is downright panty melting, but when he *really* smiles? It's hard not to get entranced, and the chin dimple that appears there? Somehow makes him hotter.

"But I'll need to figure out work. I have at least a week of work I have to do. I have meetings and a deadline for one of my clients. Is there any way I can work remotely at the lodge?" I fiddle with my hands, feeling my anxiety creep in. I know I took a couple weeks off because of the holidays already, but I can't afford to take another week off.

"I'll make sure you have your own space set up to get some work done for that week. There are enough rooms at my parents lodge that we can get you sorted somewhere you can focus on work." Xavier reassures me, so quickly and easily, that the butterflies in my stomach from earlier return. I squash them just as quickly, reminding myself that this is all for show. We aren't really dating, and he's doing this to display the good boyfriend role. I force a smile. "That would be perfect, thank you."

Xavier looks like he's about to say something when Penelope bursts into the room with a huge smile on her face. "It's all settled! We will be leaving next Friday, so make sure you're all packed up and ready to go! Oh, this is just perfect!" She clasps her hands together with a dreamy look on her face. "I'm so excited to have the whole family together at the lodge this holiday!"

"Are you serious!?" Chloe sneers. "We're just going to all spend time at the lodge together like some big old happy family? Like this isn't just a ruse they're playing at?" She's glaring at me as she takes a step toward where Xavier and I are sitting on the couch. Dalton grabs Chloe by the elbow and quietly says something to her. His eyes quickly dart to me before returning to Chloe. It's too late. Chloe saw the shift in his attention. She makes some sort of angry screech before she stomps toward the exit. "*Fine!*" she shouts. "Come on Dalton. We're. Leaving." She has his hand gripped tightly and is dragging him out the room before he even has a chance to say goodbye.

"My goodness, what is up with her? I mean, honestly." Penelope shakes her head before sitting on the arm of Theo's chair, as he quickly wraps his arm around her. "Anyway, I'm so happy you guys will be coming to the lodge!"

"Yeah about that, Mom," Xavier starts and the look on his moms face begins to fall. "No, no. We're still coming," he clarifies before continuing. "While I will be able to move things around to get the time off, Harper still needs to work for at least the first week we're there. She's an editor, so she can do it remotely. So she's going to need a space of her own for the first week so she can get work done."

"Oh, absolutely no problem, we can make that work! Especially if that means you're still going to be coming!" She sends hopeful eyes in my direction.

"If I can get my own space where I can work for a couple hours a day, then absolutely." I give her a genuine smile, happy my work doesn't have to suffer for this, and relieved at the load of stress I no longer have to face.

We spend the next half hour going over the events that will be happening during our trip. The first week sounds like it's just getting ready for Christmas, with socializing and shopping. There are a few Christmas parties that Penelope informs us we will be attending. Xavier cuts in a time or two, asking about going skiing and some ice fishing. While his parents don't seem to be entirely open to that idea, they still agree to it, nonetheless.

A yawn escapes my mouth before I can stop it. Xavier catches me trying to cover it, but stands up and offers his hand. I place my hand in his and he helps me stand.

"I think it's time to head out. Thanks for having us for dinner." Xavier has pulled me into his side, wrapping his arm around my shoulder. I follow suit by wrapping my arm around his waist.

I smile brightly at his parents. "Thanks so much for having me over. Dinner was delicious."

Penelope grabs my hand with one of hers and pats the top of my hand with the other. "It was a pleasure having you here. I'm so happy to see Xavier finally bringing someone around. For a moment, I thought he would just stay single forever!" I feel Xavier's body stiffens, and I look up at him to catch the way his jaw flexes. He gives a forced smile before leaning forward to give his mom a kiss on the cheek.

He still has me tucked at his side, even after we're away from everyone. I don't let go though, because it feels like he needs this comfort right now. I begin to smooth my hand up and down his back as we walk. He seems like he's in a trance of some sort. As I continue my motions, he begins to relax a bit more. I finally decide to break the silence as we make it to the truck and he unlocks it, removing himself from my side to open my door for me again.

I get little flutters in my stomach every time he's done this. It's something you don't see anymore. I tilt my head up, studying him. His jaw is still set in a tight form, and the look in his eyes seems like he was trying to keep me at arms length. It is as if Xavier doesn't want me to see the emotions that he's holding back. I place my hand gently on his forearm, and he flinches. I remove my hand quickly, giving him an apologetic look. "Where'd you go up in there?" I bring my hand up to my temple and give it a tap. His eyes pierce mine for a minute before a soft smile appears on his face.

"It's nothing. I'm sorry." He runs his hand over his face and sighs heavily. "It's just—I dealt with some shit when I was younger, and it put me off from getting close to anyone. I'm only telling you this so you understand the reason why I mentioned the two of us fake dating after we kissed. I just need you to know that." He pauses and looks off into the distance.

"It's okay. I get it." I say with as much support as I can portray in a look. "You don't have to give me your life story. I don't expect you to do that. I do want you to know that I got you, okay? Whatever that means during this whole thing." I don't give him a chance to respond as I hop into the truck and close the door myself. He stands there for a minute before shaking his head and heading toward his side of the truck.

The drive home is quiet. The music is on low, and I watch the world pass as we drive back to my house. I begin mentally making a list of everything that I will need to pack for this getaway. It's then that I realize I have zero winter gear of any sort. Alright, then. I will be immediately ordering things when I get home. I'm sure there isn't that much that I need. Right?

The truck slows as Xavier turns into my driveway.

"Thank you for the ride. I guess I'll see you next week?" I begin to unbuckle myself, when Xavier interrupts me. "Wait." My eyes drop to the seatbelt.

"Oh no. I can get out by myself, it's fine." I hear the click of the truck as he locks it while he runs around the truck, and then unlocking it before opening the door for me. "You know I am perfectly capable of getting myself out of your truck."

That smirk that melts my panties appears on his face. "And miss an opportunity to catch you when you fall?" He says it with such amusement, and it is a stark contrast to how he was when we left his parents. He helps me down and walks me toward the front door. I'm looking in my bag to grab my keys in case Evie locked the door.

"I just wanted to apologize for how I was when we left. My mom can seem like a good person, but she knows what to say to get under your skin." When I turn to look at him, his hands are in his pocket and he's looking down at his toes, shifting his weight. When he looks up, I see the sincerity shining in his ocean blue eyes. "It's part of the reason I do my best and attempt to not attend these dinners. I try to avoid the remarks about my single life, because that seems to always be the focus. Not my successes, like the clinic."

I take a step forward and watch as his eyes focus on my movement. "For what it's worth," I pause, noticing how being this close forces me to look up at his over six foot stature. "You should be proud of your accomplishments. That clinic is amazing. You really care for these animals, and you can see it in the way you interact with them. The way you helped someone out in an emergency situation, because her poor dog got into a scuffle with a porcupine." I see the slightest twitch of his lips, and it makes my own smile grow. "You don't need to apologize for your feelings."

Xavier stares at me, the air around us heavy. There's a sense of awe in the way he's looking at me, and it makes a chill go down my body. He catches the movement before taking a slight step back. "Thank you. I appreciate that. I'm going to get going. I'll text you more details of the trip as my mom sends them over."

"Okay, sounds good! I'll talk to you later then" I begin walking backwards to my door. "Goodnight, Xavier."

"Goodnight, Harper."

I stand on my doorstep, watching as he drives off. My mind replays the night as I turn inside. It didn't go as bad as I thought it would. The look on Dalton's face when he saw me was absolutely priceless. I thought for a moment that he was going to pass out. I didn't expect the way that Chloe reacted though. I mean, I didn't interact with her that much when I would visit Dalton on his lunch breaks. She definitely was fake-friendly to me to save face, but I caught the way she looked at me with judgement. When she accused me of trying to get Dalton back? That's where she was so wrong. When I found out Dalton had been cheating on me, it broke something in me. Yes, he broke my heart, but he also broke my trust. And that's something that he won't get back. Trust is huge for me. When I give my trust, I am believing in you that you won't abuse or break it.

She seemed to be so fixated on that, so I knew I needed to say something and set things straight. The only white lie in my whole spiel was that Xavier and I didn't know Dalton would be there. And then there's this three week long vacation at the ski lodge. I feel my heartbeat pick up again thinking about spending three weeks with his family... and Dalton. That's three weeks of having to keep the charade up and act like a couple. I'd rather crawl into a hole and avoid it all, to be honest.

And dear God, if Xavier keeps kissing me the way he did tonight? I'm in for a rude awakening when this is all over. I think back to that kiss, and the way the world seemed to have slowed down when I faced him, seeing just how close we were. My breath hitched as he leaned forward and closed the small distance between us. It was soft and sweet, not rushed or demanding. His woodsy scent was rich and warm, with the undertones of spice mixed in, reminding me of a warm fire. It was perfect. And *that* was terrifying.

It *is* terrifying.

I'm not able to think much more about it as the front door swings open, and Winnie barrels through the doorway, right into my side. I let out a small grunt as he collides with me. I bend over to greet him, laughing as he circles around me, wiggling his whole backside in happiness. A loud clearing of her throat informs me that Evie is standing there in the doorway. I peek through my lashes and am met with Evie in her favorite band t-shirt and shorts. Arms crossed over her chest, her golden locks are pulled up into a messy bun. The spacers in her ears are a plain white silicone, and when I look at her moss green eyes, they're looking at me questioningly.

"Get your ass in here, and spill." She demands, as Winnie runs past her back inside. I stand up and follow into the house, putting my things away and taking off my boots.

"Let me get into something comfier first," I grumble as I make my way into my bedroom. She's quick on my heels though, as I knew she would be. I go across the bedroom and quickly change into my favorite purple cami set.

Evie's sitting on the end of my bed, her legs crossed underneath her as she leans back on her hands as she waits. I quickly go into the washroom to wash my makeup off and brush my teeth. When I return to the bedroom, Evie's in the same exact place I left her, and this time, Winnie has joined her.

"Okay, so. It wasn't as bad as I thought it was going to be." I join her on the bed. "Dalton's face was worth every moment. He looked like he was going to pass out."

"I would have loved to see the look on that fucker's face." There's a devious smirk on her face as she motions for me to continue.

"The thing I wasn't expecting was the way Chloe lost it and then accused me of being there only to get him back." Evie's face scrunches in disgust. "Chloe gets shut down. Dalton says *nothing* while she's having this tantrum. It was their dad who told her to cut it out."

"Xavier didn't say anything?" Evie asks with a raised eyebrow.

"Well no. But he had me, like possessively pulled to his side and he was stiff as a board. Evie, if you could have seen the look in his eyes. Well, you would be dead" I take a minute to remember the look on his face. It's around the time I started rubbing his back. I wanted him to know I was fine, but I don't think he got the message until I said something. "Anyway, I came out and said she had nothing to worry about, and that I met Xavier by happenstance, and we hit things off. I even said that we didn't know we would be running into Dalton or Chloe...or that I knew Chloe when he invited me to dinner. You should have been there. You would have been pleased with the speech I gave." I smile over at her proudly. She looks at me with one of her own.

Then, like a freight train, it hits me. "And *oh my God.* I forgot to tell you the craziest parts!" I yell.

"Dude chill. I'm literally right beside you–" Evie winces.

I interject before she finishes her sentence. "Dalton and Chloe are *engaged.*" I say with a straight face.

Evie's mouth drops open quickly, before she snaps it back shut. "Excuse me? I'm sorry I think I blacked out for a minute." She sticks a finger in her ear like she's trying to clear it out.

I shake my head, continuing. "You heard me. Apparently, it just happened though, so they haven't announced it. I totally forgot to try and get a look at her finger to see the ring. Their mom dropped the bomb, but then Chloe continued on her tangent so I didn't get the time to fully digest it before we moved on to the next thing."

"That's fucked." Evie says, as she crawls over to the headboard and tucks herself under the blankets.

"You're telling me." We lounge for a bit in silence, before I put *New Girl* on the TV. We watch an episode before we dive back into the evening. I tell her about the comment Penelope made, and how it seemed to set Xavier off. I mentioned that I tried to talk to him about it. He didn't completely shut me out, but he told me it had something to do with his past and why he's never been in another relationship. While I appreciated the honesty and sincerity there, it just has me wondering what he went through. He was not open to discussing it at all so I respected his wishes and dropped it.

"Now, let's circle back to this ski lodge." Evie says before gracing me with a huge yawn.

"What about it? I'll be gone for three weeks. I'll leave Winnie here with you, you get free range of my house." I roll on my side to face her as I pull the duvet up to my chin. She mimics my movements, and raises her eyebrow in question.

"We're just going to ignore the fact that you're walking into a one bed trope romance novel?"

I scoff. "Yeah okay, you're delusional." I feel my eyes roll.

"No, think about it! Stuck up in a ski lodge. It's snowing, so it's going to be cold, and you're going to need to keep warm. Wouldn't you know it, you guys have to share a room – with a bed. We both know you won't let him sleep on the ground or anything, so you're going to have to share." Evie grins at the thought.

I give into her fantasy for a minute before I shake it off. "That seems nice and all Evie, but we don't live in a romance book."

Evie huffs. "That may be so, but I wouldn't count the idea out as impossible."

We lay there in silence. I circle back to earlier, and think of packing again. "I don't think I have clothes for this trip. Especially anything like snow pants."

"Sounds like we're going to have a besties shopping day tomorrow!" Evie starts quickly clapping her hands with excitement at the idea. I chuckle, feeling better than I have in awhile.

"A besties shopping trip sounds like the perfect way to end the weekend. Night Evie." I end with a yawn, my eyes beginning to feel heavy.

"Night bitch, love you." is the last thing I hear before oblivion takes over.

Chapter Fifteen
Harper

"**A**BSOLUTELY NOT." I SAY to Evie, as I grab her hand and drag her past the lingerie store. "I don't need anything from that store. We have a list of things I *need* for this trip."

"Come onnn, Harps!" Evie begs. "There is nothing wrong with a couple of hot pieces to take along with you, *just* in case." She pulls on the hand I have grasped to turn me around. She gives me her best puppy dog eyes. "Please! Can we at least go in there to look at bathing suits? You're going to need one anyway as I'm sure they have an indoor pool or a hot tub or something."

We stand there facing each other before I huff out my defeat. "Fine. But only bathing suits. Nothing more, you hear me?"

She uses her pointer finger to trace a X on her chest. "Cross my heart." She then turns, and practically skips into the store. I shake my head as I follow her.

Here's the thing: I'm not much of a lingerie wearer. I find it too revealing, and I become self conscious of all my lumps and rolls. Where other women find confidence in them, I don't. Any woman who feels confident and sexy in these pieces, no matter what size, more power to them. I, on the other hand, only see my physical negatives when I wear something like that.

I stroll through all the sections of the store. My eye catches on a few items that I love, but would never buy for myself. When I finally make it to the swimsuit section, I find a simple, black one piece. The way the straps are designed is what attracted my attention. It comes with a front cross structure that I'm just obsessed with, and it allows for enough coverage that makes me feel comfortable with showing a little skin. I don't need to look at any other suits. I grab my size, holding it up against my body to ensure that it will fit. Moving toward the register, I keep an eye out for my best friend. Evie has been bopping around the store, and I catch her just finishing up at the register.

"You found some stuff for yourself?"

She whips around to face me as she snatches the bag from the counter and holds the handles out in front of her. "Well, of course. I can't let you have all the fun with buying new things." She gives me a wink before moving to the side for me to buy my suit.

Minutes later, we make a couple more stops before I have everything I need. We pop into Ruthie's for a hot drink before heading back to my house. Evie and I haul everything I bought into the living room, and I don't unpack it because that's a later-Harper problem. We take advantage of the nice fall day and I start a fire.

We play fetch with Winnie for a bit before taking a break. He was not a fan of stopping, so in pure Winnie fashion, he sits there with a grumpy look on his face while the balls lays at his feet. When he realizes that we truly are done, he picks up his ball and goes and lays down in the middle of the yard. Evie snorts. "Wow, he really hates when we stop playing, eh?"

I smirk at her before looking over my shoulder to the furball laying in the yard. His head down is in his paws and he's looking over in our direction. *Poor baby.* A huff leaves his mouth before he begins to close his eyes. Evie and I settle back into our chairs around the firepit.

We finish our drinks while the sun begins its descent over the horizon. We barbecued some burgers for supper, and decided Evie was going to spend the night again as she didn't work until the evening tomorrow. I still have to work bright and early, but Evie being here while I work has never been an issue. She lets me be while I work, and I seek her out when I need a break.

"I'm not looking forward to packing." I put my elbow on the arm rest and place my cheek on my fist. I look over at Evie, who has curled herself up on the chair. Somehow, she has fallen asleep. Her hands are tucked under the side of her head, blonde hair in a messy bun on the top of her head. There's one of my plaid fleece blankets thrown over her body. A quick snort comes from her body as she begins to mumble. My lips press in a line to try and hold in any laughter. "But why does the bunny need a pocket watch? He's still going to end up late, he can't tell time." Turning my face to bury it in my shoulder, I snicker over Evie's latest sleeping rants.

I stare into the fire, entranced by the way the flames shape-shift as it crackles around the burning embers. The colors of orange and white cascade, and the heat from the fire envelopes my body as the evening starts to grow colder. Winnie had come closer to the fire as the sun set, curled up at my feet.

I start to think about how the next couple of weeks are going to go for this trip. The unknown of what to be expected of this trip is weighing on my nerves. I glance at Evie, and see that she's still out cold. I make note to wake her up soon so we can head into the house. I grab my phone from my pocket and open it up. Before I can think otherwise, I text Xavier.

> Harper: I'm getting nervous about this trip.

> Xavier: I was just thinking about you. What's going on? Why are you nervous?

My stomach does a little flip at the thought of him thinking of me. Before I read too much into it, I answer him.

> Harper: I'm just getting nervous about what this week is going to entail. If I packed enough clothing and supplies. What if we get snowed in? What if everyone decides after spending a couple days with me that they hate me?

The message is marked as read, and three dots appear then disappear a few times. The bubbles repeat as he types something and then deletes it. In the next moment, my screen changes to show an incoming call from Xavier. I take a deep breath before swiping and accepting the call.

"Hello?"

"Talk to me," Xavier murmurs, his voice low and husky on the other side of the phone.

" I am talking to you, aren't I?"

A deep chuckle rumbles through the line, the sound sending a shiver down my spine. It causes a low heat to unfurl low in my belly, the sensation melting down in my core. I press my thighs together, trying to ease the feeling that I should *not* be entertaining right now.

"Okay, smartass. You know what I mean– but to answer your questions. While I can't confirm we won't get snowed in, I can guarantee that we are well equipped to handle a potential snow-in."

"That's reassuring." I grumble, picking at a loose string on my shirt.

"I'm just being honest with you. Our place isn't anywhere close that would be affected by an avalanche or anything. But if we get a good amount of snow, and the roads are closed, the lodge is built to handle an extended period of time while we wait to be cleared out."

"I guess as long as everything is well stocked."

I swear I hear the smile on his face as he continues, "As for hating you, that's impossible. They'd be crazy not to like you."

The heat creeping up my neck has little to do with the fire in front of me, and everything to do with the words coming from the man on the phone.

"Well, you're not too bad yourself." A yawn escapes my mouth before I'm able to catch it.

"You should get some sleep. If you ever want to talk about what it's like out at the lodge, let me know. We can go have lunch one day this week before we leave, and I can come with the floor plans and everything so you're well prepared." The teasing tone becomes strong as he finishes his sentence.

"Okay, okay," I chuckle, but pause before I continue, debating if I should finish my thoughts. Eh, fuck it. "But yes please, to lunch and the floor plans."

A boisterous laugh crackles through the phone, I can't help the smile that forms on my lips from the sound. "Anything you say. How's Wednesday at Ruthies?"

"Sounds great."

"Sweet dreams, Harper."

"You should know, people close to me generally call me Harps."

"Is that so?"

"It is," I confirm, as I begin chewing on my thumb nail, a smirk playing on my lips.

"Alright then. Sweet dreams, Harps."

"Goodnight, Xavier."

It's quiet for a moment before the call disconnects. I look back at my phone, before I shut the screen off and slip it in my pocket. I get up and put the fire out, letting the water extinguish the flames. Once that's done, I place my blanket in the storage ottoman I keep outside and wake Evie up.

"Eves, get your ass up and get to bed."

It takes a couple tries before she finally gets up and drags herself to the house. I finish the quick clean up of the backyard before I call Winnie in and head in for the night.

***

I have most of my stuff packed and ready to go for the end of the week. Evie and I sat down together, going over what she needs to do for Winnie while I'm gone. He's pretty easy to take care of, but with this being my first long stint without him, I'm a bit worried. I don't want him to feel like I'm abandoning him.

Xavier and I have been talking almost daily, and end the night on the phone now. It's crazy that a couple weeks ago, I had literally fallen into this guy's lap. Now, I'm heading on a trip with him and his family a couple hours north to stay in his family's ski lodge. How did my life take this turn?

Like he knew I was thinking about him, my phone rings.

"Well, hello."

"Hey," he greets, his deep baritone washing through me. "How was your day?"

I roll onto my side, putting the speakerphone on, resting my phone on the pillow next to me. I tuck my hands under my head as I respond. "It wasn't too bad. I had a couple meetings and finished off my final round of edits for one of my people. How about yours?"

I hear some shuffling on his end of the phone, and the open and closing of a fridge, indicating he's in his kitchen. I check my phone, seeing it's nine thirty. "It was busy, but that seems to be the norm. I had the vet who is covering for me come in today so I could go over what the schedule should look like in the next couple of weeks. But, it's the holidays, so you still can't truly know what the place is going to look like. My only saving grace is Todd being there to run the front desk and keep everyone alive. I don't know what I would do without them." He barely gets the last word out before a yawn comes from him. "I just got in after locking the crew up for the night. So, I'm about to grill up some chicken and veggies to scarf down before going to bed."

"That does sound like a busy day, but at least it was productive!" I feel movement on the bed and look down to see Winnie army crawling up the bed. His tail is thumping on the bed as he looks affectionately at me. Once he moves his body to melt into mine, I throw one arm over to embrace him. I kiss him lightly on the head. He huffs before he buries his head into my blankets and gets settled. I'm absentmindedly petting him, when Xavier's voice comes in after I hear a clatter on the floor.

"Ah fuck," he grunts.

Lifting myself up on my elbow, I let my curiosity show. "Is everything okay?" Pulling my phone toward me, I switch the call to video chat. When he doesn't answer right away, I think the worst. There's the clanking sounds again, and then a minute later, I hear the water running. It's then that he accepts my call, having his phone leaning up against the wall facing him at the sink.

"Yeah I'm fine, I just wasn't paying attention as I went to grab the dish out of the oven and I was using a dish cloth instead of my oven mitt, so I just burnt my thumb a bit. I'll be fine though."

"Jeez, yeah that sucks. Did you save your dinner at least?"

He chuckles. "You would be hearing a lot more swearing if I dropped my food along with it."

There's a comfortable silence as I watch him move around the kitchen, eyeing the flex of his arms as he puts on his oven mitts and then takes his dinner out of the oven. When he reaches above him his shirt rides up a bit, giving me a teasing glance of the patch of hair that starts from his belly button and works its way down into his shorts. He really is a delicious looking human being, and I'm still trying to figure out how this arrangement turned into something so—effortless.

For the last week, we've drifted between casual conversations about our days at work and what we're doing. One night, I convinced him to watch *Is it Cake?* because he didn't believe me when I said there are some people who do such a good job, you can't tell which item is the cake. That night, we watched three episodes before I fell asleep, our call on the phone still connected. I woke up that morning to drool down my cheek and a message from Xavier saying I fell asleep and he hoped my sleep was great. I find myself smiling about that moment, when Xavier interrupts.

"I actually wanted to talk about tomorrow. With it being a couple hour drive, I don't feel comfortable with you driving up there by yourself. You haven't been there before, and sometimes the road to the lodge can be confusing." I hear utensils working over a plate before it stops. "So, I'm going to pick you up."

"Oh that's really okay, I don't mind driving my—"

"I wasn't asking Harps, I would feel better if you drove up with me."

I pause there for a moment. His tone leaves no room for arguments, but he does it in a way that shows that he cares. It doesn't take me long before I agree with him. "*Fine.*"

"Good girl." There's a momentary pause when he takes a bite to eat. My eyes linger on the way his lips wrap the fork. I watch the tines as they disappear before slowly being pulled back out. I briefly remember the feel of his lips on mine, and I wish I knew what his lips felt like on other parts of my body. I tell myself to get a grip. I don't know what it is, but being around him makes me feel like a horny teenager.

It has to be because I haven't been laid in a few months. I actually don't remember the last time I even orgasmed. *Well, that's depressing.*

"So I'll pick you up around noon tomorrow?" He asks, effectively snapping me out of my orgasmless turmoil.

"What? Oh yeah. That should be fine. I'm basically all packed, and Evie said she would be over once she's finished her shift at the office tomorrow. Winnie should be good alone for that long." Evie had just started a new temp job for the Christmas season. It was a small little office that needed someone to cover reception while the normal receptionist went on holiday. It's perfect for Evie; she never likes to stay in one job longer than needed. She's always been free spirited like that. Her family is super supportive, no matter what she chooses to do with her life. Her parents took me in as a second daughter, and I'm forever grateful to have some form of consistent parental figures because of them. I truly don't know where I'd be today if it wasn't for them.

"Are you still nervous about going?" Xavier asks, bent over the counter, peering at me through the screen, his head cradled in one hand.

I shrug my shoulders. "I mean a little, but I've been feeling a bit better about it over the last couple days." I go to say something else, but a huge yawn breaks free from my mouth, effectively silencing me. When I collect myself and look back at him, he has a soft smile on his face. It's not a smile I've seen before, but I definitely put this to memory because I don't know if I've ever seen him this relaxed.

"What?" I muse, tilting my head.

He shakes his head, that smile still on his face. "Nothing, I should let you get to sleep. I'll see you tomorrow?"

"Sounds good, I'll be ready." I feel a smile of my own forming on my face. "Goodnight, Xavier."

"Night, babydoll." His voice is gentle as he hangs up.

I pull my bottom lip between my teeth, shock mixed with a soft yearning floods my mind. He just called me babydoll. *Me*. I hate pet names, but when Xavier purrs one unexpectedly? That does something to me. I roll onto my back and blink up at my ceiling, spiraling about this revelation.

My mind plays dirty and my thoughts turn to his mouth. Those firm, but delicious, lips pressed against mine as we kissed last week. I sink into the mattress, letting myself imagine those same lips trailing down my neck, skimming between my breasts as they nip and kiss, descending lower. Liquid warmth begins to pool in between my legs. I picture Xavier, on his knees, settling between my thighs.

My hands begin to slowly move their way down my body, tracing where I picture his lips have been. I cup my breasts together, imagining Xavier's massive hands kneading them before moving to pinch my hardened nipples, dipping his head down to pull one between his teeth. A hiss releases from my mouth at the pinch of pain that comes with the pleasure. The ache grows stronger, and I need more.

I throw the blankets off my body, reaching over to my end table. I grab one of my toys stashed in the drawer. I've always had them, but I swear, these things have dust on them because Dalton never really was a "team player". He always figured that he was good enough, and if I'm honest? I think he was threatened by silicone. My hand lands on one, and I smile as I pull it out. I got this suction cup dildo from Evie as a gag gift a few years ago. It's never been used. Hell, I never even took it out of its packaging.

I can't rip the box open fast enough. My pulse picks up in anticipation. I make my way to the bathroom. I could have continued on the bed, but Winnie is there, and that just seems…odd. I shut the door behind me and lock it. Why did I lock it? Honestly I don't know, but I feel like I need to.

Placing the flesh-colored silicone toy on my vanity, I quickly strip my clothes off, leaving a messy pile on the floor. Scanning the room for options, I decide on the tub for convenience. Grabbing the toy and throwing my legs over the edge, the chill of the porcelain immediately brands my ass. I inhale a quick breath preparing myself for another chill to zip up my spine before attempting to sit down again.

My breathing has evened out, but the weight of the toy in my hand sends my heart rate spiking again. Bringing the toy up to my collarbone, I take my time trailing it down to the valley of my breasts. Using the tip, I circle my left nipple until the peak hardens. I slowly run the toy along my skin before switching to the other nipple and doing the same. My chest is flushed with arousal, and I start moving the dildo down my stomach, directly toward where I throb. *Ache.*

I've never used a dildo before, but the size of this one is familiar. I spread my legs wide, bringing the tip lower, until I feel the moment it brushes over my clit. A shock of pleasure runs through my body, causing me to shudder. I run the tip over my clit again, and I buck up at the sensation. *Fuck, yes.* I continue the ministrations, starting at my clit and pushing through my folds. When I pull it away and look, the shaft is glistening with my arousal. Exhaling, I drag it along my core again, relishing the way it feels. My body isn't ready for me to slip the dildo inside, but the feeling of it rubbing against my clit? The way it soothes the ache? *That* is pleasurable enough, and I continue chasing that movement, over and over again.

I slowly slide from the side of the tub until I'm in a squatting position. My hand never stops moving the dildo over my throbbing clit, again and again. I begin thrusting with each pass, craving more friction. The pressure has been slowly building, but as I grind over the hardened silicone, I feel myself climb higher, chasing the edge faster. I cannot control the way this feels, my breath barely more than panting, a gasping of air as I give into what I crave.

The pressure almost seems unbearable, the need for release is crushing. "Oh yes," I moan, throwing my head back. My eyes close as I try to focus on what I'm doing. My mind shoots to Xavier's lips once more. The way his shirt lifted when he reached above him on the call earlier tonight. The definition of his Adonis belt carved perfectly into a V shape. The way it makes me want to trace the lines down with my tongue. I burn with the ache of needing *more.*

The thought of him pushing my legs apart as he thrusts into me, pinning me with hard and thorough snaps of his hips, is all I need to tip over the edge. Everything turns white, my body consumed by my release. A heady gust of liquid rushes from me as I drop the toy, my fingers taking over, rubbing myself through my release. I never want it to end. As my vision returns, I feel the way my clit is incredibly sensitive, overused in the best way. My knees are in the pooling of my release, and I lean forward. Placing my forehead on the cool porcelain, I attempt to get control of my breathing.

I stare down at my mess. My inner thighs are damp, but it's the puddle at the bottom of the tub that has my focus. I have *never* squirted before. I never thought it was possible. Yet, here I am, coming down with one of the best orgasms to date... in a mess of my own making. While I try to wrap my head around it, I decide to shower since I'm already here. I quickly wash my body and hair before I step out, dry off, and get back into my pajamas.

I crawl into bed and roll onto my side, my eyes heavy with exhaustion. My body is relaxed from my time in the tub and I don't fight the urge to sleep.

Chapter Sixteen

xavier

THROWING THE LAST OF my things in the truck, there's a bite to the air from the fresh coat of snow from last night. Cupping my hands together, I breathe into them for warmth before heading out to check on the animals one last time. I paid to have heated water barrels, but that doesn't mean I can always trust and rely on them. The one time I don't check is going to be the time that they're broken, and then there will be no water available.

I hear Clyde bray before I even make it around the corner. He can hear the sound of my boots crunching on the gravel, and I know he wants his morning pets. I don't care what you hear about donkeys; they are such affectionate creatures. Clyde is just a big attention whore. He will take any, and all, forms of affection. "Hey there, big guy!" I say, pulling out a carrot from my jacket pocket and presenting it to him. He chews on it happily as I scratch behind his ears. "I'm going to be gone for a couple days. Now, it's going to be Todd who's coming in and checking in with you. Don't give them any trouble. I want to hear that you were on your best donkey behavior."

Yes, I talk to my donkey like he's a human. I swear it works, and I have a soft spot for the ass. He rubs his snout up my chest and bumps my chin in affection. I laugh as I give him a few more scratches before moving on to the next area. Once the ducks are fed, and I'm satisfied with my final walk through, I head to the truck. Removing my phone from my pocket, I type out a quick message.

Xavier: Hey, I'm leaving in a few. I'll see you shortly

Harper: Hi! Sounds good! I'm just finishing my lunch so that's perfect!

Tucking my phone into my pocket, I hop into my truck. Before I know it, I'm pulling into her driveway. My stomach does a little flutter of nerves, and I feel my hands begin to sweat. This feeling is foreign to me. I don't get nervous like this. I pride myself on being level-headed, but there's something about Harper that makes me unsteady, in the best way.

Knocking on her front door, I rock back on my heels as I wait. When the door opens, I can't help the smirk that grows on my face as I take her in. We've really gotten closer over the last few weeks, and I've picked up on a few of her quirks—like how she wrings her hands when she's nervous. Or if she thinks something is really funny she snorts, much to her embarrassment. I think it's adorable. *She's* adorable.

Harper stands before me, dressed in boyfriend cut jeans and a navy knit turtleneck sweater. Her jet black locks are pulled up into a messy bun. It looks like one of those styled messy buns versus when you just quickly pull your hair up. Her green eyes pop with just mascara on her lashes.

"Hey," she says, almost breathlessly. "Come on in, I was just throwing the ball in the backyard with Winnie." She waves me in, closing the door behind me before leading the way through her place. I try to take in my surroundings, pinpointing the spots that I've only seen on video chats.

Aimlessly, I follow behind her, my eyes strain as I try to keep them above her shoulders.

I lose the battle as my eyes trail downward, and I admire how the jeans fit her body. The fabric frames her ass perfectly, like it was meant to be a part of her. The all-consuming temptation to reach forward and caress her plump ass nearly overpowers reason. With an extreme amount of self control, I manage to tear my gaze away, focusing on my surroundings just as we arrive in the kitchen. With ease, she glides through the space and continues out the sliding doors.

As soon as the doors are open, Winnie flies through, heading right toward me. I'm already bending to his level when he collides with me, effectively knocking me on my ass. A twinge of pain shoots up my back at the impact of the fall, but overall, it isn't that bad. Before I know it, there is a wet tongue moving all over my face. I try to escape it, but he is on a mission.

"Oh my God! I'm so sorry! Winnie, off!" She runs forward, grabbing Winnie by his collar and pulling him back. "That is not how we greet our guests," she whispers, scolding him gently. " He must really like you." Winnie starts barking, his whole back end swinging back and forth with excitement, making me chuckle.

Once Winnie has mellowed out, we set out to the backyard. Harper begins throwing the ball for him, but he gets distracted a couple times with the fresh snow. We watch as he begins tossing his ball in the air with his mouth, then going after it. "Sometimes, I feel like he really doesn't need me to play fetch, but just does it for my benefit." She giggles as she watches him. I take that moment to look at her, the sparkle of amusement in her eyes as she watches her dog goof off in her yard. Her cheeks have a slight tint to them. There's a small smile gracing her mouth. Her arms are crossed under chest, giving her breasts a little lift. Despite them being fully covered, I would be lying if I said I didn't take a moment to appreciate them.

I must be staring too long because a moment later, Harper's eyes connect with mine. I give her a small smile, trying to play it off like I was just looking at her for a moment, and not taking in as much as I could.

"Uhh, yeah it looks like it, eh? He's having fun though either way."

She sighs with contentment. "Yeah, he does."

There's a slight pause before she continues. "So, all my stuff is packed and ready to go. I think Winnie has burned off enough energy that he should just nap until Evie gets off work." There is a slight tremor at the end of her sentence. She tries to blow it off like she's clearing her throat, but when I look down, her arms are uncrossed and she's started wringing her hands.

"What's going on?"

Her eyes come to me and she takes a breath before blowing it out slowly. "It's just this is my first long stint away since I got him. We're still new, and I don't want him to think like I'm abandoning him." I step up next to her and grab her hands. "It's going to be okay. I've dealt with a lot of rescue dogs, and Winnie is doing good." I briefly look toward the dog in question before turning back and looking into her eyes. "How about this? We head up there and check in with Evie daily. If Winnie isn't eating or interacting with her, I will personally come here, pick him up, and bring him back to the lodge."

Her eyes go wide, disbelief and awe shining through. "You'd—you'd do that for me?"

I shrug my shoulders. "If it makes you feel better, of course I would. I don't want you to be stressed out and worried while we're there. If this is something I can do to make our time together better? I'll do it."

Her mouth opens slightly before it closes, and she nods her head. "Thank you."

A smile forms on my lips as I take a step back, heading toward the door. "It's really no problem." I hold open the door, watching Harper and Winnie go through before following. Winnie runs to his water dish to take a drink, and Harper walks toward her fridge. "Do you want something to drink before we go?"

"No thanks, I'm good. If you want to show me where your bags are, can I load them into the truck?"

"Uhm, yeah. They're just by the door. I'll meet you out there in a minute, just going to go do a final walk through to make sure I didn't forget anything."

I make my way back to the front, seeing her bags and I grab them. By the time I have everything loaded up, Harper is out of the house, and her back is to me as she locks the door. Opening the truck door, I watch as she climbs up into the cab.

"You know– I'm a big girl, I can open the door myself." She quips, a hint of amusement lacing her tone. My right hand flexes in my hand, and I barely resist the urge to pull her down and smack her ass. Her sass will be the death of me over the next three weeks.

Clicking my tongue, I remind her just who I am. "What kind of gentleman would I be if I left you to fend for yourself?" I ask, the corner of my lips twitching in amusement. After closing the door, I round the hood, I run my fingers through my hair, tugging slightly when I reach the base of my neck. A zing runs down my spine. I feel the way something gnaws at my chest, heavy and unmoving. Anxiety sinking its teeth into me as I am reminded what happens when I let someone get that close to me. It's something I promised I would never let happen again. Jumping into the truck, I quickly buckle myself in and pull out of her driveway.

"We've got about two hours ahead of us. You can pick whatever you want to listen to." Passing my unlocked phone to her so she can pick the music, the cab is filled with brief silence before the musical tones of Twenty One Pilots filter through the speakers. Leaning back in my seat, I settle in and enjoy the company.

The next couple hours are filled with a mixture of listening to music and playing rounds of twenty one questions. With every new piece of information I learn about Harper, I find a hunger for more. Her favorite color is purple. She believes in ghosts and spirits, and would love to have an opportunity to go ghost hunting. Until today, I can honestly say I've never realized that was an actual thing people do. I just thought it was something that was made up, like *Supernatural.*

Before we know it, we're coming to the road that leads up to the lodge.

"Now, I have to warn you," I start.

"That doesn't sound too good." She says, chuckling.

"It's really not *that* bad. I just—with Chloe and Derek here—there are probably going to be moments that are going to be tense. Chloe is treated like a princess, and she usually gets what she wants."

"Okay…" Her hesitance is palpable in her tone. "So is this an every man for themselves speech, or?"

"What? No!" I turn my signal on and slow down on the side of the road before I put it in park, spinning to face her. "I wanted you to know that I'm in your corner. I know how my sister can be, and I know whatever she tries to throw your way is with the purpose of bringing you down. I want to say it's a defense mechanism, but honestly she's just a self-centered bitch."

A guffaw leaves her mouth at my bluntness.

"Her and I have never gotten along. I know there are some siblings that do, but we aren't one of them." I face the road again as a sigh leaves my lips. "I haven't been to the lodge in a while myself. I wouldn't be going if you weren't coming, to be honest." I look over at her, the green of her eyes are focused on me with such intensity. I offer a small shrug before I start to pull the truck back onto the road.

It's quiet for a couple minutes. I think the conversation is over and I'm glad she knows I've got her back. I really do. I won't let her take the words my sister might spew at her seriously. It wasn't hard for me to figure out how deeply the actions of my sister and her new boy toy cut Harper and impacted her self-worth. I'll be damned if they try to make her feel worse.

"You know I have your back too, right?" It's a simple sentence, but the weight of it is heavy on my chest. I glance at her, nodding so she knows I heard her. I don't think I'm able to respond otherwise.

Just then, the lodge comes into view, pulling Harper's focus as she takes it in. "Wow," she whispers in awe "This place is fucking huge."

Pulling up to the house, I press the door opener on my visor, glad I remembered to grab it before leaving. Moving forward to the first open spot, I throw the truck in park before sliding out. I snake around the front, opening Harper's door. There's a smirk on her face as she hops down, but she doesn't argue with me. She won't win that argument.

My hand intertwines with hers as we head toward the door that connects with the main lodge. "Wait. What about our bags?" Her steps falter as she looks back at the truck.

"Don't worry about those. My parents have hired staff to grab the bags and take them to our room."

A garbled squeak leaves Harper's mouth. My arm that's connected to her is jolted back. Turning, I see her wide emerald eyes connect with mine, shimmering with panic. "Our room? – like one room. One bed. You and me?"

My lips twitch as I try to hold back the amusement that washes over me. "Uh yes. Generally that's what I mean by our room. It's a California King bed though, Harper. We can take our respective sides when we go to sleep." I say, stepping toward her, trailing my hands from her shoulders, down her arms before dropping them back to my side. "I can promise you this. I'm not expecting anything to happen behind closed doors." *Unless you tell me otherwise, which I really hope you do.*

I keep that last part to myself though.

Her eyes flick between both of mine, and I briefly catch them jump to my lips. Raising my eyebrow at her, her cheeks bloom with heat. I don't think I could get tired of making that color appear on her face.

"C'mon." I encourage, nodding my head toward the door. "Let me show you around and where you can set up your office for the week."

The next half hour is spent showing her where everything is. The kitchen, which Harper stated was a wet dream with all the industrial equipment and marble countertops, followed by the living area that leads to the back deck. There is a hot tub and a fire pit surrounded by big wooden chairs. I see the way her eyes light up at the hot tub. I make a note to take her out tomorrow, after we've had some time to settle in.

I show her the pool and sauna area that includes an indoor gym before taking her upstairs. Stopping briefly at the top of the stairs, Harper looks around before my hand tugs on hers insistently, leading her to my bedroom. It's the opposite of where Chloe and my parents usually sleep. I like the silence and being in my own space, which I think Harper will appreciate too. You tend to learn what your Chloe limit is and crave that distance.

My room's the third door to the left. Opening the door, I step back to let Harper take the first step into the room.

The room is nothing too crazy, covered in a grey color scheme. The California king bed is on a four poster canopy frame. Opposite the bed is a wall to wall bookcase. The shelves are lackluster, a few books here and there on the shelves. If I were to come up here more often, maybe the shelves would look a little fuller. Walking up to the floor to ceiling windows, I pull back the curtain, and the room is instantly bathed in amber hues from the sun. Sometimes, I just sit in the arm chair that's right by the windows, close my eyes, and soak in the sun like a cat.

"Oh my God! This bookshelf is gorgeous!" I turn around and find Harper, running her hand along the length of the shelf as she surveys the minimal books I have on there.

"If you think that bookshelf is great, just wait until I show you your office for the week." I start to walk toward her as she spins around to face me.

"You really didn't have to set me up in a full office. I could have totally worked from the bedroom. I don't want to inconvenience anyone."

Shaking my head with a tsk, I close the distance between us. My height causes her head to tilt up, as I loom over her. There's tension filling the room, but I'm unsure if it's one sided.

"Absolutely not. You need to have separation from the place you sleep and where you're going to work. Plus, there are eight rooms in this lodge, and we're only using three. It's not an inconvenience, okay?" My eyes bore into hers, waiting for her to argue with me.

I see the moment she realizes there's no point in arguing. She grumbles and throws her hands up. "Ugh, fine. Show me the room, then."

Chapter Seventeen
Harper

THIS OFFICE SPACE IS heaven, and it has everything that I need. The room has matching floor to ceiling windows like Xaviers, my desk facing the view. Out the window is a clear view of the ski slopes. The powdery white mountain tops are dusted with the green of the forest. The movement of the chair lifts moving in a mesmerizing loop, standing there I watched its movements. Shaking myself out of the trance, I head toward the leather chair. Sitting down, I run my fingers over the cool leather, and the buttery soft material feels soothing on my skin. My body sinks further into the plush chair as I take in the rest of the room. The neutral beige and browns are balanced throughout the room, but there are slight pops of blues scattered throughout. There's even a modern desk that is so gorgeous. A modern desk that looks brand new. Wait. I sit up straighter, turning my attention to Xavier, who has been standing in the doorway watching me this whole time.

"Did you buy this stuff *just* for me to work here for five days?"

Xavier just shrugs his shoulders, "I wanted you to have your own space to work." He says with such nonchalance, I sit there with my mouth open.

A smirk dons his lips, and his arms reach up to the top of the door frame as he leans forward. "I think the words you're looking for babydoll are '*thank you*.'"

My mouth snaps shut, and I watch as the mischief dances in his eyes. *Okay, two can play at that game.*

I saunter my way over to him, making sure to put an extra sway in my hips as I move. I watch his eyes trail down my body as the distance closes between us. I stop right in front of him, tilting my head up with my bottom lip between my teeth.

He's still leaning on the door frame which gives me a little advantage as I go up on my tip toes, bringing my lips to his ear. "Thank you."

It comes out breathless, and if I'm honest, I couldn't stop myself from checking him out as I moved across the room. His dark jeans hang low on his hips, the material hugging his thighs. Damn, he's mouth-watering. His blue henley shirt fits deliciously across his chest, and the way his biceps bulge out of the sleeves is damn near sinful.

I'm broken from my thoughts as I feel his nose trailing along the side of my face. My eyes flutter closed, and I tilt my head away to allow him more access to my neck. The brush of his warm breath sends noticeable shivers down my spine. Angling my face, his face shifts until his lips are so close, I feel the warmth of his breath on mine.

"Oh, there you two are! I saw your truck and was wondering –" Penelope's words fall off as she takes in how we're standing. "Oh goodness, I'm so sorry!" She quickly turns around like she walked in on us naked. A quiet chuckle leaves him before he closes the distance, quickly pressing his lips to mine. He leaves my space, turning around and giving me his back. "Hey, Mom." Penelope turns back, embracing Xavier before turning to me.

She opens her arms and rotates her body like she's showcasing the room. "Well, what do you think? Xavier told me exactly what you needed, so I made sure it arrived and was set up right away!"

My eyes go to Xavier briefly before they go back to Penelope. "It's wonderful. You guys really didn't need to go to all this trouble for me."

"Oh, pish-posh dear! It's truly no trouble. I'm just glad you were able to make it and drag my son here along." She grabs at Xavier's arm and gives him a loving squeeze as she looks up at him. He returns her smile, but it's not his real one. There's care in this smile, but it's guarded.

A moment passes, and Penelope clears her throat. "Yes, well, dinner is in the works, and it should be ready at five! I'll leave you guys to get settled in, and I'll see you at dinner!" With that, she saunters out of the room, the door closing behind her.

We stare at each other, the air tense. "You know, she seems to really be excited that you're here." I start watching as Xavier's posture changes slightly.

He shoves his hands in his pockets and clears his throat. "Uh yeah, like I said I haven't come out here in a long time. Not that my mom hasn't tried."

My mouth opens to say something, but he continues. "I'm going to leave you to get the office set up so it's ready for Monday. I'll be in the gym getting a quick workout before dinner." His body still faces me as he begins to step backwards toward the door.

"Yeah – that's fine. I'll see you later, then?" Worry begins to make its way through me. He looks at me, and gives me a soft smile before nodding and heading out the door.

❧❦

Finding my office stuff was simple. However, dragging it over to the office was a workout I wasn't prepared for. The brunt of the work is done, and I'm standing there as I do an inventory of everything I need so I'm prepared for work. The only thing left to do is get the Wi-Fi password, and then I'm golden.

My skin was sticky with sweat, and I decided I'd feel better once I cleaned myself up. Now, I'm standing in front of the bathroom mirror after the shower, feeling like a million bucks. Quickly throwing a black sweater dress over my head, I check my phone.

Xavier never responded back to the text asking for the Wi-Fi password. Biting my lip, I begin debating whether I wait for him so we can walk down together or go down alone.

I bite the bullet, heading downstairs by myself. Making my way through the hall, I go down the stairs. The dark mahogany floors contrast the eggshell cream color of the walls beautifully. There's a centralized table in the middle of the foyer that has a vase filled with fresh flowers.

I try to remember which way it was to get to the dining room, but I get turned around. I don't know where I am, and when I turn the corner I run right into a wall. No. Not a wall. My whole body freezes as hands hold on to my biceps to keep me from falling over. I wish it was Xavier who I ran into, but I'd recognize that pine needle and cinnamon scent anywhere. I close my eyes, willing this nightmare to disappear.

"Oh, sorry." Dalton mumbles, his hands quickly pull away as soon as he realizes I'm steady. I open my eyes but I keep them on the floor. I can't look at him.

Before he can say anything else, my worst nightmare comes into play. "Dalty baby, what are you doing just standing– oh."

Fan-fucking-tastic.

"Ugh, I thought it smelt like desperation over here. Back off bitch. He doesn't want you anymore."

A scoff leaves my lips before I can stop it, and I decide at that moment that I'm not going to take any of her shit. "Trust me Chloe, he's *all* yours. I hope you enjoy my sloppy seconds." And with that, I turn around, heading in the other direction. I turn down a different hallway, pushing through the next door. I find myself in the kitchen, and there are people in here working. They pay me no mind as I walk through, eventually finding myself at the door to the back deck.

My heartbeat is pounding in my ears, and my chest grows tighter with each breath. My anxiety is taking the wheel, and I can't stop it. The last thing I was expecting was a confrontation. My body moves on autopilot, stepping out the back door and onto the deck. The cool air hits my face, and a shiver tears through my body. The bite of cold on my cheeks is a welcoming distraction.

I open my eyes and look around. Five things I can see: snow, the hot tub, the fire pit, a tree, and my breath. Four things I can touch: the ground, my sweater, my face, the chairs around the fire pit. I close my eyes. Three things I can hear: the wind, my breath, and wind chimes in the distance. I open my eyes again. Two things I can smell: the trees and the faint smell of chemicals from the hot tub. One thing I can taste: I can taste a hint of crisp, resinous pine, a hint of an earthy undertone.

My heart rate has settled as a chill runs over my body. "Shit, it's cold" Mumbles from my lips as my hands move up my arm, trying to keep myself warm. "Why did I rush out here? Such a stupid choice." Looking down, I see that I also failed to put shoes on. I should probably head inside. As I turn around to head back inside, I run face first into another hard wall. "Oh, for fuck's sake!" I grumble, taking a step back, and look up at the wall of muscle that just blocked my retreat inside. This time, when my eyes connect with the person, it's not my ex but my current fake boyfriend.

A rush of relief leaves my body, "There you are. I was trying to find the dining room, and I got all turned around. Then, I got all flustered when I ran into Dalton and Chloe. *Then*, I just needed some air– so, here I am." I shrug, semi-exaggerated.

"What did she say to you?" he asks firmly.

"What?"

"It's my sister, and I know her. She wouldn't waste an opportunity to say something if—where are your shoes?" He's looking down at my feet, which I have been bouncing back and forth on.

"Well–" a yelp leaves me as I'm lifted into the air. I look around, and all I see is the ground and legs. "What are you doing? Put me down!"

"You have no shoes on, and you've been standing out here for God knows how long. I'm carrying you inside, and we're warming you up." We're heading inside before I even get another word out. I feel like my top half is bouncing on his shoulder, which is ultimately making me feel sick to my stomach. I grab hold of his lower back and support myself up. It doesn't help. Not because my stomach still hurts, but because I now have a focused frame of Xavier's ass, and I don't think I've ever been so attracted to a man's ass.

The way his ass looks in those jeans though?

Criminal.

I'm snapped out of my trance when I'm plopped onto a chair. Getting my bearings right, I realize that we're at the kitchen table.

"Stay." He sternly tells me as he straightens, moving around the kitchen. The water in the sink begins running, and he reaches under the sink, pulling out what looks like a water basin before testing the water with the inside of his wrist. When the basin is filled to his satisfaction, he takes it out and walks my way. He kneels down in front of me and places the basin to his side. Next thing I know, he's grabbing my right foot and stripping off my sock before doing the same to the other.

"Seems like this is becoming a pattern." Looking down at him on his knees stirs something in me. When it first happened with my ankle, I was in too much pain to notice anything. This time around, I'm starting to recognize the sexual tension that it stirs in me by seeing this big bulky man kneeling for me, and I flash back to that night in the tub.

He looks up at me with a raised eyebrow in question, and I chuckle. "You know...you, on your knees in front of me." I wave my hand in his direction. "This isn't the first time." His face morphs into a smirk that I swear causes a flood in my panties. He leans forward, and his voice is dangerously low as he says.

"Trust me dollface. When I'm on my knees for you, the only pain you'll feel is when it's followed with pleasure." My mouth drops open, my brain short circuiting at the words that just came out of his mouth. I've only confirmed that it's real when a chuckle falls from his mouth as he continues to place my bare feet into warm water. My feet begin to tingle as the cold dissipates from my bones.

Xavier stands and leans forward, causing me to fall backward on my chair until his hands rest on either side of me. I have to tilt my head back to keep eye contact with him as he begins to speak.

"Now— I'm going to go upstairs and get you some clean socks. You're going to stay here and wait for me to come back. Then, we are going to go make an appearance at dinner." All I can manage to do is nod my head, because his closeness is intoxicating, and if I'm honest, I still haven't fully recovered from the comment he made earlier.

That damn smirk appears on his face again before he leans closer. His lips are so close that all I'd need to do is lean forward slightly and they'd be connecting. His lips smash with mine in a quick, punishing kiss. I'm still registering that we're kissing as he pulls away. "Good girl," he murmurs, before he straightens and turns away from me. I watch him as he walks away in pure astonishment. My fingers reach up and graze my lips, still feeling the tingle from that kiss.

What was that?

Chapter Eighteen
xavier

I HAVE TO ADJUST myself as I make my way out of the room. The mere mention of being on my knees made my cock painfully hard, and I don't think she realizes just how willing I'd be to be on my knees, worshipping her. My control snapped when I pushed my lips onto hers. I've been thinking about her mouth since the first time my lips pressed against hers on Thanksgiving.

It took every ounce of control not to deepen our kiss, nipping and pulling her plush lips into my mouth.

But I couldn't do that, especially not in front of my family. Besides, this is our agreement. We'd agreed to display affection so the plan is more believable, but this is something more.

Why did I find myself kissing her when no one was around? Was it the way she felt as I was carrying her? How she stared up at me, joy shining in her eyes? A wave of possessiveness rolled over me when I saw her out in the snow with no shoes on. The only thought in my head was getting her feet warm.

Skipping steps, I make my way up to my room. Once I'm there, I go to her bags that are...empty. She must have put her clothes away already. I look through the dresser drawers before I find what I'm looking for. Once I grab the thickest pair I can find, I make my way back downstairs.

Reaching the kitchen, Harper is exactly where I left her. Something in my chest tightens at the fact that she listened to me so well. She seems to be off in her head, her eyes fixated on something. As I close the distance between us, her eyes shoot to me, and a small smile forms on her mouth.

"How are your feet feeling?"

"They're good."

"Good. Feet out." I pass her a towel to dry them off, handing her the new socks as I empty the basin, putting it back under the sink where I got it. I turn back toward her, and she's standing rubbing her hands over her thighs before she throws her thumb over her shoulder. "Should we head over to dinner? We're *definitely* late now." A nervous chuckle leaves her lips.

"It's fine, I told my mom that we were going to be late. She pushed dinner to five thirty. So," I grab her hand and head to the next room over. "We're actually just on time," I whisper in her ear.

We enter the dining room to find only my parents seated. My dad is whispering something in my moms ear as she leans into him. There's a soft smile on her face before she laughs, lightly smacking his chest with her hand. When she looks over and sees we walked in, her face shines.

"Come! Sit, sit!" She encourages us to join them.

Leading Harper, I have her sit in a seat across from my mom, and I sit beside her. When I look up, I see my mom staring at me with affection that I haven't seen from her in a long time. Unsure how to take that, I readjust in my seat, putting my arm around Harper's chair. My mom and Harper begin talking about Christmas traditions. As their conversation deepens, I excuse myself to mix us a drink. My dad slides up beside me and begins to refill his own.

"You seem different, son. Lighter." He comments before turning and resting his elbows on the bar, looking over at the table where the girls are deep in conversation. I smile as Harper talks animatedly, hands flying everywhere as she speaks.

I mimic the position my father is in as I take in the scene. "I mean, I am different. A lot of good has happened lately." There's a brief silence before I continue. "I was doing well with just focusing on the clinic. The new addition was going to be my main focus for the foreseeable future. But then, Harper came in with her dog, and she fell into my life – literally. She went to introduce herself and fell *into* me." Chuckling, I take a sip of my drink before releasing a sigh. "We ran into each other later that night." I shrug. "We talked, and I just decided to take a chance."

"Well, it looks good on you. I'm happy you decided to let someone into your life since –"

"Don't, Dad. Please."

He puts his hands up in surrender and doesn't say anything more. He pats me firmly on my shoulder before he returns to his seat beside his wife.

Returning to my own seat, I pass Harper her drink. She smiles at me in thanks. I throw my arm back around her shoulder, and she sinks into me with ease as she takes a sip. We sit there for a couple minutes before I check the time. We should have started dinner already but my sister has yet to make her presence.

"Are we going to start supper?"

Just on cue, Chloe comes barging into the room, face in her phone as she plops down in the chair dramatically. She's typing away furiously, and the silence is pungent as Mom looks past Chloe, presumably waiting for Deke to come through the door next.

"Chloe, dear. Where's Dalton?"

Her eyes leave her phone as she huffs. "He's on some work call. Something stupid." Her response is short, eager to be back furiously typing on her phone. The silence stretches on for a couple minutes before the doors open, and the kitchen staff come in with dinner. We start with a spring salad topped with slices of fruits, feta cheese, and a raspberry vinaigrette, paired with fresh dinner rolls. A warm puff of steam escapes the roll when I tear it open.

The table is relatively silent as we eat. Chloe hasn't spoken much, but she's also still glued to her phone, despite the multiple attempts my parents have tried to engage with her. When the salad is cleared, the main course of roasted pork loin, flame-roasted vegetables, and mashed potatoes is placed in the center of the table. My mouth begins to water at the smell of it all mingling together.

We all work on filling our plates, and I didn't realize how starved I was until the main dishes were placed down. Peering at Harper, I see that she has barely put anything on her plate. She's looking down at her food as she takes small bites. I begin to eat my own meal, but I can't stop watching her, seeing what she's doing. I don't want to interject because she might not be a big dinner eater, but her stiff posture says otherwise.

"So." Chloe starts, her phone placed beside her plate, her eyes zeroed in on Harper. I sit up straight as I wait for what's going to come out of her mouth. "I'm just *curious* Harper– where you got the nerve to try and butt yourself into my life and my family."

My mom begins to choke on her drink. "*Chloe!*" she scolds. "What is wrong with you? This is not how we speak to our guests!"

"Oh please Mom. I still don't believe these two just randomly met and got together. When she was so desperate to get Dalton back when he ended things."

Harper laughs, full of sarcasm. Shaking her head, she wipes her mouth with her napkin before tossing it on her plate. "Desperate to get Dalton back? What exactly did he tell you because that's not the version that I lived through. I do *not* want him back. He burned that bridge the moment he decided to sleep with you while we were *still together.*" I snap my teeth together on the t's, and she flinches.

There is a tense silence as the news that was just disclosed sinks in. My moms eyes are the size of saucers as they bounce between Harper and Chloe. My dad's face has turned a shade of red that only arises when he's pissed. Chloe, of course, is just pissed that she was called out for taking someone's boyfriend. Harper pushes her chair back and stands up. "If you'll excuse me. I've lost my appetite. I'm so sorry" Before I can get her attention she's out of the room.

"Do you always have to be such a bitch Chloe?" I snap at her, pushing my plate away from me. Appetite gone. Standing abruptly, quickly glancing at my parents, "Mom, Dad I'm sorry."

My moms mouth opens and closes a couple times. She looks like she's still trying to comprehend everything that just happened. It's my dad who responds. "No need to apologize. Clearly, we need to have a chat with our daughter." His eyes whip to Chloe who is finally starting to look a little ashamed of her actions. At least, I hope that's what the look on her face is.

"I'm going to go check on Harper." My Dad nods as he turns his attention to Chloe, yelling at her before I even get out of the room.

"How embarrassing! To find out that my own daughter ruined a relationship! Not to mention, you worked *under him*! I went out on a line to get you that job, Chloe! And this is how you act?—" The conversation turns muffled as the door closes behind me, but I could care less as I race toward our room.

Entering the room, I see that the bathroom door is closed. Pacing the room, I start to think of what I can do to make this better. The overwhelming feeling to go to her wins out as I stride toward the door. I knock and wait for a response, but there's nothing. I take my chance and try the knob. It's unlocked.

"Harper?" I open the door just enough to allow my voice to travel, but also giving her a chance to tell me not to come in if she really doesn't want me there.

"Yeah," she grumbles.

"Can I come in?"

There is a garbled noise that sounds like a yes, so I don't hesitate and walk in. She's there, sitting on the edge of the tub, her elbows on her knees and head in her hands. I make my way over, leaning on the vanity as I take her in. There is definitely something going on.

"What's going on? *Talk to me.*"

She takes a breath before she sits up, resting her hands on her knees. "I'm sorry. I didn't mean to air any dirty laundry at dinner. I just– I couldn't just let her sit there and fling false accusations. Making me seem like a crazy obsessed ex trying to get him back." Her eyes meet mine, and I can see the stress in them. "I especially don't want you to think I'm trying to get him back. I do *not* want him back. I'd never trust him in that capacity again. I know we aren't serious, and like, we have this common goal. I know this is for show. But I still like you as a person. You make me laugh, and you bring this calmness that just helps my anxiety—" She stops talking abruptly. "And now, I'm rambling." She stands up and goes to walk away, but I grab her wrist to stop her. She turns to look at me, and I pull on her arm to bring her close to me. When she's close enough, I pull her into a hug.

She just seems like she needs physical contact. She's rigid for a second before her body melts, and she wraps her arms around my waist, tucking her head into my chest. I rub my arm up and down her back in a soothing pattern. Eventually, she pulls back and tilts her head up to look at me. Looking into her eyes, I can see that she's no longer in her head. She needs to take her mind off things and relax.

"Go get your bathing suit on." I keep my voice firm, giving her no room to have a discussion.

She raises her brow in question.

"Let me handle things for the rest of the night, alright?"

She pauses for a second. "Okay." Harper spins, walking out of the bathroom. *Shit.* Now I'm stuck here while she's in the other room getting changed into her bathing suit. I try to keep myself busy for the appropriate amount of time. I brush my teeth and use the washroom. I stand there for a couple more minutes before I make my way to the bathroom door, pausing before I open it. I decide to put my hand over my eyes to be respectful. "Is it safe to come in?"

There's a giggle from somewhere on my left. "Yes it's safe- thank you for asking."

I remove my hand from my eyes and she's standing over by the bed. She has her phone in her hand then shuts off the screen and puts it down. She's wearing this black one piece suit that accentuates her curves. My hands itch to run over her hips and grab a handful of her ass as I pull her against me. My mouth waters as she turns to face me fully. The cross straps of the bathing suit pushes her breasts together in a way that makes me want to rest my head there and never move.

I walk toward the dresser with my clothes in them and grab my trunks. "I'll be right back, and then I'll take you to sit in the hot tub." Her face splits open into a big smile.

"Really? I was wondering when I would get a chance to go there!" She claps her hands together a couple times. "Okay, I'll let you get dressed. I'm just going to text Evie quickly to check on Winnie."

I make my way back to the bathroom and close the door. I take my shirt off quickly, tossing it into the corner of the bathroom. My pants and boxers follow after. I grab my trunks, sticking one foot in, then the other, before pulling them up and tying the strings. I move over to the closet, grabbing two of the world's softest towels. When I head back into the room, Harper is still in the same spot as when I left. She smiles at me, quickly finishes her typing then crawls off the bed. She reaches out, and I grab it with mine. A blush crosses her face, and it's then that I realize she was trying to grab one of the towels. Oh well.

I pull on her hand, leading her to the deck where the hot tub is. Thankfully when we get out there, there's no one else with us. I didn't want to run into my parents, or Chloe, at all for the rest of the night. I especially didn't want Chloe near Harper. A roll of protective instincts kick in at the thought of Harper being spoken to like that again. My grip on her hand tightens as we head toward the tub. I put the towels off to the side where we will be able to grab them easily when we get out, and I lead her to the stairs attached to the hot tub. I hold her hand as she steps in and submerges herself into the heat.

A groan of satisfaction leaves her lips, and I clench my jaw as my dick twitches hearing that sound come out of her. Focus. I just need to get into the hot tub so that my dick can be hidden in case it continues to have a mind of its own...especially if she keeps making those noises.

I lower myself quickly into the hot tub. The heat working over my body and relaxing my muscles. I look across the water and see the woman who has slowly been making me crazy. I lost control in the kitchen earlier, and now that's all I can think about as I sit here across from her. It plays on a constant loop in my head. With her jet black hair in a messy bun on the top of her head and the steam of the hot tub clouding around her, it almost seems like I'm lost in a fever dream.

The emerald of her eyes are so captivating, and there's a twinkle in her eyes as she looks back at me. "So," she starts. She begins to trace her hands along the top of the water, moving them back and forth over the surface. "What are some of the things you like to do around here?"

I think about that for a minute. "I mean it's been awhile since I was here last." I lean back in the tub and spread my legs as I get comfortable. "There's this cute little village bakery I loved to visit. The owners are this couple that have run the place for, like, forty years. They have hands down *the* best chocolate croissants I've ever tasted in my life."

"Oh, those sound phenomenal. Can you take me to check it out?"

"Absolutely. We can make it the first thing we do once you're done with your work week. How does that sound?"

"Perfect!" Her smile spreads wide, joy illuminating her face at the prospect of a decadent pastry. It makes a smile spread over my own face, and that warm feeling begins to start in my chest again. I find myself bringing my knuckles to my chest to rub.

Spreading my arms across the back of the hot tub, I take in the beauty before me. Harper sits across from me, her eyes fixated on the movement of her hands moving through the water, soft smile on her face. The calmness that she emanates settles something in me that I didn't think I could feel again being here. With her in this hot tub. Here in a place I haven't been in years. I thought that being back here would be suffocating. That I would be thrown back to the pain and loss that happened so long ago.

I feel something on my knee, snapping me out of my swirling thoughts. My eyes snap to hers, and her head tilted to the side as she studies me.

"You alright?"

I shake my head before bringing my hand up from the water and wiping my face. "Yeah sorry, my mind just took off there for a moment." Her foot is still on my knee. So I lean forward, hand grasping around her foot before I pull. A yelp leaves her lips as she slips forward slightly.

"Come over here," I say with a chuckle. "I promise I won't bite."

She removes her foot from my lap and slides along the bench of the hot tub, inching closer. Just then, she returns her feet to my lap, and I instinctively grab them. I don't hesitate to make her feel good, and a foot massage sounds like the perfect idea. As I bring my thumb over the balls of her feet, I see her head drop back. A moan leaves her lips.

I pause in my movements, and take a deep breath. The sounds she's making are testing my control. "Babydoll," I warn.

"Hmm?" Her head lolls to the side as she opens her eyes. They're hooded as I continue my motion on her feet.

"If you keep making sweet noises like that, I won't be in control of what I might do."

Her body straightens.

Shit. I went too far.

Then, I notice how her eyes are dilated. Keeping our gazes locked, I graze my hand up her calf, massaging her there. Her mouth opens, and a gasp falls into the air.

Her lids narrow, that stare of her becoming more lust-filled with each pass of my hand. I feel her body soften, becoming pliant under the pads of my fingers. Another breathless moan leaves her lips, and my hands tighten on instinct on her calf. My cock is hard as a rock, straining against the front of my trunks. Removing one hand, I try to readjust myself without her noticing, but that fails miserably as her eyes zero in on my movements under the bubbling jets. I clench my jaw as she slowly takes her plump bottom lip between her teeth.

"Harper," I say sternly.

"That's not my name," she breathes.

Oh.

A low growl releases from deep in my chest as I lean forward, my hands trailing up the outside of her thighs. "Babydoll. My restraint is barely more than a thin string. Be very careful what you say next."

A breathless laugh leaves her lips before she pushes up on her arms to lean into me, bringing her lips to nearly touch my own. The mixture of mischief and lust swirling in her eyes tells me exactly what she's going to do next.

She pulls back just painfully enough, and lets out a moan. *Fuck it.*

My lips crashing onto hers, swallowing the sound as my hands move to cup the backside of her thighs. I drag her to me, placing her legs on the outside of my thighs, forcing her to straddle my lap. Her arms have wrapped around my neck as she intensifies the kiss. Her tongue grazes across my lips before I open, allowing her access. Our tongues tangle together, as my hands skim her curves.

Her hips rock into me, grazing over my hard cock. I grab hold of her, pulling her down as I thrust up. Her hands grip the back of my hair tightly as another moan slips from her lips, and her forehead resting up against mine. "Fuck," she whispers. "That feels so good."

I continue to thrust up into her. The friction is intoxicating, and the lust swirls between us as the pleasure builds. Harper has taken over grinding her core over me, and she picks up the pace.

"That's it" I huff. "Grind that greedy little pussy over my cock. Make yourself come for me, babydoll. Use me." Harper's breathing has started to pick up as her hips begin to falter. I can tell she's close. The way her bathing suit is designed, I can't gain access to her breasts the way I want to, but I'll make it work. I lean forward, taking her covered nipple into my mouth and suck hard.

"Oh, fuck." She moans, her hands on the back of my head holding me in place.

"Don't stop. Please," she whines. I need her to come, and I need her to come now, because the way her pussy feels? Even with the layers between us?. I'm going to come in my swim trunks. I bite down on her nipple, and she detonates. She tugs the back of my head, and as I release her swollen nipple, she crashes her mouth onto mine. My orgasm rushes through me. I keep thrusting up into her to prolong our pleasure as long as I can.

Her body begins to relax as her orgasm finishes. Our kissing has slowed to a casual pace. My hands run up and down her back as her hands play with my hair. When she pulls back, her eyes bounce back and forth between mine, and my mind starts to clear from its foggy lust filled haze. I follow her, pressing my lips to hers in a soft kiss.

"Let's get out of here, and get ready for bed."

She nods her head as she starts to climb off of me. I watch her step out of the hot tub, my eyes following the sway of her hips before she wraps her towel around her body. I grab my towel and wrap it around my waist before coming up behind her, placing my hand on her lower back as we head inside.

We make our way up to the bedroom and take our turns getting ready for bed. I let her go first and take the moment to quickly check my work email, making sure everything's in order for my absence before plugging my phone in the nightstand.

Harper steps out of the bathroom in a beige two piece pajama set. Her dark hair is falling around her face as she makes her way to the other side of the bed. I grab my pajama pants and shirt before I take my turn in the bathroom.

As I come back to the bedroom, Harper is sitting up on the left side of the bed, the bedding pooled around her waist, and her laptop sits on her lap. Her brows furrowed in concentration as she reads. I love to see how concentrated she is when she's fully consumed in her work. I walk up to the right side of the bed, and only when do I pull back the covers, does she notice I've come out of the bathroom.

"Oh, sorry. I just thought I'd get a head start on editing one of these manuscripts. I tend to do this sometimes before bed. It just helps me wind down. I hope you don't mind? If you do, I can put it away." She goes to close her laptop when I shake my head.

"No, that's fine. If this helps you wind down for bed, I won't interrupt you. I can usually fall asleep under any conditions." I chuckle as I climb into the bed and lay on my side facing her, watching her do her thing. Occasionally she highlights something and begins typing rapidly, before she continues on.

The calming notes of her working away and the sound of her typing are the last things I hear before sleep takes me.

Chapter Nineteen
Harper

I T FEELS LIKE I'M in the warmest cocoon and it is *lovely*. God, I don't remember when I got these sheets, but I'm forever thankful for them. As I attempt to stretch, I register the weight around my midsection. My eyes fly open, and as I look around, it dawns on me. I'm at Xavier's parents ski lodge. Which means...

I look down, and see a muscular tattooed arm wrapped around me. Before I can appreciate the artwork, my bladder begins to scream at me, demanding relief. Slowly and carefully, I grab his hand, moving it behind me to release my body from his grasp. I slowly slip out of bed and quickly grab some leggings, a baggy sweater, bra and some underwear. Then I make my way to the bathroom, closing the door and locking it. Placing my clothes on the vanity, I go through my morning routine, not skipping a single step. Braiding my hair, I quickly brush my teeth before unlocking the door. As I open it, I immediately spin around, a yelp echoing in the space.

"Oh my fuck. I'm so sorry."

"Shit." I hear a thump, and then shuffling from behind me. "Okay, you can turn around."

My cheeks and neck flush as I face him. He's got on a pair of loose basketball shorts with a grey Henley shirt. *Much* more clothing than when I opened the bathroom door. I was not expecting to see Xavier's full ass. "I am so sorry." I apologize, bringing my hands to cover my face.

"No, it's okay. I figured you were going to be in there for a bit, so I thought I'd change quickly. It's poor timing on my part." When I peek through my fingers, he's got his arms crossed over his chest, and he's looking at me with his head tilted.

I pull my hands away from my face, rocking on my toes. "So. I was about to head down and get something to eat. Did you want to join me?" I slowly start walking to the bedroom door, while I wait for him to answer.

"Nah, you go ahead. I'm going to get a quick workout before I eat. I meant to wake up earlier, but I slept like the dead last night." He's sitting on the bed now, lacing his runners before he stands. "But, I'll walk you to the kitchen before I go to the gym."

We make our way downstairs in silence. I don't miss the brush of his fingers against mine as we walk. The heaviness of what happened last night hangs between us. Should I bring it up? Should we talk about it? That definitely wasn't done for show. What started as a relaxing hot tub soak soon turned into a hot and heavy make out session. Okay, it wasn't *just* making out. I dry humped the shit out of him in a lust filled haze until my orgasm slammed into me so hard, I was seeing stars for what felt like hours.

I'm so lost in my own thoughts, and I don't realize we've arrived in the kitchen. Xavier leaves for the gym, and I make my way to the fridge. I've never been much of a breakfast person, but what usually gets me through is a smoothie. I make my way around the kitchen, finding the blender and grabbing the ingredients that I need to make the perfect smoothie. I'm pouring it into a cup when Penelope walks in, a smile gracing her face when she sees me.

"Oh Harper! Good morning! How'd you sleep?" She walks around the island I'm standing at and comes beside me.

"It was good! Those sheets are to die for, they're so comfortable. I felt like I was sleeping on a cloud." I take a sip of my smoothie, humming with satisfaction.

"Those are my favorite sheets too! I loved them so much, I bought a set for all the beds!" She walks over to the cupboard and pulls out a glass herself. "I hate to ask, but do you happen to have any leftover smoothie? It looks delicious."

I look into the blender, seeing there's quite a bit left. "Yes absolutely, I truly don't know how to make a single serving smoothie unless it's in one of those bullets." Picking up the blender, I fill her cup before going to the sink to rinse it out.

Penelope and I spend the next hour chatting about the plans for the next couple weeks. She asks me what my work week will look like so she can plan the rest of the week accordingly. I give her the general idea of what my schedule looks like. I don't have too many things booked, but there are a few things I want to accomplish.

We part our ways shortly after, and I head over to my makeshift office and begin working.

A pang of hunger brings me out of focus. My body is screaming at me that I've been hyper-focused on work longer than I should've been. A quick glance to the clock confirms what I already know. I worked all day with no break, skipping lunch. One meeting turned into another, while spending what little downtime I had squeezing in editing. When I wasn't doing edits, I was answering emails from potential clients and scheduling consultation meetings for the upcoming year.

I look at my phone, seeing that I have six messages. There are a couple from Evie giving updates on Winnie. He seems to be handling everything well, although I feel like there were a lot of goodies given to him in bribery. That's just something I'll have to deal with when I get home.

The other messages are from Xavier. They start off casual, checking in on how I'm doing. As the time lapses between the messages, they become more concerned.

Xavier: How's it going in there? Do you need anything?

Just as I'm about to answer him, the office door swings open. Xavier enters with a plate of food and a bottle of water in his hand. His hair looks disheveled, as if he's run his fingers through them multiple times. He's got an olive green sweater paired with grey sweatpants. I mean, he has to know what he's doing wearing those, right? How torturous that is? Does he know that's how you make the girls pant?

He stalks toward the desk, placing the plate and water bottle beside my computer. When he straightens and crosses his arms, I can't help but take in the way his biceps bulge and his forearms flex. The cords of his muscles move the ink that's plastered up his arm, shifting them in a way that makes them dance.

He looks down at me, and I can't entirely read the expression on his face. There's a combination of concern and irritation, but I don't know what the issue is. I won't find out unless I say something.

But when I'm about to talk, he's already speaking.

"Did you eat anything today?"

"Of course." I say defensively. Of course I ate, he just doesn't need to know that it was this morning...or that it was only a smoothie. I lean back in my chair, matching his energy when I cross my own arms over my chest. I catch his eyes drift quickly down toward my breasts, and I smirk.

"Are you sure about that?" He asks, as he uncrosses his arms, leaning forward on the desk toward me.

I place my hands on either side of my chair before I stand up, placing my hands on the desk lined up with his, mirroring his movements.

"Yup." I put extra emphasis on the 'p'. His eyes narrow on me, and he doesn't say anything. I begin growing uneasy with the silence. I shift slightly, but refuse to break eye contact.

He moves closer, bringing our faces until they're just a breath apart. He tilts his head as if he's going to cross the distance. I inhale sharply before he whispers against my lips. "Liar." Xavier steps backward with a smirk on his face and nods his head toward the plate of food on my desk.

My mouth drops open, which just earns me a chuckle. He sits in the armchair that's placed by the window before he continues. "Eat your supper, and tell me about your day." He brings his right foot up, resting his ankle on his left knee. I sit back down and pull the plate toward me. I look down and see a chicken pot pie on a medium-sized plate. The steam rushes out as my fork cracks through the crispy crust, releasing its contents onto the place. The smell of comfort envelopes my senses as the first bite touches my lips. My eyes roll to the back of my head as I savor the rich, creamy taste.

"Why is everything that's made here so delicious?" I'm already getting my fork ready for my next bite. Xavier doesn't answer me. He just watches me eat. If it were any other situation, I would find this creepy, but there's an almost satisfaction coming from him as I do as he's asked.

I spend the next thirty minutes eating and telling him about my day. He tells me about his, although it sounds like he was mostly doing the same and checking in with the clinic. When I'm done eating, we go down to take my dishes to the kitchen.

We run into his parents in the living room where they are snuggling up to each other watching a movie. Xavier tries to sneak us by, but his mom catches us and *insists* we join them. To Xavier's reluctance, we join them. He leads me over to the other couch, and plops himself down the length of the couch. In the next moment, he's pulling me down onto his lap. A small squeak leaves my lips as I try to get off him.

"I shouldn't be sitting on you. I'll hurt you," I grumble, trying to shimmy off him.

His grip on me tightens as he leans forward into my ear, whispering through clenched teeth. "If you keep moving like that, we'll have a whole other problem on our hands." I go still as the realization of what he says washes over me. So instead, I slide down between his legs, making it so that I'm not actually on him, I lean into him so my back is to his chest.

It's some sort of romantic Christmas comedy that's on, but I can't fully pay attention. Xavier has been rubbing circles on my stomach since he wrapped his arm around my belly. He started it a few minutes after we got comfortable, and it's been a consistent motion since. My stomach has been clenching as warmth slowly builds between my legs.

When the movie is over, I jump out of his lap, saying goodnight to his parents before I quickly make my way to our room. I just need a cold shower before bed. Xavier is keeping pace with me as we walk back to our space. I glare in his direction as he moves down the hall with such nonchalance, while I'm low-key trying not to breathe heavily from the exertion of energy it's taking to get into the bedroom quicker.

Xavier beats me to the door and opens it for me to go in. "You and your incessant need to always open my freaking door," I mutter as I move past him. I grab my pajamas before I beeline for the bathroom. "I'm just going to shower and get ready for bed." I close the door, flipping the lock before resting my back against it as I take a couple deep breaths. When I open my eyes again, I'm a bit calmer, but there's still an undercurrent of need that's pulling in my groin. I toss my pajamas on the counter before grabbing a towel from the cabinet. I grab my toothbrush and put toothpaste on it, shoving the toothbrush into my mouth as I start aggressively brushing my teeth. My reflection only confirms the growing flush crawling along my skin. I begin to think of the way Xavier growled in my ear as he told me to stop squirming. Ashiver runs down my spine. I bend over and spit in the sink, rinsing off my toothbrush and putting it away. I turn the shower on and strip out of my clothes.

Stepping into the cold shower stream, I hiss as the cold water shocks my system. "Motherfucker, that's cold." I mumble as I quickly rinse my body down, effectively using the heat that has slowly been burning me up all evening. Grabbing the knob, I turn up the heat, and I grab the shampoo to begin the process of washing my hair.

Ten minutes later, I'm stepping out of the shower, toweling off before beginning my nighttime routine. Do I go through the motions a bit slower than normal? Perhaps.

I take one last look at myself in the mirror, breathing deeply before I head for the door. I step through to see Xavier laying on his side of the bed. his back on the mattress and his hands behind his head as he stares up at the ceiling. He looks deep in thought, but as soon as I start walking to the bed, he's turning his head in my direction, watching me.

"How was your shower?" He keeps his tone casual, but there seems to be a hint of amusement in his question.

"It was exactly what I needed. I'm beat though so I can't wait to crawl into these sheets." As I go to grab the sheets to pull them back, they're already on the move. Xavier had already flung the blankets over so all I'd have to do is crawl in. I give him a quick smile as I adjust the pillows to where I want them. Two pillows on my side, so I have a pillow to hug. One pillow goes underneath my knee.

However, I find myself copying his posture and laying on my back as well. There's a moment of silence before either of us speaks.

"Goodnight, Harps."

"Goodnight, Xavier."

As soon as I respond, he leans toward the nightstand and turns off the light, blanketing us both in darkness.

Chapter Twenty

Harper

X AVIER AND I HAVE quickly developed our own routine. He goes for his morning workout while I'm working. He checks in around lunch time, when he brings me something to eat, and we sit and chat. He sometimes spends the afternoon in the office with me, just doing some check-in calls or sending emails for the clinic, while I continue on my work day. If I have any video meetings, he leaves me alone. To be honest? It's been nice.

The evenings are always different. We don't always gather for dinner, but when everyone does, it's slightly tense. I can usually ignore both the daggers that Chloe sends my way, and the way Dalton looks at me, almost as if he wants to say something. He's tried to talk to me alone a few times. After the second attempt, Xavier hasn't left my side very often in hopes of discouraging him from approaching me. I have nothing to say to Dalton, so I don't understand why he's trying to get me alone to talk.

When there isn't a family dinner, I find myself having a girl dinner. Xavier has taken note of that, and sometimes has a plate made up with all my favorite healthy snack foods. I usually take those with me and sit in the hot tub with an audiobook in my ears to relax.

It's Friday night, and Xavier and I have made plans to watch a movie followed by playing card games. It's not the most thrilling night to most people, I'm sure. But I would choose these nights over one out at the bar any day.

Speaking of going out and partying, it seems to be like all that Chloe and Dalton do. They have gone out almost every night. I'm not complaining because the less run-ins with Chloe, the better. There are still two weeks of our vacation, so anything can happen. The optimistic side of me hopes that everything will work out, and we will be able to coexist. But the cynical part of me just laughs in my face.

I'm in the kitchen looking for some popcorn or some type of snacks for the movie. I was able to find some popcorn kernels, so there *has* to be a popcorn maker here somewhere. There is a pantry door I haven't tried yet, so I head in there.

Bingo.

This room has all the extra appliances, ready to be grabbed and used. I do a quick scan, spotting the popcorn maker on a shelf at the back of the room. As I make my way over there, I feel a presence behind me. The back of my neck prickles, and instantly I become a bit uneasy. I grab the appliance and turn around. There, standing in the frame of the door, is Dalton.

Fucking great.

I sigh heavily. "What do you want, Dalton?"

His mouth thins for a minute, as if he's pondering what he wants to say. "I just–I wanted to talk to you. I've wanted to talk to you for a while."

"Have you ever thought that I don't want to talk to you, Dalton?" I bite back, not policing my tone. Walking toward the door, I am forced to stop a few feet in front of him. "Can you move, please?"

You'd think I'd kicked his puppy based on the look he gives me before stepping back. I move past him quickly before getting to the counter where I have everything set out. I plug the machine in and turn it on. The machine roars to life, and I begin to dump the kernels, watching them disappear from sight. Familiar popping fills the kitchen, and as I place a bowl in front of the popcorn machine, Dalton lingers.

"Harps."

"Don't call me Harps. You lost that privilege when you broke me."

Devastation rolls over him, followed closely by defeat, as my words clearly resonate. "I'm sorry. Harper, if you can just give me a couple minutes to talk to you."

Turning around, I grab the bowl of finished popcorn and move over to the microwave to melt the butter before throwing it on. "I don't want to talk. I've already told you. Just drop it." I focus on the numbers counting down on the microwave, hoping he'll get the hint and leave me alone.

"How can you not give me just a couple of minutes, after all this time? You won't listen to anything I have to say?" His voice becomes more irritated as he continues, and I really don't want to be having this conversation, let alone be in the same room as Dalton. He's not getting the hint. What do I have to do? A dark, deep tone rumbles from behind me.

"She already told you. She's not interested." A chill runs down my spine as Xavier's presence fills the room.

"This really isn't your concern, Xavier." Dalton snaps at him.

The room turns cold, and I turn around to witness what's happening. Xavier stalks forward until he's toe to toe with Dalton.

"I think when it involves my girlfriend," he growls, his tone lethal. "It sure as fuck does concern me. Especially when I've heard her explicitly telling *you* to drop it." Xavier looking down at Dalton, despite being nearly the same height.

The tension is thick. I don't think Dalton is going to back down. Maybe one day, I'll want to let him have his minute, but he isn't going to get it right now. Just as I'm about to diffuse the situation, Dalton's jaw flexes. I watch his eyes dart over to me quickly before putting his arms up in surrender, and he steps back from Xavier.

Once he's gone, Xavier turns toward me and walks over. Placing one hand on the side of my face, he tilts my head up to meet his gaze. His thumb grazes my cheek as he looks back and forth in my eyes, checking if I'm alright. Concern swirls in his eyes, reminding me of the way the ocean dances with the shore; I immediately begin to relax. A smile slowly spreads across my face, and I lean into his palm.

"You okay?" he asks quietly.

I nod my head in response. "I'm good. Thank you." My tongue slips between my lips, moistening them as I try to redirect the mood. "Let's get set up, and then pick a movie. I can't wait to just lay on the couch," I suggest, pulling Xavier toward the other room.

I feel like I'm floating on a cloud, and the warmth surrounding me feels safe as I try to stay asleep. It doesn't work, and I find myself slowly becoming aware of my surroundings. I don't know what's happening, but I am moving through the house, and my head is resting on a firm spot.

Recollections of this evening flood my mind. After the encounter with Dalton, we made our way to the living room, where we set up our movie night. After arguing about what to watch for over a half hour, I convinced him to watch *Vampire Diaries* with me. He doesn't get the hype, and I think he only agreed with me so that we would just watch *something*. As we got into episode three though, I could see he was beginning to enjoy the show too.

Xavier's mom popped in at one point to invite me down to the village and visit the holiday market. I agreed, because it dawned on me that I still needed to find something for Xavier for Christmas. Fake dating or not, I can't be sitting there on Christmas morning, empty handed. I should probably get something for his parents too.

Once she left, we got back into the show. The last thing I remember is shifting from sitting on my own couch cushion to having my feet tucked into Xavier's lap.

"What are you doing?" I mumble, feeling the dryness in my mouth, and it makes me smack my lips together a couple times.

"You fell asleep on the couch, and while you did look adorable, I figured you'd appreciate sleeping in our bed." I pull my head from his chest, peering up at him. His focus is on making sure I make it to the bed, so I take a moment to take him in fully. His brow is slightly furrowed with concentration as we move up the staircase. I'm more awake now, but he doesn't put me down. I don't protest, and I don't entirely mind it. When I'm with him, I don't find myself worried about my body—or my weight. Xavier makes me feel secure, and I don't feel like I'm too much. The emotions surrounding these feelings are new...and terrifying.

My attention returns to the man cradling me in his arms. I see his strong jawline, scattered with a five o'clock shadow. I imagine how it would feel under my fingers if I were to reach up, gliding my hand over his jaw. Being this close, I'm able to see the faint freckles dusted over his nose and his cheeks. He has slight crows feet at the corner of his eyes, showing me that under his usual serious state, he still laughs and enjoys himself.

As we make it to our bedroom door, I pat on his chest, "You can let me down. I'm perfectly capable of taking it from here." He grunts in dismissal as he leans down with me still in his arms, and opens the door before kicking it closed. Xavier crosses the room and gently sets me on the bed.

He stands, stepping back and puts his hands in his pocket. "I'm going to go take a shower. Did you want to use the washroom before I go in?"

I shake my head and smile. "Uh sure, let me just go brush my teeth real quick, then it's all yours." Darting into the bath, I take care of business quickly. When I come back out, Xavier is grabbing his clothes from the dresser.

"All yours."

He quickly passes by me, grazing his hand across my hip. I hear him mumble a thanks before the shower turns on a moment later. Heading over to the dresser, I grab my own pajamas, changing into them quickly. I'm just pulling up my pants when I hear a noise come from the bathroom. I whip my head, seeing the door to the bathroom had never closed all the way. The light streams from the door, with a little billow of steam curling through the opening, and the water is noticeably louder now.

I settle into bed, dipping beneath the sheets but another noise makes me pause. A deep moan filters out of the bathroom, sending a chill down my body, and reminding me of the noises that came from him as I straddled him in the hot tub.

I should go close the door.

Yep, that's exactly what I should do. I quietly make my way to the door, but when I reach forward to close it, I indulge myself, taking in the view that is reflected in the vanity mirrors.

Xavier is standing in the shower, his weight held up by a hand pressed to the glass door. His eyes are closed, wet hair slicked back, and his brows are furrowed in concentration. There's tension in his neck, and as my eyes make it down his body, I notice the shift of his other arm. My eyes quickly move past his chiselled chest, down his toned stomach, as I zero in on where his bulging forearm is working. The grip on his shaft is firm, gliding smoothly along his cock before twisting at the crown. The motion is in languid succession, like he's trying to stave off finishing too soon. A soft grunt leaves his lips as he continues to fuck his fist, his hips chasing his hand.

My heart is drumming in my ears, and I feel like it's a million degrees. I have one hand over my mouth as I watch in fascination...and lust. The longer I watch, the wetter I get, and I'm unsure what to do.

I move my hand over to my forehead. "Jesus Harper. What are you doing?" I talk quietly to myself, trying to convince myself I *shouldn't* be here. A long and low groan comes from the shower and my eyes shoot back to the mirror. The look of euphoria on Xavier's face as he comes has my insides clenching for more, wanting release where I stand. His strokes slow as he squeezes out every last drop from the tip, and his forehead now rests against the glass door. He stands there for a moment shutting off the water.

A garbled squeak escapes my mouth as I spin around quickly, rushing to the bed. Tossing the blankets back and diving in, I roll over, closing my eyes to pretend I'm asleep. The silence is unbearable as I wait for him to exit the bathroom. I'm throbbing between my legs, but I can't ease the ache without telling on myself. I squeeze my thighs together, begging for this need to subside. Tonight is going to be torturous.

A hint of the bathroom light crosses my eyelids before the room goes pitch black. Apart from my own breath, the only thing I hear is Xavier coming to bed. The blankets shift, and then I feel the slight dip of him crawling into his side. He rustles around trying to get comfortable, but he struggles. Waiting, I hold my breath in anticipation of Xavier mentioning what just happened, but it never comes.

<h1 style="text-align:center">Chapter Twenty One</h1>
<h1 style="text-align:center">Harper</h1>

I WAKE UP ODDLY refreshed, and I decide to take things slow this morning. There isn't anything planned until eleven, giving me plenty of time to dip downstairs and make a smoothie. The thought of it makes me giddy.

I spend the next forty-five minutes getting ready. Armed with my smoothie, I soak in the moment, embracing the ease that is washing over me. Since I have extra time, I make the decision to curl my hair. I don't normally style it this way; it takes so much effort and there is very little payoff. The curls never last, no matter how I set them. As I drain the remainder of my smoothie, I fluff out my curls and smile. They turned out better than I had anticipated. After putting on some light makeup, I check the time and see I still have about thirty minutes. *Perfect.* I decide to call Evie and check on things. It rings twice before she picks up.

"Hey bitch. How're you surviving over there?"

"Oh you know. Just had Dalton corner me in the kitchen last night stating he just wanted to *explain himself.*"

A gasp comes from the other end of the line. "*Please.* He really thinks after the shit he's pulled, he deserves a moment of your time? Be so fucking for real."

I snort, swiping a layer of gloss on my lips. "I know, right. He wasn't getting the hint either. He kept pushing and pushing. He didn't back off until Xavier appeared in the kitchen, telling him to get lost."

"Fuck yes!" Evie squeals. "Please tell me you've sucked him off in thanks."

A gasping choke leaves my lips. "*Evie!*"

"What?!" She cackles loudly. "Oh, come on Harps. That man is built like a god. And then you tell me he basically defended your honour, and you didn't show your appreciation?"

"No I didn't– I mean, I did say thank you. But I didn't like, *service* him or anything."

Evie's chuckling stops, and a pause stretches between us. I check my phone to double check the call is still connected.

"Evie?"

"What *did* you do with him?" She asks, and I can hear her smirk come through the line

I freeze. "Uh– what? What are you talking about? I just told you that I thanked him."

"No, no, no. I heard that, but your *tone* says there is something you're not telling me."

God damnit. I hate that, even through a phone, this woman can tell when I'm not telling her something. I don't know whether I should tell her about the other night in the hot tub, or if I should tell her about last night with what I saw him doing in the shower. I'm so in my head with deciding what to tell Evie, I don't even hear her continue her line of questioning. It's not until she speaks louder that she breaks through my concentration.

"Hello? Earth to Harper."

Sighing, I start putting all my makeup away. "Sorry. Yes, there is something I need to tell you, just –" I pause, looking out the bathroom door to ensure I'm alone."There may have been some – *moments* that happened the other night that I haven't told you about yet."

Evie squeals so loudly, I have to remove my phone from my ear, waiting until she stops. "Oh my God, please tell me every juicy detail. How big was he? What did you do? What did *he* do?"

"Okay firstly, ouch to my ear drums." Looking around the bathroom, goosebumps break out along my skin as I think about what happened here, not even twelve hours earlier. I take a deep breath before I continue, "Secondly, there may have been a moment of...friction between us."

"What the hell does that even mean? Have you guys done anything or not?"

A laugh escapes from my mouth before I can stop it. "So impatient. We were in the hot tub, relaxing and talking. Then, he told me I could sit closer so we didn't have to talk so loud."

"Sure. Makes sense," Evie says, keeping things light as she encourages me. "Go on."

I spend the next couple minutes explaining what happened. How he told me to watch the noises that come out of my mouth or he wouldn't be able to control himself. The way he called me Harps but I reminded him that wasn't my name. That I wanted 'babydoll' to fall from his lips, I tell her the moment he pulled me onto his lap, guiding me as I ground myself on his shaft, and my orgasm hit me so hard, I saw stars.

"*Shiiiiit.*"

"I know, right. It's been crazy, and the tension is crazy." I pause for a moment, taking a breath before I continue. "I know this is supposed to be fake dating, but the moments we're alone? When there's no one around? It feels so *real*. It's hard to tell the difference between the lines, you know?"

"You're falling for him, aren't you?"

"*What*? Noo. No. I'm not. We're just getting along so well. It just gets confusing."

"Mhmm." Evie doesn't believe a word coming out of my mouth.

It's true, though. Xavier and I get along so well, and the need for us to present as a fake relationship only takes up eight percent of our time together.

"Evie. Stop. I can't have you in my head right now, making me question everything. This is for show. It's to get his mom off his back, and a little rub in the face to Dalton." I don't bother keeping the bite out of my voice. "That's it. There's no way he feels anything more."

"Okay well. When you're ready to admit your real feelings for him. I'll be here. I can't wait to tell you I told you so."

I huff. "I gotta go, Eve. I'm heading to a Christmas market with Xavier's mom, and I gotta find gifts. I promise I'll message you later. Give Winnie all the kisses for me. I love you!"

"Yes, I love you too. We'll catch up later."

Once I'm off the phone, I take a moment to collect myself. This is for show and nothing more. There's no way he feels anything more. Everything that's happened has just been because we get caught in the heat of the moment. It's just us sticking to the facade we agreed on.

It *can't* be anything other than that.

⁂

This Christmas market is something else. There are so many local crafters, I don't even know where to start. Not to mention, I don't even know how to begin finding the perfect gift for everyone. Originally, I had planned to wander the booths, making notes on what could be a good gift. I quickly realized that I'm not sure what anyone, and in particular, Xavier, likes.

I managed to sneak off and buy something for Penelope when she wasn't looking. She had shown interest in these cute little handmade blown wine glasses, so I bought her a set of those. I'll ask Xavier what kind of wine she drinks and get her a bottle. I still have a couple days before Christmas, so there's time.

To my utter disappointment, when I catch up with Penelope again, she isn't alone. Chloe is standing beside her. As I get closer, I hear how she went for a morning nap but woke up in time to leave with us. She drones on, telling us how the baby makes her so tired. I mean, that could be true, but part of me wonders if she's tired because she went out last night. *Again.*

Chloe looks at me with disdain on her face, and she barely acknowledges my existence. I'm boxed out as we walk down the aisles because she makes it her mission to prevent me from walking alongside her and Penelope. I try not to let it get to me.

We're about to leave for lunch, and I've all but given up on hope of finding something for Xavier as a Christmas gift. I notice a little table off the exit that has a display full of crocheted little plushies. There's an adorable little donkey grabbing my attention. It has an uncanny resemblance to Clyde, and I can't stop myself from buying it. I smile to myself as the vendor hands me the bag to take him home in.

This is perfect.

I hear a snort come from just ahead, looking up to find Chloe looking at me in pure disgust and disbelief.

"Who the hell are you even going to give that ugly thing to? Wait. Please don't tell me you're giving that to *us* for the baby. I'll save you the time. We don't want it." She says to me, whispering so that Penelope doesn't hear. She's a couple steps ahead of us, and when she turns back she smiles at us. She probably thinks we're trying to get along, when in reality, her daughter is just being a bitch.

"I know it's hard for you to believe this, but trust me when I say that I wouldn't waste my money getting you—or Dalton—a present." The snapback feels so good. God. I still can't believe this is who Dalton left me for.

Chloe's steps falter slightly before she bristles and spins on me, stopping me in my tracks.

"Oh please. I know how desperate you are. It's so sad. Dalton upgraded from a desperate fat leech, and now she's trying to worm her way into his life again. What is your game? Pretend you're over him by dating my brother and lure him back?" She takes a step closer as she leans in to whisper in my ear. "My brother has to be delusional. There's no way he genuinely is attracted to someone like you. Not with your...looks." She leans back, crinkling her nose as she peruses me from head to toe.

"If I were you," she continues, as she grabs a compact mirror from her bag to check her makeup. "I would just give it up and admit defeat. Pack your bags and take your miserable excuse of a person back to your pathetic little life." Chloe closes her compact with an aggressive snap. "Stop trying to butt your way into my family."

She gives me a serene smile and then walks off in the other direction, telling her mom she can't stomach food right now and needs to go home instead. Penelope and I still go to lunch, but the time blurs. I order a small salad but can't bring myself to finish it. My stomach is in knots, and everything Chloe plays on a loop in my head.

The instant we get back to the house, I run upstairs. I do my grounding exercise to try and center myself, but it only does so much, and I still feel off-centered about it all. Maybe doing some laps in the pool will close off my mind. I'm not a professional swimmer, but the weightlessness of swimming in the pool has always calmed me.

I dig through the dresser and find the two-piece I'd brought. The high waisted black bottoms pairs nicely with the deep red formed bikini top. I braid my hair so it's out of my face before grabbing a towel, and heading toward the pool. The area is unoccupied when I arrive, and my shoulders instantly relax at the idea of having the area to myself.

I need to feel the hurt and build up my walls again. Chloe wasn't wrong. I don't have what most would consider the ideal body. Newsflash: I'm well aware of it. I've put in the work to be confident in my skin, but sometimes, the cracks allow the pain to seep through.

The moment that hit hardest today was when she attacked me, saying there wasn't any way that Xavier actually found me appealing. It's something I've been questioning myself over the last week as things have progressed between us.

I place my towel down onto one of the chairs before heading to the pool. I sit on the side, dipping my feet into the water. The water is cool, and I inch forward slowly, before fully lowering my body into the water. The air hisses out of my body as the chill coasts up my body.

When I have acclimated to the water, I push off toward the deeper end of the pool. My arms cut through the water in a breast stroke, propelling me forward. When I'm in the middle of the deep end, I turn over, floating on my back. The surrounding noises become muffled as my breathing becomes louder with my ears being underwater.

I let my mind focus on the different sounds from underwater. The gentle humming coming from my immediate surroundings starts to help slow my heart rate and relax. I spot movement in my peripherals, so I bring myself into an upright position before wading in the water to see what the movement is.

I see Chloe and Dalton putting their towels down. The calmness that I had acquired while floating by myself diminished the moment I realized it was them. Chloe is wrapping herself around him, pulling him down for a kiss. My lips curl in annoyance. It's fine. I don't need to talk to them while they're here. The pool is big enough for us all to have a relaxing time.

"Dalty babyyy," Chloe simpers. "Come swim with me." I can hear the sickly sweet tone in her voice. I don't hear him reply, but a couple moments later, I hear the uneven rhythmic sounds of the water moving, telling me I'm no longer alone in the pool.

Over the next couple minutes, surprisingly, nothing really happens. Chloe and Dalton don't stay in the water for long, as Chloe begins complaining of wrinkles. I swear my eyes almost roll all the way to the back of my head.

Soft music plays as they both just sit there, looking at their phones. Deciding I've had enough of this whole *socialization*, I make my way to the edge of the pool, climbing out. As soon as I'm standing up straight, I hear it.

"Mooooo."

My back straightens as Chloe begins to cackle.

All I can hear is the beating of my heart in my ears, the distinct sting coming to the back of my eyes.

"Fuck" I mumble to myself, turning my body from them as I start to head back to my room. I can't deal with this right now. Staring at my feet, I move quickly, not paying attention to the world around me.

I run face first into Xavier.

I avoid eye contact as I try to move around him, but he grabs my chin with his finger and thumb and brings my eyes up, meeting his. A storm of blue threatens to break loose as he maintains eye contact with me. His nostrils flare and his mouth forms a thin line.

"What happened?" He demands in a tone that would normally send a shiver down my spine. Right now? I just want to disappear.

I try my best to put on a convincing smile. "It's nothing. I'm just not feeling the greatest, so I was going to lay down."

"Babydoll, " He begins, a level of concern softening his face.

My bottom lip begins to tremble. "Please don't. Just let me go." The words are no louder than a whisper. "*Please.*" His jaw tightens, running his gaze over me once more before he nods, and lets me go.

I slip past him, high-tailing it as fast as I can.

Chapter Twenty Two

xavier

I WATCH HARPER WALK away in defeat. There's only one explanation as to what happened, and I need answers. I need them right now. I spin in the other direction, zeroing in on Chloe and Derek. Chloe looks fucking pleased with herself. I take slow and methodical steps toward them, like a predator approaching prey. "I don't know what the fuck you said to her," I growl out. "But so fucking help me, if I hear anything else out of either of your mouths, it will be the last thing you do." I'm up in Deke's face, a sneer on my lips. This guy may have some muscle to him, but it's nothing compared to mine. Moments pass before Dalton backs down, dipping his head.

"Pathetic." Spinning around, I take off in Harper's direction.

It doesn't take long to catch up to her. Her pace is brisk, with her shoulders slumped and head down. I don't need to spin her around to know she's crying. My suspicion is confirmed when I hear a sniffle and see her hand move toward her face before falling down to her side.

"Harps!" She jumps at the sound of her name, but the sound of my voice only makes her walk faster. I adjust my pace to match hers. It doesn't take me long to close the distance, and I place my hand on her elbow to stop her.

"Hey, I was calling you." She pulls her arm out of my grasp.

"Just leave me alone Xavier." The trembling in her voice fucking kills me. I look around where we are quickly, spotting the sauna a few feet ahead. I place my hand on her lower back. "Come on, in here."

The saunas a decent space. There are two layers of cedar benches that are in an L shape. The oven that holds the coals is directly across the space from the door. Harper goes to the far side of the sauna, although the room isn't big, so she doesn't go far. I step toward her, but she doesn't look up at me. She's staring at her feet, wiggling her toes as if to keep her focused. I reach down, placing my pointer finger and middle finger under her chin, and lift her face until her eyes lock with mine. My chest seizes as I see her emerald eyes filled with tears, and I die a bit more inside as they begin to stream down her face. She tries to pull her face away but I add my thumb to hold her still. "Enough." I say sternly. Her eyes dilate slightly, a hint of lust shining in them before it disappears. Her bottom lip begins to tremble.

"What's going on, babydoll?"

Another tear tracks down her cheek. I cup her face in my hands, kissing her cheek gently. The taste of her tears will be my ruin. "Talk to me. Please." Desperation is heavy in my voice, and despite reminding myself I shouldn't be here, I can't bring myself to walk away.

Harper makes all logic fly out the window. When she was working during the week, I found myself needing to know what she's doing. It started with texting her a few times, but I easily learned that when she's in the zone working, she doesn't answer personal messages. I started bringing her lunch. The next day when I brought her lunch, I ended up staying and we talked. There have been days I pretend to answer emails on my phone, when in reality, I was watching her the whole time through my peripherals.

The silence continues before she finally gives me something, "It's not something I'm not used to." She takes a deep breath before continuing. "I've always been the big girl. I own it, I'm not ashamed. But," her voice breaks, "that doesn't mean the words still don't hurt, you know?" Tears are streaming down her face. I keep kissing each tear. Her hands run up my forearms, and she holds on to my wrists as her eyes close. I place my lips softly onto hers. As soon as they connect, Harper begins pushing forward, deepening the kiss.

I pull away before I get too carried away. "I want you to tell me what they said, babydoll." I look deep into her eyes and try to portray how I need to hear this right now.

"Like I said, it's nothing I haven't heard before."

"Doesn't matter. What. Did. They. Say. Harper." I say through clenched teeth. The thought of them tearing her down enrages me, especially after I've seen how much more comfortable she's been in her own skin this past week. My heart is thundering in my chest as I wait for her to say the words.

I take a deep breath. "Now, Harper, or I can't be held responsible for what I do if I have to leave this room to find out for myself." Her grip tightens on my wrists.

"Please don't." Her eyes search mine. "Stay." She takes a deep breath. "I'll tell you, just – give me a moment okay?" I nod my head in understanding. She goes up on the tips of her toes to give me another kiss, which I eagerly accept.

"When I was at the market with your mom, Chloe appeared. She apparently was invited the whole time, but needed a nap or something, so she didn't leave the house with us." Her hands begin to twist in each other, and then she tucks her loose hair behind her ear. "I was buying something for a gift, and she made a comment about it. I told her off- obviously. But then, she talked about how you must be delusional for wanting me, period." My whole body stiffens. "What?" I say, with a calm death would envy. Harper's lip begins to tremble again, and I can't stand it.

"You are fucking beautiful. You have had me obsessed since the mo- ment you fell into my lap– literally." A sharp inhale comes from her. "Is there anything else?"

She sighs, pausing briefly. "Well, after we got back to the house, I decided to clear my head and go for a swim. The feel of just floating in the water calms me, you know?" She begins to readjust her bathing suit bottoms, wrapping one arm around her midsection. "When Chloe and Dalton came into the pool, I decided to ignore them at first. But I wasn't really enjoying the water anymore, so I wanted to go inside and shower before settling in with a book. As I was getting out of the pool- well- Chloe moo'd at me." Harper licks her lips. "Like I said, it's nothing. Shit like this doesn't normally get to me. I think it did this time because I already had a confrontation with her earlier today, and I was still processing what happened. But when she did that, something in me cracked, and I just needed to get out of there. And here we are." She shrugs her shoulders as she finishes.

"You listen to me, babydoll, and you listen to me carefully." I pause to make sure she understands what I'm asking. When she gives me a quick nod, I continue.

"I can't stop thinking about you. I can't stop wanting more. Fuck I can't *breathe* without knowing when I'm going to see you, touch you...taste you. I never thought I'd feel like this about anyone ever again, but you came in here, and you obliterated it. And I don't ever want to go back."

I watch as Harper's eyes dilate with lust, internally smirking at how her breathing has increased. An idea hits me. I bend down and wrap my hands underneath her knees, lifting her up. She squeals, wrapping her thighs around my body. Her arms loop around my shoulders, holding tight. She pulls back slightly before her mouth crashes into mine.

Our lips move together frantically as the urgency of our need begins to increase. This isn't what I have planned. So I quickly move forward until I place her juicy ass on the top bench, and pull away. A whimper leaves her lips as I retreat, and she actually pouts.

A deep chuckle leaves my throat, my eyes trailing the length of her body. Feasting on the sight of her, and her swollen lips, I'd be a fool not to dive in for more. Her chest lifts and falls in quick succession. Under my stare, she begins to squirm, thighs clenching together trying to ease the need.

"Can you be a good girl for me, Harps?"

Harper nods her head fast as her bottom lip pinches between her teeth.

"Both feet up, and spread those legs for me, babydoll." She goes to do what I say, but I tsk. Harper stops, confusion on her face. "I wasn't finished. Now, take those bottoms off before I rip them off your body. I mean, unless you want to walk out of here without bathing suit bottoms?" I ask with a raised eyebrow. She quickly stands up, whipping them down her thighs and leaving them on the floor. She takes a deep breath and sits back, taking her time to rest her hands on the bench behind her, and placing both feet on the edge of the bench. My body ignites the moment she spreads wide for me.

I groan. "Such a good fucking girl. Look how pretty your pussy looks up there, on display for me." I begin to rub at my hardened cock. I've been hard since before I picked her up, but the way she looks right now is fucking devastating. God, she is beautiful.

Her eyes flick down as she watches the movement of my hands. I see that her eyes are blown wide with lust. I move my hands to my side, refusing to touch myself further.

"Touch yourself." My demand is rough, but I will not allow her to shrink herself.

Her eyes connect with mine as her hand starts moving up her inner thigh. A slow and torturous pace that brings a low growl rumbling out of my chest. When her hand reaches the apex of her thighs, she begins to spread her glistening pink lips. Not once do her eyes leave mine, not even as she swirls a finger around her swollen clit. I hear her breath hitch.

"That's it. Show me how you please yourself," I say through gritted teeth. This is all we can do. I can't think about how her sweet cunt would taste, or the way she'd feel wrapped around my cock. This is the closest I will come to heaven. My fist clenches as I resist the urge to pull down my trunks and grasp my cock.

She moves her hand down, plunging two fingers into her pussy. With her mouth dropping open, a desperate moan leaves her lips as she continues to push her fingers in and out. I can hear how wet she is. It pulses in the quiet space of the sauna. Each new noise that comes from her drives me closer and closer to snapping.

I'm such a masochist. I shouldn't be doing this. And yet, I can't keep myself from continuing to put myself in these situations.

I continue to watch her pleasure herself, bringing herself up higher and higher. The closer she gets to her release, the closer I get to losing my composure.

"Tell me babydoll. Are you going to come for me?"

She nods her head eagerly. "I-I'm so cl-close," she stutters, ending on a whimper. She's pushing up on the balls of her feet as her hips forward with every plunge of her fingers. Her legs begin to shake.

"Oh fuu-uck." Her words fade into whimpers as she removes her fingers, coated with her arousal. The pads of her fingers move quickly in a back and forth motion over her swollen bud. She lets out a high pitched moan as she gushes, soaking the cedar beneath her. Harper coaxes her body to ride out her orgasm, plunging her fingers back into her soaked core, fingering herself a few more times. Turning her attention to her clit, Harper comes once more, squirting again.

Holy shit.

That was the hottest fucking thing I've ever seen. My resolve snaps. In three quick strides, I'm in front of her. My heartbeat is pumping so loud, it's all I can hear in my ears. I take her in her blown out eyes as they stare at me. My eyes track the flush pink of her cheeks as it bleeds down her neck, spreading across her chest. Her breaths are coming in pants as she tries to get her composure back. She goes to sit up straight and close her legs, but my arms snap out. I place my hands on each leg and hold her open, my eyes zeroing in on her swollen pussy. My eyes dip, connecting with the bench below that's absolutely drenched from her release.

"That was the most breathtaking thing I've ever seen." I whisper in a husky tone. I'm waiting for her to tell me to let her go. My grip on her thighs are firm as I hold them in position, keeping her spread wide. Every second she stays on display like this, the closer I get to dropping to my knees.

"So…" Harper starts, "Are you just going to hold me spread open like this for your viewing pleasure, or are you going to do something about it?" Her brow quirks up, emeralds dancing with her dare.

I'm silent for a second before my resistance shatters. "Fuck it." I fall to my knees and dive in.

Tasting her for the first time is like finally taking a bite of a forbidden fruit. She's warm, juicy and so fucking satisfying. I know instantly this taste won't be the last, that I've just taken the first hit of my new addiction. I want to spend the rest of my night feasting on her pussy, licking and sucking until she's putty underneath me. My cock is painfully hard, and she gasps and moans coming from her are just as addicting as her taste.

With one hand I release my cock from my trunks and I grasp it tightly, giving it one hard stroke. I can't come in my hand like a teenager. Each noise that comes from her spurs me on to do more, to give her more pleasure. I need her to come again.

I need to feel her release on my tongue.

I move my other hand to her opening and begin to slowly ease in a finger. She gasps as her core tightens around me. I quickly add a second finger, working her over. Her wet core clenches, as if she's trying to pull me in deeper. I curl my fingers, searching for –

Harper jolts. *There we go.* I continue to stroke, slowly and deliberately, as her legs begin to shake again. She tries to close her thighs around my head. I release my cock, using both hands to hold her thighs open. Her hands grip into my hair, and she begins to strangle me with her pussy. Not the worst way to go, if you ask me. I growl in encouragement. Pressing one of Harper's knees to the bench, a silent reminder coming from my hand, I reach down and stroke my cock again. I feel the zing in my balls, and with two more pumps, I explode all over the bench. Stroking myself a few more times, I relish at the thought of my release mixing with hers.

When her grip loosens, I go to look at the mess we made. The sight is better than I could have envisioned. I reach down, running a finger through the mess. What a shame that I'll have to clean this up.

A smirk forms on my face as I glance back up at her.

Chapter Twenty Three

Harper

OH MAN, I'M IN *trouble.*

That smirk is laced with promise...and desire. His eyes are fully dilated with thirst and desire. Without breaking eye contact, his fingers move down to the bench below. Before I know it, he's moving his two fingers in front of my mouth. He pauses a second before murmuring, "Open."

I don't think twice as I open my mouth, and he places his two fingers into my mouth. "Suck." I twirl my tongue around his fingers, pulling them further into my mouth. The mixture of my own tangy release with his salty is a combination that I find myself enjoying more than I thought I would. His eyes don't move from my mouth. Xavier pulls his fingers from my lips slowly before replacing them with his own.

My heart races again as I lean back to accommodate him. Xavier moves with me, settling between my thighs, before running his hands up the side of my body. One hand rests on my rib cage, while his other hand travels between my breast and up my collar bone. When he reaches my neck, he slides it around the back before his hands tangle with the base of my hair.

Shivers dance through my body as he devours my mouth, keeping me exactly where he demands I be. Breaking the kiss, Xavier angles my head to allow him access to my neck. He begins working his way up the column of my neck, kissing and sucking in places that make my toes curl. A slight whimper comes from my lips as he nips just under my jaw. His nose traces up the side of my jaw, before pulling back slightly. His blue eyes are shaded, a mix of feelings shifting within them like a stormy sea wave—chaotic and untamed.

"Now that I've tasted you, I don't think I'll ever be able to stay away." He whispers before smashing his lips with mine. I happily reciprocate, our tongues battling as they tangle together.

When we pull apart we're both panting. I watch the storm continue to brew in his eyes. His nostrils flare and I see the tick in his jaw as if he's still trying to hold himself back. Neither of us speak.

The moment dissipates, and Xavier straightens, tucking himself back into his pants. He scratches at his jaw before he wipes his mouth with his hand. I quickly bring my legs together.

"I'm- sorry." The statement is so quiet, I almost miss it. I pull my bottoms back up and go to say something to him, but he's already out the door. My head begins to spin, thinking about what just happened, and how we got here.

All I wanted was to hide, and if I'm honest, cry. No better time to cry than in the shower since the tears just blend with the water. Next thing I know, I'm being pulled into this sauna.

I was shocked stupid at the dominating presence he took when he told me to listen. My body shivers when I think back to what he said, and the emotion I felt coming through those words? It was like he was a man starved. I saw the moment the resistance snapped, and it was electrifying.

Whatever just happened, it didn't end the way I was hoping it would. The way we came together was bewitching. I thought at that moment that maybe my feelings toward him were reciprocated. But, just as quickly as it happened, it stopped, and he's back to pushing me away.

He says he's got a past, and I don't want to push him into telling me anything he's not ready to. But it's starting to feel like anytime we move a step forward, we're moving three steps back. I sigh in frustration, collecting myself. I toss a bit of water over our mess and make my way upstairs.

As I enter the bedroom, I notice I'm alone. I'm not sure where Xavier went, but I honestly don't think I'm up for seeing him after that. My mind is in a very confused state, and I need to sort out *all* my feelings before I talk to anyone.

Normally, this is where Evie comes in. I would call her and tell her everything that happened, from the Christmas market to the sauna. I would get some reprieve from her commentary about everything. At the end of it though, she'd help me sort through my feelings, and what's going on in my head. Sometimes she's even just stayed silent as I talk, and talk, and *talk*.

I just don't have the spoons to talk with anyone tonight. I shower quickly, braiding my hair and washing my face. I spend a bit of extra time moisturizing my face and brushing my teeth before I enter the bedroom. There is still no sign of Xavier, so I grab my headphones and my phone. I check my messages, seeing the pictures Evie sent me of Winnie. I tell her I miss her, and I'll call her tomorrow. Slipping under the covers, I find my comfort show and begin to sink into the mattress.

I don't know when I fell asleep, but a dip in the bed tells me that Xavier has returned. Removing my headphones, I remain still, waiting to see if he'll say something. Silence wraps itself around us, and I roll to stare at the ceiling. Our breaths are deafening, and I debate whether I should say something first. Sneaking a glance at Xavier, all I see is his muscular back, and I don't know if he's asleep. I close my eyes, losing myself to sleep...and the wish that I could get the man beside me to open up.

Chapter Twenty Four

Harper

THE DAYS LEADING UP to Christmas are...tense. Xavier has been distant, and if we aren't around his family, he is working out, or he's skiing. It's all messing with my head. This last week with his family has been as smooth as I could hope, all things considered. I spent some time with Penelope, and overall, she seems to be ecstatic that Xavier brought me.

I avoid Chloe and Dalton like the plague. But since the whole incident at the pool, I haven't seen much of them. I'm sitting in the chair in the office, reading when I hear a knock at the door. "Come in!" I shout, as I mark my spot in my book. When I look up, I see Penelope smiling at me.

"Hi dear! I was just going to head into town and get my nails done. I thought I would pamper myself before our Christmas dinner, and I wanted to extend that offer to you."

"Oh, that's so thoughtful!" I pause slightly, out of shock. "I'm sure they won't have a walk-in spot open with how close it is to the holidays. Thank you so much for inviting me, though."

"Okay, I have a confession." Penelope looks somewhat bashful at her admission. I don't know whether to find it adorable or be apprehensive. I've been scarred from previous experiences. "I actually booked these appointments when Xavier said you guys would join us for the holidays. I know that was very presumptuous of me, and I should have asked in advance, but Xavier can be a flighty one. It all started back when he was eighteen." She crosses the room, settling herself against the desk, and crosses one foot over her ankle. "I won't go into too much detail, because it isn't my story to tell and I won't air his laundry out like that, but he went through something unimaginable at such a young age. I wish I could have protected him from it. There's nothing more painful than seeing your flesh and blood suffer in such a manner. We did therapy, and that seemed to help. He started focusing on his studies. He has always wanted to be a vet."

She smiles softly as she reminisces of a younger Xavier. "We are so proud of what he's accomplished. When he discussed how he wanted to open up his own clinic on his property, his father and I wanted to help fund it. But he refused, saying he wanted to accomplish this on his own. That just made us more proud. He never really wanted to use the family wealth that we have, which I don't fault him for. His sister has relied on us a lot financially. She's always needed more of a hand holding than our Xavier. He's always been so independent." She gets quiet for a moment.

"*Anyways*," Penelope waves her hand. "I'm sorry, I'm rambling. What I'm trying to tell you is that when I saw him with you, my son seemed lighter. And then he agreed to come out to the ski lodge here, after declining for so long. So, I booked these appointments hoping that I can get some one-on-one time."

I take a minute to collect my thoughts. Xavier's mom has been so open and welcoming, and that's something I'm not used to. "That was very thoughtful of you, Penelope. I'd love to go!" A smile takes over my face, and excitement stirs inside my belly.

Penelope claps her hand with excitement. "Oh perfect! The appointment is in an hour! So, I'll leave you to get ready, and we'll meet downstairs!" She is up and out of the room in a flurry, leaving me to get ready.

Penelope's light is the perfect way to bring myself back for the spiral I've been going down. The way Xavier has described his mom, I thought she would be more closed off than how she's been. I can see how she cares deeply about the people she loves. It also becomes evident that she has given more attention to Chloe, which can explain why Xavier is feeling the way he's feeling.

I wish he would just talk to me.

I've been laying on my bed for the last hour talking with Evie on the phone. I need my best friend now more than ever. I think she could sense it too, because I have been laughing for the last ten minutes as she tells me about another disaster date of hers.

"*Then*, she leaned forward. I thought maybe she was going for a kiss right? Or even a hug, since clearly she had to know the date went as terrible as I thought it went."

"Oh God– which did she do?" I snort, wiping away a tear that collected from laughing so hard. This date was a disaster from the start when Evie's date showed up– *with* her ex...who joined them on their date.

"Neither! She booped my fucking nose, Harps. Pressed it like a fucking button. And then she *giggled*. Told me she had a great time, and she'd love to do it again. Her ex was still in the backseat!"

Laughter explodes out of me. I drop my phone, rolling around on the bed in a fit, and a snort leaves me. This girl has zero luck dating anyone.

Muffling noises drift from my phone, so I grab it and bring it to my ear again. "I'm– I'm sorry. But that has to be the most disastrous date I have *ever* heard you go on. Please tell me you blocked her."

"Blocked, deleted. Gone. Never again, Harps. Also remind me to *never* agree to be picked up on the first date. As soon as I tried to dip and remembered that she was my ride, I wanted to simply fucking pass away."

A snicker leaves me. "Noted."

"What about you, babes? How are things going?"

My mood immediately diminishes at the question. "It's alright."

"And what's your real answer?"

I *want* to talk to her about this. I just don't even know where to start with it. "I don't even fully know where to start. The place is beautiful. There are so many cute trails to walk, and the easy access to get to the town is so ideal. I tried this bakery that Xavier told me about. We were supposed to go together but...it never happened. So, I just went by myself, and I tried their chocolate croissants. They were to *die* for. They were the perfect combination of flaky and fluffy. Xavier's mom and I went to a spa and got our nails done today. I got them done in this pretty emerald green color that's going to go so well with my dress for the Christmas Eve dinner party they have planned."

"That sounds great! But where has Xavier been during all of this? And what about that bitch Chloe and that scumbag?"

"That's where things get complicated."

"... Complicated, how?"

That was the only encouragement I needed before proceeding to tell her everything. There wasn't a moment from the last few days that I left out.

I'm panting by the time I finish, feeling more confused than I was when I first started.

I hear the sound of her letting out a breath. "Fuck, that's a lot to unpack here."

"Try living it." I scoff.

"Well, first. Chloe's a bitch, and I think she is Dalton's karmic retribution so good luck to *him*. It sounds like she's an attention slut and hates anything that isn't revolving around her. That's a her problem, not a *you* problem. So, I don't want you wasting any more time thinking about her. If she starts to talk shit, just walk away. It's not worth your time, and she *will* get hers."

"Yeah I know, and normally I can deal with her shit, but that one day was just...too much."

"I know, and I think you still handled it well because you didn't let her see it. Secondly, I don't know what it is with Xavier, but it's clear he's battling with something. I know you want to try and fix it, because that's who you are, Harps. I love you for that. I just think you need to give him that space."

I sit there, thinking about what she's saying. She's right, of course. But that doesn't mean I have to like her answer.

"But, that doesn't mean you can't look fine as hell for this Christmas Eve dinner." I hear a beep on my phone, and I look down. It's Evie requesting a video chat. I accept and her face comes on the screen. Her blonde hair is down, reaching past her shoulders, framing her heart shaped face that currently is sans any makeup. Her blue eyes shine with mischief, telling me she has something planned.

"That's better," she says, a devious smirk forming over her face. "Now, what did you pack in terms of outfits for this dinner?"

I show Evie the green dress I had packed. She instantly agrees that I should wear it, silencing any second guessing I had.

"Before I go," Evie starts. "I packed you a present in your suitcase. I don't know if you've found it or not, but it's at the front of your bag."

I look at my screen, raising my brow in question.

"Oh, just go look!"

I make my way over to where my bag is. I look in the front of my bag, and when I reach my hand inside, I connect with something. I pull it out, seeing that it is a tiny gift wrapped box.

"Is this it?" I ask as I show her the gift box in question. She nods her head enthusiastically. "Yes! Now open it!"

I quickly unwrap it and open the lid. My mouth drops, and my eyes fly to the screen, looking at my best friend, who gifted me none other than lingerie. "This was what I was looking at when I was buying my bathing suits. You're a sneaky bitch."

"Well, you weren't going to buy it, and I know you'd look hot in it. You should wear it under your outfit tomorrow. You know," she wags her eyebrows at me, "just in case."

I shake my head, but I feel the smile spreading on my face. I look down at the box, appreciating the black lace and how it forms the sheer bra. The matching thong that looks like a small piece of scrap fabric. I know they're meant to look hot, and I'm not complaining about how my own ass will look in it, especially matched with my floral back thigh tattoo. They're just not the most comfortable.

"You're evil Evie, and that's exactly why I love you."

"I love you too, babes. Now, I'm off to bed. I have a busy day tomorrow! Tell me how the dinner goes!" She presses a kiss to the receiver, hanging up before I can even say goodbye.

Quickly, I get myself ready for bed, then crawl in. I get comfortable in bed feeling lighter than I have in awhile.

Evie truly is the best.

Chapter Twenty Five

Xavier

I ADMIT IT.

I've been an asshole.

After the moment we shared in the sauna, I completely shut down. I felt like I couldn't breathe, like steel was banded around my lungs. My fight or flight kicked in, and at that moment, I needed to get out of there, as fast as possible.

I've been avoiding Harper as much as possible. I'm getting up before she wakes, and staying in the gym until I know she's cleared out of the bedroom. I quickly run into the bathroom and shower when she leaves before gearing up to spend the afternoon on the slopes. I haven't skied in years, it took me a long time to be at peace with skiing again and get back on the hill. But the familiarity of the motions keep the demons at bay.

Of course, when we have to all be together as a group, I play the part. I play the boyfriend. I remind myself that we're fake dating. That this is for show. I indulge in the feel of her by my side, the way it feels holding her. Placing kisses on the top of her head, here in front of everyone it's safe. It's all I can allow myself.

If I start to think of anything more happening, then *she* comes back, reminding me why I've closed myself off all these years. She was the one who broke me, and I don't want to be in that position again.

I cannot truly care for Harper, because that only leads to one thing. Heartbreak.

I won't be able to survive another one.

My workout this morning is focused, the music in my ears matching the vibes.

Ten minutes later, with sweat dripping down my back, I hop off the treadmill, and make my way over to the weights. I'm grabbing two dumb-bells for a seated shoulder press. I sit down and when I look at my reflection in the mirror, I make eye contact with Deke. His posture is awkward, as if he isn't sure how to move around the gym with me here.

Removing one headphone from my ear, I ask, "Can I help you?"

Derry stands up straighter "Uh, no. I was just hoping to get a little workout in, but I can go." He throws his thumb over his shoulder pointing in the direction of the exit.

"I don't need the whole gym to myself. You're free to use it as well." I lean forward and begin my first set.

We workout together in silence in our respective areas. I focus on my workout, reveling in the burn that comes with every set. It's only when I finish my last set that Dane speaks again.

"You know Harps– ahem, Harper."

"I don't think you really have the right to speak about Harper anymore," I grunt, adjusting my grip on the weights, before redirecting my eyes to him. "Wouldn't you agree?"

A sigh escapes him, placing the weights back down on the wrack before turning. He looks like shit. It's more than the exhaustion that comes with dealing with my sister's antics. My dad has worn that look before. No, this is different. He looks bone deep tired; the bags under his eyes are prominent. "You look like shit."

He laughs. "Yeah, I guess I deserve that." He shuffles in place for a minute. "I know you won't believe this, but I truly didn't mean to hurt Harper. I've got a lot of pressure at work and with my family. I let it control me, and I let my parents talk me into things I normally would never agree to." He sits down on one of the workout benches, resting his elbows on his knees as he looks down shamefully. "I fucked up. I'll own up to that. I just want a minute to talk to her. I don't know exactly what I'm expecting from it, but she was my best friend. I would talk to her about everything. I just miss her."

I mean, I feel for him. I can understand the pressures of work and parents. I've never met his parents, but I have a somewhat idea based on the little that Harper has told me. I'm not a stranger to fucking up either. It's what I'm currently doing, and I'm trying to figure out how exactly to fix this too. Perhaps this is something we could help each other out with. An olive branch, if you will.

I sigh heavily. "I'll talk to her."

Dylan's head shoots up, and he looks at me in awe. "You–you will?"

I shrug. "Yeah, but I could actually use your help too. I have this idea for Harper's Christmas gift, but I need to talk it out."

"Absolutely, anything! What do you have in mind?"

"Okay, so here's my idea."

***

Dwight–I mean–Dalton and I spend the rest of the afternoon putting everything into place so that my surprise arrives just on time. I was trying to aim for it to happen on Christmas morning, but when we were able to figure it out for tonight, I jumped on the idea.

I'm nervous. What if she hates it? What if this is something she doesn't want? My palms begin to sweat, and I wipe them on my pants. I'm in uncharted territory right now. I've told myself that I was going to stay away, but here I am, doing this big grand gesture. Why? Because I hate the fact that I've been so cold to her.

I decide to push down my emotions like I always do, and focus on what I need to do right now: getting ready for dinner tonight. I shower quickly, pulling the outfit I've chosen from the closet. I'm keeping it simple with a pair of beige slacks and a black dress shirt.

My parents' Christmas Eve parties are pretty low key. It usually consists of my parents, some of their close friends, and colleagues. I invited Josie and Monty to come out with the kids, and suggested they bring their parents so they have someone to watch the kids. I've spent the last couple years with them for the holidays. I've been to every Christmas since Shiloh was born, and I don't plan to miss a single one. Plus, I want to see the look on Monty and Josie's face when they see I got Shiloh an inflatable bounce house...and added a jumbo bag of plastic balls to go with it. A smirk forms my lips as I think of tomorrow morning watching him open it up.

A knock interrupts me, and Monty walks in. His strawberry blonde hair is slicked at the sides, his curls controlled on top. He's wearing his tortoiseshell square glasses, and light stubble frames his face. He's never been one to have a full beard, but he often sports a bit of scruff. He's wearing a light grey dress shirt, and dark grey slacks with a matching jacket, his collar open revealing his collar bone. My eyes drift behind him to see if Josie is tagging along, and sure enough, a couple seconds later she comes into the room, huffing and puffing.

"I swear to God, if this baby doesn't come out soon, I'm going to lose my mind." She finds the closest chair, lowering herself while shooting daggers at her husband. As she looks over at me her eyes soften and she opens her arms. "Now, come over and hug me, because, well, I'm stuck here until further notice."

A chuckle leaves me as I stride over to her. I embrace her in a hug, kissing her cheek. "You look stunning," I tell her as I look over at her. She's wearing a maroon, wrap up dress. Her chocolate hair loosely curled with it pinned up to the side. Light makeup dons her face, with a deep nude on her lips. Being so close to her due date, I'm amazed with how well she's doing. A woman's body is amazing, and I am in awe at how it can change into a house for life.

"Oh please. I'm as big as a house, and I'm ready to pull this kid out myself if they don't come out soon." There is nothing but warmth on her face as she gently rubs her hand in circles around her belly. She blows at a piece of hair that's fallen over her face, trying to maneuver it out of the way. "How are *you* doing, big guy?" Seriousness falls across her face as she looks me up and down. I give her a small smile and look over at Monty, who's looking at his wife like she is the very breath in his lungs. When I think of that kind of love, my mind instantly goes to Harper. My heart rate jumps, and a pressure begins to form in my chest. A wave of guilt and grief flow through me at the thought of having these feelings for anyone other than *her*.

I feel a hand gripping my shoulder. When I look up, Monty has a concerned look on his face. "Hey." He starts, as he lightly taps the side of my face, to make sure I'm listening to him. "It's okay, you know? To move on." My brows furrow as I listen to him, and I feel the pricking of heat at the back of my eyes. "Have you told Harper about her?" *That's a loaded question.* If I would have let her in, I wouldn't have put this huge barrier between us the last couple days. It also means that I would have to admit to myself that I'm starting to love someone else.

I sniff, running my hand down my face. "No– I can't. Telling Harper about her means admitting I have feelings. Admitting I have feelings means…" My voice fades as the tightness in my chest squeezes so tight, I forget how to breathe.

I feel something in my hand, and when I look down, Josie is holding my hand. Tears are welled up in her eyes as she looks up at me. "It means letting a part of her go." Josie finishes for me. "Just because you're moving on doesn't mean that she's gone forever, Xavier. You honor her. Telling Harper about her will allow you to keep her memory alive." I give her a curt nod. I try to suck in a deep breath of air, but it's hard.

We stand like that for a couple minutes. The comfort that I receive from them is palpable. I need help to get through the emotions that are crashing through me in waves. Just as my heart rate has settled down, the bedroom door bursts open.

"Uncle Xavy!" Shiloh comes barrelling through the doors toward me. A smile spreads over my face, and I quickly wipe my eyes before bending over to catch him as he collides into me. "Hey, there's my best buddy!"

"Hey!" I hear Monty grumble in the background.

I chuckle. "Who's excited to come to a fancy party tonight?" I lean closer to his ear, dropping my voice to a whisper. "I hear there's chocolate cake too."

"CHOCOLATE CAKE!" Shiloh exclaims, throwing his hands in the air and wiggling around in my arms. I let him down as he grabs his moms hand. "Come on Mumma, let's go get some cake!" After a few attempts, she gets up from her seat and follows along after their son, but not without throwing daggers at me as they leave.

"You're going to pay for that, you know." Monty chuckles, as he watches them leave the room.

"Yeah, but it'll be worth it." There's a pause as we stand in my room. I fix the cufflinks of my sleeves. "Is everything in order for tonight?" I finally ask.

"Yes. Yes, the package safely arrived, and Dalton said he put it in Harper's office." Nerves begin to flutter in my stomach at the realization that my plan was executed perfectly. I wouldn't have been able to accomplish this without Dalton's help...and the help of my best friends.

"Perfect. Thank you Monty."

"Anything for you. Now, let's head on downstairs and socialize a bit, eh?" He smacks my back before heading out the door. I reach for my phone and send Harper a text, before putting it back in my pocket and following Monty downstairs.

Chapter Twenty Six

Harper

I READ OVER THE text a couple times. That's the most vague text ever. Part of me wants to tell him to just tell me what it is, because I'm not the biggest fan of surprises.

Curiosity gets the best of me though, and I find myself heading toward the room that has been deemed my office. I'm putting in my gold hoop earrings as I open the door to the office. Next thing I know, a heavy sack of slobber plows into me. It takes me a second to realize that my dog is here.

"Winnie?!" I get down to his level and hug him as he wiggles with joy around me. "Oh my God, baby! You're here! How are you here?" I pull back to look at his face, his tongue hanging out as he pants, and his back end wags, showing his pure joy of being reunited.

"Uh, what am I chopped liver?" A voice comes from further in the office.

My eyes snap up and connect with my best friend. "Evie? What the hell are you doing here!?"

I jump up and make my way across the room toward Evie. When I get close enough, I throw my arms around her, squeezing her tightly in a hug. I pull back. "I can't believe you're here. How are you here?" A wave of relief flows through me.

"I'm your Christmas present!" There is a sly smile on her face. "That *fake* boyfriend of yours pulled some strings to get me and Winnie here at the last minute to celebrate."

I stand there in shock, my brain swirling at the fact that Xavier went out of his way to bring me my best friend and my dog for Christmas. I don't think he understands how much I appreciate this.

"Oh my God," I whisper.

"What?" Evie asks. "What is it? Are you okay?"

"He did this. for me?" My eyes move between her hazel ones. They shine with understanding.

"Yes babes. He did." She takes a step back, checking me out before letting out a low whistle. "And can I just say– damn girl. You look smoking!"

Throwing back my head, I laugh. The way she validates me and doesn't let me spiral is some magical voodoo shit. "You're looking pretty hot yourself."

I take my best friend in. Her blonde locks are pulled up in a styled bun, with braids running along the side. She's in a silver spaghetti strap slip dress that comes down to her knees. The neckline plunges to just below her breast, and when she turns around, the back ends just above her ass. She looks at me over her shoulder and winks.

"You think so?" She spins back around, linking her arm in mine. "Come on, let's go drop Winnie off into your room and head downstairs, yeah?"

Taking Winnie to the room, he happily runs to the bed, jumping up before circling and laying down. We make our way down to the party. "This place is fucking bonkers. You've been staying in this place for almost three weeks?"

"Yup." with an emphasis on the 'p'. "It's a crazy, but surprisingly homey, feeling."

My stomach begins to flutter. I scan the small crowd, taking in everyone who's here. There's a little boy who's running around with some chocolate around his lips. The act itself makes me smile, especially once I see a man with blonde curls and glasses chase after him.

"*Hello Daddy.*" Evie comments beside me. I slap at her arm.

"Evie, no." I shake my head, chuckling.

"What? I have eyes! I wonder if he's a single dad." She begins to look around like she will somehow be able to establish if he has a wife by staring at everyone at the event.

"Oh, keep it in your panties." I pull her with me to the drink table. She just replies with a shrug of her shoulders, giving me a mischievous glint. She's going to be up to no good tonight.

I grab us a couple flutes of champagne, available at the bar. Passing one to her, I bring my glass up to my lips, taking a sip. The crisp taste of the champagne washes over my tongue, the perfect balance of sweet and acidity settling over my taste buds.

I spot Chloe and Dalton across the way. Chloe's wearing a fitted sweater dress that perfectly highlights the little bump, as she's over half way through with her pregnancy. She hangs off Dalton, who is trying to have a conversation with Theo and some other man who looks to be the same age as Xavier's Dad. I don't linger long on them before I'm scanning the crowd, trying to find the one person I want to see most right now.

My eyes finally connect with Xavier. He's laughing as he talks to a pregnant woman, who's laughing with him and holding her belly. The blonde man that we saw earlier chasing the little boy walks up next to them, the crashed out boy in his arms. He leans down and kisses the pregnant lady's cheek.

"Oh poo. I guess he isn't a single dad." Evie pouts beside me.

A snort leaves me as I side eye her, "I actually think those are Xavier's best friends. Monty and Josie. They've been together forever."

"How unfortunate for me." She grumbles, "Well, let's go say hello shall we?"

She hooks her arm in mine again and begins to lead me to the group. As we approach, I see the moment Xavier notices us coming toward him.

He stands up a bit straighter, and a small smile forms on his mouth. He looks at Evie and nods in her direction before returning his gaze to me.

Josie looks at me and a smile spreads over her face. She gives me a little wave, and then her eyes look over to Evie. I see the way she takes Evie in. There's slight interest in her eyes, and then her arm comes around her husband's bicep, squeezing it. Monty was looking down at his son but moves his eyes over to us. His eyes roam over Evie's body, and when he locks eyes with me, a slight flush creeps on his cheeks as he realizes I was watching.

"Hey," I lean forward and offer my hand. "I'm Harper, you must be Josie and Monty. This is my best friend, Evie." We take turns shaking everyone's hands. I walk over to Xavier and stand by his side, looking up to him. He offers me a small smile.

I lean up on my tip toes, and bring my hand to the back of his neck, pulling him down to me. I plant my lips against his for a light kiss. When we pull apart, I thank him for bringing Evie and Winnie up for the holidays.

His eyes soften. "It's the least I could do."

"You guys are fucking adorable."

I turn my head and glare at my best friend. She just smiles back at me with a shit eating grin. "So," she continues, "what does this party entail?"

"Nothing too crazy. It's a bit of socializing, and there will be finger food coming around in the next bit."

Monty and Xavier begin reminiscing of previous Christmas Eve parties they went to when they were teenagers and what they used to get up to. Xavier's arm has been around my waist the entire time we've been talking, rubbing slow circles on my back. After a while, Monty goes off with his parents to get Shiloh, their son, off to bed. Evie and Josie are chatting about anything and everything. They seem to hit it off, and even though Josie is married, it doesn't stop Evie from harmlessly flirting.

I lean over to Xavier to whisper in his ear. "Do you think Monty is going to be pissed when he comes back to see Evie flirting with his pregnant wife."

A smirk forms on his lips. "Nah, believe it or not, they're quite the adventurous couple. They've had people join their relationship before. They haven't brought anyone in since Shiloh, though."

My mouth opens and closes a couple of times. That wasn't the answer I was expecting from him. He chuckles low at my reaction. "Yeah, I know it isn't something you'd think of looking at them." He brings me in closer to his side. "I'm sorry I've been an ass lately."

I look up at him and I see the sincerity in his eyes. "It's okay." I bring my hand up to his face, letting my thumb run along his cheek. I watch his blue eyes dance with emotion as they bounce back and forth between mine. A smile spreads on my face before I bring his lips to mine in a kiss.

He eagerly accepts the kiss, his hand on my hip tightens in his grip. When his tongue grazes the seam of my lips, I eagerly open for him. Our tongues tangle together, and when we break apart, our breathing is heavy. The tension between us is drawn so tight, but I won't be the one to take the next step. He's clearly struggling with something, and I don't want to push him too far.

"You look tired. Let's head upstairs." The statement is anything but true, but the underlying message is saying so much more. I don't think I can speak at this moment, so I just nod.

He breaks eye contact. and looks at our friends. "It's getting late, and we're going to call it a night."

His hand moving to my back as he leads me away from the group before anyone responds. We quickly exit the party, forgoing goodbyes. Xavier tugs me up the stairs, anticipation thrumming between us with every step. We don't make it to the door before my body is whipped around, his tattooed hand wrapping around my neck as I'm pinned to the wall and pinned to the wall. A gasp leaves my lips, as I note the hesitancy in his eyes.

"We don't have to–" I don't get to finish my sentence as his lips are crashing into mine. My hands shoot up, grabbing at the front of his shirt and pulling him closer. My tongue pokes out and grazes his lips. A growl comes from him as he opens up. The hand on my neck tightens briefly before he tears his mouth away.

His forehead rests against mine as his eyes close. We both are panting, and my hands begin to roam up and down his chest. "I haven't been able to stop thinking about you." Xavier's voice is gravelly. "I know– I *know* I have been distancing myself the last couple days. I just– I got scared." His thumb runs aimlessly over my jaw. "When I realized my feelings for you were more than our agreement, it hit me with such force, I forgot how to breathe. I didn't think I could feel like this, I *haven't* felt like this in a long time." Leaning down, his lips ghost over mine before he places a gentle kiss on my lips.

"I thought breathing was a natural instinct." My brows furrow at his words, and he chuckles. "Something my body does without thinking. When you came into my life, I realized that I haven't taken a *real* breath before. Everything else was just the bare minimum for survival."

My mouth parts at his words, the wheels turning to understand what exactly it is that he just said.

"Are you saying," I lick my lips, trying to form the words in my head. "You like me?" I internally groan at the juvenile response. *Of course, that's what he means you dumbass.* My hands leave his chest as I cover my face in embarrassment. "Ohmygod. Ignore that."

His hands cover mine as he removes them from my face. He's got that sexy smirk going on, there's this lightness to his eyes.

"Yes, babydoll, that's exactly what I mean." With that declaration, he leans down and hooks his arms under my knees, lifting me. A squeak leaves my lips as I wrap my arms around his neck, pressing my lips to his. Stumbling our way back to our room, we make our way toward the bed. Before he can drop me, something cold and wet grazes my leg. I yelp, tearing lips from Xavier as I look down and am greeted with the beady eyes of my American bulldog.

"Oh Winnie. I forgot I left you in here to nap," I climb out of Xavier's grasp and scratch behind my dog's ears as his tail thumps against the bedding. Xavier hasn't stopped touching me, his hands roaming over my sides. He leans down and begins kissing my neck. Moving southward, he gently grazes his teeth along the column of my neck. My whole body shivers. I am pushed up against the bed as he gets to the bottom of my dress, slipping it over my curves.

Winnie jumps off the bed and trots off to one side of the room. My focus is brought back to the man in front of me when my dress lifts up over my ass. The cold air washes over my skin. My hands fly to the front of his shirt, and I begin hastily unbuttoning his shirt. When the last button is unclasped, I run my hands up, pushing the shirt over his shoulder and letting it drop to his feet. Xavier stops his movements. "Turn around." Damn, the man can growl.

I quickly turn and look over my shoulder, and if my panties weren't already soaked, they would be now. Xavier's eyes are darkened with lust as he takes me in. He quickly unzips my dress, and it falls to the floor. His arms wrap around me as he brings my back flush to his chest. His hands roam over my stomach. My arm snakes up and wraps around his neck, tilting my face toward his as I pull his lips to mine. His hand lowers, delving beneath my thong as he cups my pussy. Instinctively, I rock my hips into his hand. His fingers glide between my wet slit with ease, and it makes him pause. His lips are wrenched from mine as it hits him.

"Are you wearing a crotchless thong?" He asks, fighting for control. I hum, a knowing smile dancing at the corner of my mouth. A deep growl of satisfaction leaves him as he slams his lips back against mine. Continuing his pursuit, he starts teasing my opening before he pulls back, circling my clit. A moan leaves my lips. "God you're soaked." He dips a finger into my core, and I tighten around the intrusion. Just as quickly as he fills me, he pulls out. A whine leaves me as he turns me around again.

"Get on the bed."

Chapter Twenty Seven

xavier

MY EYES DEVOUR THE desperate look on her face, her chest heaving as she sits her plump ass on the bed. Her tits bounce as she shuffles backwards. Her taut nipples are obvious through the sheer lace, and my mouth waters, wanting to take them into my mouth.

She lays there in the middle of the bed, resting back on her elbows staring back at me. This time is different. I can feel it down to my core. There's still grief there, but guilt doesn't consume me like it did last time. There's something else in my chest.

Hope.

I think back to the talk I had with Monty and Josie just hours ago. How it's okay to move on, that her memory won't disappear. While I'm not ready to share that part of my life with Harper yet, I know I will eventually, and that's all the motivation I need.

With renowned confidence, I crawl over Harper. I settle myself between her thighs as I lean down and kiss her. This time it's slow, with deep, measured movements. When we go to pull apart, Harper bites down on my lip and tugs. The sensation causes me to grind into her core, but the friction between our layers isn't good enough. I quickly get off the bed stripping the last of my clothes.

I fist my cock as I stand at the end of the bed, deciding what I want to do next. I don't get to make a choice when Harper slips her body around, crawling toward me. Her eyes are fixated on my length. Precum begins to form on my slit as I give myself one tight stroke up. Taking my other hand, I collect it on my finger and hold it out in front of her. "Taste."

Harper doesn't disappoint as she grabs my wrist and pulls my finger toward her mouth. Her lips wrap around my finger, swirling her tongue around. I watch as her perfect lips continue to suck on my digit as I pull it out.

"You like how I taste, babydoll?" Her head nods in quick, short movements. "Do you want to taste it again?" I grip the base of my cock, looking at her tilting my head in question.

"Yes," she pants.

She loosens her grasp on the hand that was just in her mouth and goes to grab my cock. She whimpers when I take a step back. It's the sweetest of noises, but I'm even hungrier for her moans. She looks up to me, confused, sitting back on her heels to kneel at the end of the bed.

"You'll get your taste." I walk around the end of the bed, approaching the side. Her eyes follow my movements, turning her head to ensure she doesn't lose sight of me. I climb on to the bed with her and lay down on my back with my head pointing in the direction of the headboard. "But I need to taste you too. So, get over here, and sit."

"Oh. I don't think I should."

I lift my head and raise my brow in question. She has turned her whole body so she is facing me now, her bottom lip between her teeth. She looks cute when she's nervous.

"Well, I don't think I should given my si–"

"Don't you finish that sentence." I can see the insecurity behind the nerves. I don't want her to think for a second that the size of her body is unappealing. So I sit up, curling my finger at her in a beckoning motion.

"Come here, babydoll."

She pauses only for a moment before she begins to crawl toward me. She settles herself on my lap, her legs outside of mine. I graze my hand up to her laced nipples and pinch, coaxing a gasp from her mouth as she leans forward, attempting to alleviate the pressure. The pained look on her face turns into pleasure, as I release. I only give her a moment's reprieve before I pinch her other nipple.

"Let me tell you how this is going to go, okay?" I continue, letting go of her nipple. I move my hand and grip her chin, forcing her to keep her focus on me. "I'm going to lay back here, and you're going to put that pretty pussy over my face. Got it?"

I watch as she nods her head. "I'm going to need the words, babydoll."

"Y-yes."

"Good girl. Then, you're going to wrap those luscious lips," I emphasize by licking across her plump bottom lip. "Around my cock and suck. And the entire time? You *will* be *sitting* on my face."

"But I don't want to suffocate you."

A chuckle leaves my mouth. "You never could, babydoll, but ah, what a wonderful way to go it would be. My face buried in my girl's pretty cunt."

An audible intake of breath comes from her, followed by a shiver that tracks down her body. Her pupils are fully blown with lust, that plump bottom lip caught between her teeth. Her cheeks are flushed, and I map how it travels all the way down to her chest. I release her chin and trail my hands down her body. I cup her ass and give it a quick squeeze before I swat it.

I flop back on the bed, briefly lifting my head and eyebrow in question. She hesitates only for a second before she positions herself over my face. My body is thrumming in anticipation as she lowers herself. In the next moment, I feel her tongue glide over the head of my cock. I close my eyes briefly, savoring the feel of her tongue as she tastes me.

My cock is enveloped by warm, slick heat, causing me to groan. I don't wait another second as I reach up to her and pull her down to my mouth. Spreading her wide, my first lick starts from her swollen bud, and travels all the way down to her puckered hole. I feel a gasp around my cock as she tries to pull away, but I hold on to her tight, not letting her move an inch. I lick and suck her folds, savoring in her taste. Her tangy sweetness coats my tongue with every lap. I drag my tongue up to her opening before plunging it in, releasing a groan from her. The vibrations roll along my cock into my balls and she quickens her pace sucking me in a frenzy. The tingling starts low in my balls, my orgasm beginning to build. I need her to come first though. So I double down my efforts, fucking her with my tongue I bring one hand around and put pressure on her clit as I rub circles around it.

She pops off my cock, gasping. "Holy shit, yes." She's panting with one hand gripped at the base of my cock, the other hand beside my hip on the bed holding herself up. Her hips begin to move as she grinds her pussy down on my face. Her arousal grows wetter, she grows hotter, and I growl my encouragement as I continue to tongue fuck her.

Her movements begin to falter. Her pussy contracts around my tongue, trying to suck it in deeper. She's so close, she just needs a little more. When I pinch her clit between my thumb and forefinger, she screams as her pussy gushes over my face. I lick with fervor, wanting to taste every last drop of her orgasm.

Her body softens, but she's still trying to hold herself over my body, as she lifts her leg over, flopping to the side and laying on her back. She has a hand on her forehead as she stares at the ceiling. Her breathing is finally starting to slow down. I get up on my hands and knees, and I crawl over her.

Her swirling emerald eyes connect with mine, and then a small smirk forms on her face. I lean down and kiss her. She opens up for me so easily. Our tongues tangle, and she shows no aversions to tasting herself on my tongue.

When we part, I stay mere inches away from her lips.

"You didn't finish," she whispers.

A soft chuckle leaves me, and I cup her cheek in my hand. I trace my thumb along her jaw, watching the movements before I reply. "Oh babydoll, I'm not done with you just yet."

I quickly jump off the bed and go to my nightstand where I put my condoms. I pull one out quickly and toss it on the bed before I join her again. Her eyes stay locked on me as I resume my position. The hand that rests at her side begins to grip the sheets, the anticipation of what comes next adding to the tension in the room. Her eyes dart back and forth across my face, her eyes wide, so dark and intoxicating.

"We don't have to do this if you aren't ready." I understand the shit she went through, and how that might make her hesitate to be intimate with me. "I won't push you. I want things to go right when this happens. If now isn't the time, then that's okay."

Her hand that was gripping the sheet moves up to grasp my side.

"No," she says, exhaling. "I want this...I'm just a little nervous."

"Nervous is okay. We can go at whatever pace you want," My dick is screaming, wanting its release, but I pay it no attention though, not when this beautiful woman lays beneath me. Her flushed cheeks, and tousled dark locks that fan around her. She is the definition of sin.

Her body lifts toward me, and her lips crash with mine. Our kiss isn't frantic this time. It's comfortable with just the right amount of pressure as my pulse begins to race again. I feel something touch my hand, and it's then I realized that Harper has grabbed the condom, passing it to me. I quickly sit up on my knees to put the condom on. Harper lays beneath me as I sheath my cock, and when I bring it to her core I feel my chest tighten.

This is it. After all this tension, all the times I've not only denied myself, but denied her when I let the guilt win. It all led us down to this moment. I notch myself at her entrance, my eyes connecting with hers. I begin to push myself in. Her tight cunt is squeezing me like a vise. Her mouth drops open, and a soft whimper rushes out, seductive and heady. When I'm fully seated in her, I take a minute to look down at where we're connected.

"Fucking beautiful." I pull out and snap my hips back forward. I begin to set a steady pace, watching my cock disappear into her. I bring my hand forward, rubbing circles around her swollen bud. She immediately tightens around me at first contact, and Harper moans loudly.

"You look so fucking good right now," I pant.

"Kiss me. Please, Xavier."

My lips tug up at the corner of my mouth. "I can't say no to you, baby."

Descending onto her, swallowing her whimpers. I continue to thrust into her. Her hands roam all over me, like she can't decide what she wants to do. Releasing her lips, I pepper kisses down her jaw, until I reach her ear.

"Fuck Harps. You feel so fucking good, squeezing my cock just right." My teeth graze the bottom of her ear, causing her body to shudder. "This pussy was made for me, babydoll."

I roll my hips, angling myself so my pelvis is rubbing against her clit. She responds to the change of pace with a throaty moan. "Such a good girl." I lay the words upon her skin, increasing my pace. Her hands snake around my neck, gripping my hair. Her hips begin to move in tandem to mine. Each time we connect, it fills the room with the slap of our skin.

I begin to feel my balls tighten, my teeth grinding as I hold myself back. I'm driving full speed toward spilling over, but I need to see her come on my cock more than I need to breathe.

"Let go for me, Babydoll." My hand slides down to her clit, as I begin to circle it firmly. "C'mon, Harps. Give me what I want."

I feel her squeeze around me, but she needs more. I can see it in her eyes as they drip with desperation and lust. Her mouth parts as she sighs, her hands moving above her head as she grips the sheets. She watches as my fingers continue to work her.

"Do you need more?"

Her eyes connect with mine before she nods. I stop the movements of my hand briefly, a growl of protest leaving her lips before I take my thumb and forefinger, pinching her clit.

"Oh *fuuuuuuuuck!*" She screams into the room, as her pussy clenches down on my cock, pulling my orgasm to the forefront and slamming into me. I topple forward, catching myself on my forearms as I continue to thrust into her. We ride out our orgasms together.

When our breathing begins to even out, I sit up, pulling out of her slowly. My eyes rake over her body as she stretches her arms over her head. Leaning forward, I place a quick kiss on her lips before rolling off the bed. I make my way toward the bathroom.

"Come on," I holler from the bathroom. "You need to use the washroom so you don't get a UTI."

Grumbling comes from behind me as I take my time removing the condom and tying it off before tossing it into the garbage. Turning around, her soft emerald green eyes meet mine with hesitation as she stands in the doorway.

Striding toward her, I close the distance that I've already grown to hate even though she's right here. My hand reaches up, and I trace the side of her face before cupping it in my hand. Leaning forward, I press a kiss to her lips. Now that I'm allowed to have her wholly, I don't know if anything will ever satisfy me again.

"I'm going to grab us some clean clothes. Use the toilet, and then we'll shower." I direct her, noting the way her eyes are soft and wide as she looks at me. Stepping to the side, I give her room to walk past before I return to the bedroom.

When I return, I find Harper standing in front of the mirror as she removes her makeup. Walking past her, I set our clothes on the vanity, and turn the shower on. Stepping up behind her, my eyes connect with hers. The corner of her mouth tips up as she leans back, resting her head on my shoulder.

My arms circle around her, one hand snaking up through the valley of her supple breasts, until my hand lightly wraps around her neck. Using my thumb, I tilt her head so it's facing me before leaning down to press my lips against hers. Harper melts into me.

Why did I deny us this for so long?

I know exactly why I did. I should have talked to her sooner, told her everything.

I'm not going to stress the *what ifs*. I'm going to spend the rest of my time showing her exactly how much I want her.

Stepping back, I tap her ass. "Come on, get in. Let me wash you."

She steps in directly under the stream, a satisfied groan leaving her lips. Tilting her head back, my fingers comb through her hair, ensuring it's wet. Reaching past her, I grab her shampoo squirting a healthy dollop into the palm of my hand.

"Alright babydoll, turn."

She looks up at me with curiosity in her gaze, hesitating for a minute before turning her body.

My fingers methodically comb through her hair, massaging the shampoo to a lather. She lets out a content sigh, barely audible over the sound of the water. My chest warms with affection as I take in every relaxed movement of her body.

"Good?" I ask, turning her back around so I can rinse out the suds.

"So good." She hums as her head leans into my hand.

I repeat the process with the conditioner. While it sits in her hair, I grab the cloth draped across the shelf and squeeze the body wash on the cloth.

"What are you doing?" Harper giggles when the cloth runs down her arm.

The corner of my lip twitches as I look down on her. "I thought it was obvious? I'm taking care of my girl."

Guiding the cloth over her collar bone, I take my time dragging it over her breast before teasing the damp fabric over her nipple. Watching as it grows taut, I linger for a breath before repeating my motions on her other side. A soft whimper leaves Harper's lips, and I capture it in a kiss.

She pulls back, cradling my face in her hand. I lean into her touch for a moment, letting it ground me before I continue my descent.

The cloth follows the path of my hand as I move down her body. I drop to my knees before her. The cloth traces every delicate curve, holding me captivated as I memorize her soft, ivory colored thighs. I ache to push my hands between them, caressing her wet heat.

My gaze trailing up, connecting with the eyes that have easily become my new favorite color, as a smirk spreads across her face.

"What's on your mind?"

She catches her bottom lip between her lips, shifting from one foot to the other. A yelp leaves her as I swat her ass.

"Use your words, babydoll."

"You're just– you're on your knees."

A laugh escapes me as I remember what I told her.

"Ah yes," I murmur, running my hands up her outer thigh, before reaching round to grip her ass in my hands. I bring her forward until my nose is at her mound. I breathe her in before I dart my tongue out to taste her. A whimper comes from above me as I stand.

"As much as I would love to stay on my knees and worship you until you're nothing but putty under my hands..." My hands go to the back of her neck as I tilt her head and rinse her hair one more time, washing out the remainder of the conditioner. "It's late, and I want to hold you."

Over the next couple days, I take any opportunity I can to steal Harper away. Once I got a full taste of her, I couldn't get enough and needed more. I find myself seeking her out throughout the day, pulling her into side rooms, hall closets, just so I can get another taste of her. Feeling the warmth of her body around me the day after we finally got together was reviving. My inner turmoil didn't allow me to take this step because of the guilt of what happened to Shelby. I realize now that I was all in my head and that I *can* still honour her in other ways. I've decided I'm going to tell Harper about Shelby tonight after our day on the ski hill.

I make my way into the kitchen and find Harper there at the island getting her smoothie together. She doesn't hear me come in, so I make my way behind her wrapping my arms around her and burying my nose into her neck. I place a gentle kiss to where her neck and shoulder meet. Her body shivers at the interaction, and a small smile forms on her face.

"Come skiing with me today."

A soft laugh leaves her as she starts the blender. "You want *me* of all people to go skiing? Are you wanting me to hurt myself?"

"I wouldn't let that happen. Come on, let me teach you. We don't have to go down any of the crazy slopes either." She shuts the blender off and then spins around so she's facing me. I crowd her space more, pushing her against the counter with my hips. Her hands snake around my neck as she looks at me. She's silent for a couple minutes before she lifts on her tiptoes, placing a kiss against my lips.

When she pulls back, there is a smile on her face. "Okay."

"Yeah?" A smile spreads wider on my face, and I lean down to plant another kiss on her lips. "We'll go in a bit and get you sorted out in gear." I begin to trail my lips across her jaw and down her neck, and when I reach the sensitive spot between her neck and shoulder, I suck. She gasps as her hands grip my hair in a vise.

A breathy laugh leaves her. "Okay, you need to go and let me have my smoothie and get changed. I'll meet you in the living room in two hours?"

"Sounds good." I snag an apple from the counter and take a bite as I walk backwards away from her. "See you later, babydoll." I wink at her, watching the flush on her skin deepen. Every day with her is lighter, and I'm so grateful.

Chapter Twenty Eight

Harper

BEFORE TODAY, YOU WOULDN'T have caught me dead on a ski hill. I'm not the most graceful person, so why would I tempt fate?

But when Xavier came to me, asking if he could take me skiing? I couldn't say no.

After my smoothie, Evie and I took Winnie for a walk. I had invited Evie to come skiing with us, but she just laughed in my face and told me that she had a date with the hot tub this afternoon that she just couldn't cancel.

Now, here we are at the ski hill. I've been all suited up. We rented everything that I'd need to do this. I'm trying to learn the basics of skiing so that I can try and tackle a hill.

The first couple times we try this out, we aren't going down any big hills. But no matter where we are, it's a hot mess. My body is as stiff as a board. My knees are locked, and more often than not, my arms are held out beside me to ensure I keep my balance. I take my fair share of falls as I try to get the hang of things.

I'm determined though. Watching Xavier take the time to teach me the proper technique has made me want to learn it even more. He really is a great teacher and so patient with me as I fumble my way through.

"Come on Harper, you can do this. You've done this so many times now. This time will be better." I give myself a pep talk as we move forward to another practice run. When I make it to the end of the small run, I squeal with joy!

"I did it!" I throw my hands up in the air in triumph. Then the next thing I know, my back is on the ground, and I'm looking up at the sky. I burst out laughing because, of course. Xavier stops next to me and gives me a once over. When he has determined I look okay, he smiles at me and helps me up.

"Did you see that!?" I ask him. "I mean, not the end part, but the rest of it?"

"Yes I did, that wasn't too bad. I think a couple more runs, and we can maybe try something a bit bigger, eh?"

"You think?" The hope in my voice is obvious. I know at the beginning I thought this was going to be a terrible idea. I thought I was going to be too out of shape for this, but once I got the hang of everything, it started to become easier, and I was enjoying myself. Despite the many tumbles, which I expected anyways.

"Yeah, you're catching on quick there, babydoll. I'm impressed." He leans forward and gives me a quick peck on the lips before we get back to it.

We spend the next forty five minutes doing run after run of the smaller hill. I've been able to go down with ease, but I still struggle a bit with slowing down. I'm getting the hang of it. We head back to the lodge briefly and have some hot apple cider to warm up.

We find a nice little spot in the lodge that has a loveseat looking up at the ski hills. We sit there, at my insistence, so that I can watch other skiers and take notes. Xavier's arm is wrapped around my shoulder, his hand playing with my braided hair, apple cider in his other. He takes the time to explain some techniques to me as we watch.

We're in our own cozy little bubble, and I absolutely love it. Ever since Christmas Eve, when Xavier finally opened up and confirmed his feelings were real, things have been going so well. He's more attentive, always touching me in some way.

Christmas morning was spent deepening our conversation while snuggled in bed.

We're in bed, with Winnie sleeping soundly at the end of the mattress. The heat from Xavier's body against my back is comforting. We both just woke up, but it's still too early. I tried to get out of bed, but Xavier's arms tightened around me. "Don't. Stay in bed with me for a little while longer." He plants a kiss on my shoulder before burying his face in the crook of my neck.

"Okay, but when my bladder starts screaming at me, you have to let me go."

"Deal... also, Merry Christmas, Harps."

"Merry Christmas, Xavier." We lay like that in silence for a couple of minutes, just enjoying the feeling of being in each other's presence. My hand is drawing patterns up and down the arm he has wrapped around my midsection. "I want to talk about last night," he starts. My motions pause as I wait for him to continue. "I know I put you through a lot the last couple days, and I know I already apologized for that. I got scared, and I put distance between us. It was selfish, and it wasn't fair to you." I feel the deep breath he takes, and the air waves over my skin at his exhale. "Things were starting to get real for me, and at the time, I didn't think that you could feel the same way. I didn't deserve for you to feel the same way." "Xavier. You deserve happiness too. And the feelings aren't one sided." "They aren't?" It was barely a whisper, but I heard his response. I rolled over in his arms so that we were face to face. I cupped his cheek with my hand. A small smile forms on my lips, as I take in the vulnerable look that starts dancing in his ocean blue orbs. "No, I feel it too." My thumb traces his jaw back and forth as I try to think of how to word it. "I'm not someone who falls easily, but when I do? I fell pretty hard. With the time we spent getting to know each other before Thanksgiving dinner, and everything I was learning about you, I began to fall a little more. I had to constantly remind myself that this was something that we agreed on, and nothing more. But I can't keep denying this attraction that I feel toward you."

More silence falls between us. His brows furrow as he takes in what I've said. Nerves swim inside me, wondering if I got this all wrong. Was this just for sex? Adding a little benefit in our mutual agreement? Then I remember what he just said, and I remind myself that this man has scars, and I need to be patient.

"I don't think we should be fake dating anymore." My blood runs cold at his declaration. *"What?"* I squeak. *My heartbeat begins to pick up as I move myself away from him. I sit up taking the blankets with me to cover my body, because we're both still naked. Running a hand through my hair, I look away from him.*

"Harps, where are you goi– oh God, no." *The mattress dips and covers shifts as he leaves the bed, and leaving the bed, and then, he's right in front of me. My eyes shoot down to my lap. I can't look at him now. He wants to end this whole thing. I knew it was something that would happen, but I thought after last night, we were starting something.*

"Babydoll, look at me." *There's a hint of desperation in his voice, but I can't bring myself to look at him right now. He heaves a sigh, and then I see his hand slide over to grasp mine. I try to pull it away, but he grips me a bit tighter.* *"What I meant by that is I don't think we should be fake dating anymore... because I want this to be real."*

My head whips up, mouth agape, as I stare at the beautiful man before me. His hair is ruffled with sleep, the slight indents on his face from where it rested on the pillow. His eyes, a deep blue shining with intensity to his confession. It takes me a few seconds to fully comprehend that he just told me he wants this to be real.

"You–" *I shut my eyes and take a breath before opening them.* *"You want us to date? Like, for real?"*

That damn slow smirk begins to form on his face. *"Yeah Harps. I want to date–like for real."*

I don't even think as I surge forward, pressing my lips to his. Nothing about it is urgent, but there was a solidification that happened with this kiss. Xavier pushes me on my back, rolling on top of me and settling between my legs. My hand trails up his body before resting around his neck.

We spent the next couple minutes making out like teenagers before breaking apart. Through heavy panting, I speak my mind. *"We should probably get ready to meet with everyone for Christmas."*

Xavier groans as he buries his face in my neck. *"You're probably right."*

"If we don't get up soon then my mom will come barging in here," he grumbles. "And I'd rather her not."

Just then, there's a knock on the door, and I can't help the giggle that leaves my mouth.

I'm taken out of my thoughts when Xavier asks me if I'm ready to give the hill another go.

"I think so, yeah! I actually think I'm good to try something a bit...more?" Sitting up straighter, I'm feeling confident. I want to challenge myself, and I think the small hill we have been doing was okay.

"You really think you're ready for something more challenging?"

I sit there and contemplate for a minute. "I think so." Trying to portray as much confidence as I feel, I keep my tone light. "I really think I'm getting the hang of this!" I stand up and hold out my hand for Xavier to grab. He downs the last of his drink before he gets up and takes my hand in his, leading the way out of the lodge.

※ ❦ ※

The higher we get on the lift, the more I wonder if I made a mistake by asking to go to a bigger hill. I watch as other skiers and snowboarders make their way down the hill with ease. I'm entranced watching each person go down. Before I know it, Xavier is bumping me with his elbow, telling me that we're at our stop and need to get ready to get off.

I watch as we approach the top of the hill. I prepare myself by pointing the tips of my skis up as Xavier lifts the bar on the chair. When my skis hit the hill and they become parallel with the ground, I push up and glide forward with the momentum of the chair. When we get a bit of the way up, I begin to slow down in a plow motion off to the side. Xavier saddles up beside me with a grin on his face.

"That was fantastic the way you got off the lift, babydoll." My body hums at his praise and a matching smile spreads on my face.

See, you can do this Harps.

I follow him as he leads us to the part of the hill he wants us to go down. A spike of adrenaline washes over my body as we near the top. I never thought I would enjoy something like this, but doing this with him makes it such a great experience.

"Thank you for taking me skiing today, I'm really having the best day. I just wanted you to know."

He's silent for a minute while he looks down the hill, and when he turns to look at me, he gives me a soft smile. "I'm glad you're having fun."

There's another emotion that washes over his face, but it's gone before I can decipher what it is.

"Okay, I want you to go down first, and I'll follow behind you. This way I can make sure that you're not struggling or if you need help."

I look down at the hill and take a deep breath. I nod. "Okay, sounds good!"

"Don't forget to plow your skis if it gets too fast, Harper. This isn't a race." His tone is stern, and I just roll my eyes at him. I begin to push forward, but not before I stick my tongue out at him.

A laugh breaks free from me as I begin my descent down the hill. My speed picks up as I swerve my way back and forth, taking my time to avoid bumps or dips in the hill that might send me falling. My heart is beating fast as we begin to go near some trees. There is a clear path between two tree branches, and I can see beyond them that there is a path that goes in and out of the trees. On the other side of the trees, there is a clear path that sends us straight down.

Feeling confident with how my skiing has been going, I choose the tree-lined path to challenge myself a bit more. When I go through the first gap in the trees, I gasp out in triumph. I don't get to fully celebrate when the next opening quickly appears. I focus on my movements allowing myself to safely veer between the trees.

I'm doing it.

I'm actually doing this. My heart rate spikes with adrenaline, and buzzes through my veins as I continue my trail.

I'm doing so good, I can't wait to get to the bottom and scream with excitement about how I did it! Just as I'm preparing to go through the next opening of trees, I catch a movement right at the corner of my eyes. A white blob runs in front of me, and I panic. I try to swerve out of the way, but my movements are too jerky.

I lose my balance.

And I'm falling.

My body tumbles at a momentum that I can't slow down. I don't know where I'm heading. My boots suddenly lighter as my skis detach, not faltering the momentum as I continue to fall down the hill. The only things I can really see are white, blue and some green, as my sight spirals with the motions. Suddenly everything stops as pain ricochets up my body briefly, the heavy impact of my body hitting something dense before my head slams against something hard.

Then, all I see is black.

Chapter Twenty Nine

Xavier

N^{o.}
No, No, No.

Not *again.*

Everything happened so fast.

She was doing so well as she was gliding down the hill. I was admiring how fast she caught on to skiing. She was determined as I taught her the essentials, but I should've known better. I should've told her that I wanted her to go down the smaller hills a couple more times. That we could do the bigger hills another day. We're still supposed to be here for less than a week. There's plenty of time. There *was* plenty of time.

Then I watched as that fucking rabbit ran out of the bush and into her path. I watched as she tried to dodge it and lost her balance instead. The air in my lungs froze where it was as I watched her tumble forward, her skis flying off her boots. I lean forward, tucking into position to increase my speed, to get to her faster. To get to her before she hurts herself.

My heart is beating out of my chest as I race toward her.

I watch in slow motion as she connects with a rock settled beside one of the trees. I saw the impact it made as her back connected with it and shot her head back onto the hard surface.

I wasn't fast enough. I couldn't save her. I skid to a stop beside her, kicking off my skis as I drop to the ground.

"Fu-uck." A sob leaves my mouth as I settle in beside her, checking her over. I remove her goggles from her face so I can get a better look. Her eyes are closed, but when I get closer, I can see that she's still breathing.

Her body is at a weird angle from the way her body landed on the snow covered rock.

Black begins to frame my vision as my breathing increases. *Fuck, it's happening again.* I lightly shake her shoulders.

"Harper– Harps." The desperation in my voice is obvious as I try to get her to wake up to no avail. " *Please* look at me." The blood rushes in my ears and I can't hear anything. My chest is constricting as I fight to take in a breath. I lift my shaking hands and rip off my goggles and helmet tossing them beside me. I run my fingers through my hair as I try to calm myself enough to think clearly.

"Oh my God, are you alright!" A voice shouts from behind me, but I don't answer him. I can't. I think I'm going into shock. I hear the person close in, and if they say something else, I don't hear it. Harper is laying in front of me unconscious. It all feels too familiar, except Shelby still woke up. She woke up, and she got up. Harper isn't awake. Her eyes aren't opening.

"Help!" It's the only thing that I manage to say.

"I've already called down to the lodge, and they're sending up the ski patrol now." I still haven't fully looked at the man that came to check on us. I turn to look and I'm met with silver eyes looking back to me with concern. The man looks to be in his late fifties, his salt and pepper hair peek from the sides of his helmet. The tan color with laugh lines are prominent on his face. "Can you tell me your name?" He asks the question calmly, taking a seat beside me as we wait.

"Xavier." I take a deep breath, "That's Har-Harper." My voice cracks halfway through her name.

He puts his hand on my shoulder in support."The name's Hank."

Just then a groan comes from Harper's body, I jolt forward. "Harps, Harps, can you hear me? You're okay. I'm right here."

"W-what happened?" She grumbles, bringing her palm up to her forehead.

"You tumbled right into a rock. I think you hit your head too. Just stay still, okay?" My hands are hovering over her, wanting to comfort her, but not sure if my touch will do it. "Ski patrol is on their way, and they should be here any minute."

Harper opens her eyes slightly. Her pupils are slightly dilated, and then she squints as she tries to focus on me. "Well, that's silly. We haven't even gone to the ski hill yet." She pauses, before opening her eyes again briefly. "Or- wait." There's a longer pause as Harper's eyes furrow in concentration before she closes them again.

When she doesn't continue her sentence, I reach forward and shake her slightly on her shoulder. "Hmm?"

The tightness in my chest went away momentarily when she woke up. The moment she didn't remember that we were skiing, it was like my lungs were in a tight grasp again. Just as I'm about to shake her again and get her to keep talking, the ski patrol arrives.

"Hey everyone, my name is Pete. I heard someone took a tumble, yeah? How's everyone else doing? Is anyone else hurt?"

I shake my head quickly, clearing my throat before answering. "No, I'm fine. I was behind her when it happened. A rabbit came running as we were going down. She attempted to avoid hitting it, but when she did that, she lost control and tumbled. She landed right on this rock and lost consciousness. She just came to, but appeared confused when we were talking."

Pete looks over me quickly, before moving to Harper. I sit there and watch as he spends the next half an hour assessing Harper's injuries. He lays her on a backboard and puts her in a cervical collar, just to be on the safe side. When he's established her injuries, he checks on her pain. She complained that her head, back, and ribs hurt. That makes sense to me as those were probably the biggest impact. After he's checked her vitals and deems that she isn't in need of any additional oxygen, they load her up on the sled they arrived in.

They took her skis with her, and I was offered a ride or to meet them down at the bottom of the hill. I chose to ride on the sled with them so that they don't have to wait for me before the ambulance takes her away.

The ambulance wouldn't take me with her to the hospital, despite my fight around it. In the end, I lose and my panic begins to rise again. I abandon my skis and pull out my phone, calling the only person I can think of to help me at this moment.

The phone rings a few times before the call connects.

"Hey, big guy! How was skiing?" Josie's soft voice comes through the line.

"It's happening again." My voice cracking at the end before it turns into a sob.

I hear shuffling in the background from Josie's end of the phone. I hear her mumble something before she comes back. "Where are you? Are you still at the hill? I'm coming to get you."

Ten minutes later, I'm sitting in the car with Josie as she makes her way to the hospital. The paramedics only told me where they were taking her. I sit there, leaning forwards with my head in my hands, replaying her fall, over and over again. My mind fixates on all the ways I could have saved her. Out of every scenario that I run through my head, there are two facts that remain the same.

I couldn't save her, and it's all my fault.

I shouldn't have agreed for her to go down the hill. I should have told her another day. I should of–

I jump as a hand grasps my shoulder. Josie is looking at me with concern on her face. She opens her mouth to say something, but closes it again. Her grip on my shoulder tightens, before she pulls me and wraps her arms around me. My body slumps as it recognizes the safety of my best friend. I hear the door open behind me, and a hand grasps my neck. I don't even need to turn my head to know that it's Monty. At the realization that my best friends have dropped everything to be here for me, I let go. The burning that has been constant at the back of my eyes finally releases, and tears begin to fall down my face. A strangled noise leaves my throat.

I let all my fear, and self-loathing consume me. I allow myself to feel every heavy ounce of grief, the weight of it constricting the air in my lungs. Every inhale feels like a knife slicing against my chest. We sit there together for a couple minutes. When I have collected myself enough, the three of us make our way into the hospital.

We walk into the emergency department, and the waiting area is quiet. The plastic rows of waiting chairs are empty, minus a couple of chairs. I pay them no mind as I walk toward the reception desk. The receptionist is a middle aged woman, with her dirty blonde hair braided back. Her neutral colored scrubs look ruffled, showing signs that she's been here for awhile, but she greets me with a smile.

"Hi there. My girlfriend was brought in by ambulance – Harper Beckett."

"Let me just look her up for you." She quickly types on her computer as she looks up Harper in their system. After a couple more clicks of mouse on the screen, she returns her gaze to me. "It looks like she got here about fifteen minutes ago, but that's all I really have up here. Let me go talk to the doctor and see what I can find out for you. Go have a seat, and I'll come find you once I know a bit more."

I swiftly nod my head, but I remain where I'm standing. I track the nurse as she disappears into the back rooms where the patients are brought through. Josie comes to my side, grabbing my elbow. "Come on big guy, we aren't going to get answers any faster standing here like a big grizzly bear."

She directs me to the closest seat and tells me to sit down. When I do, I bend forward, resting my forearms on my knees as I keep my focus on the door the nurse went through.

The time seems to tick by slowly, and I feel like we've been here for longer than we have been. At some point, Josie stepped away to call Evie and let her know that Harper is in the hospital. Monty took her place beside me. He's tried a couple times to start a conversation, but I wasn't responding.

Finally, I watch as the doors open, and the nurse that left comes through with a doctor following behind her. The nurse spots me right away. I'm up and out of my seat in the next second. Anxiety claws under my skin as I prepare myself for every possible negative scenario to become my reality.

"You're here for Ms. Beckett?" The doctor asks, kindly.

"Yes, we are. I'm Xavier Hawthorne. I'm her boyfriend."

The doctor looks through his clipboard for a moment. Flipping through the papers, he returns his gaze to me. "Ah yes, I have you right here. I'm Dr. Porter. I have been the doctor that has been overlooking Ms. Beckett since she was brought in. She's been asking for you. If you follow me, I can show you where she's resting."

The air rushes out of my lungs. "She's awake?"

"Yes, she's awake! A little drowsy, but that's to be expected with her mild concussion. Please follow me, I'll bring you to her and explain more."

I turn around to look at Monty. He's running his hand through his hair, and I see the relief on his face. "Go," he says, "I'll wait with Josie for Evie to get here." I nod quickly, before turning back around and motioning for the doctor to lead the way.

The doctor leads me through the doors that lead back to the patient's rooms. The fluorescent lights flickered overhead as we walked down the aisle. The halls buzz as nurses and doctors go about their shifts attending to all the patients that have been admitted. When we reach halfway down the hall, the doctor pauses in front of one of the rooms and turns to me.

"Ms. Beckett is just over here in this room. She's currently stable, but we have her hooked up to some IV fluids just to keep her hydrated. Once the IV is complete, we can move forward with discharging her."

"What do you mean discharging her? She's not going to stay overnight to be monitored? What if it gets worse?" Both my hands are in fists as I try to calm the panic that has reappeared in a matter of seconds. How can they just send her home? What if things get worse, and she's not at the hospital to get immediate attention?

"Now, this won't happen for some time yet. The neurologist still needs to give her at least two more checks before she gets the okay to go home. She came in slightly confused, but she appears to be more lucid now."

"What if she gets worse when you send her home?" I ask.

"I can assure you she has gone through all the neurological tests to ensure that nothing more serious is at play. She went for a CT when she arrived, which showed no signs of brain bleeds, swelling or fractures. All her symptoms point to a concussion—and a mild one at that. We can discuss the care that she will need at home during discharge."

I flex my hands a couple more times, taking another deep breath. "I need to see her." I won't believe anything this doctor says until my eyes are on her myself. I walk past the doctor and make my way to her door.

"Mr. Hawthorne, she's resting. She needs to rest, both physically and mentally, to allow her brain to heal."

I take that moment to collect myself before I enter her space. When I have a little bit more control over my emotions, I walk through the door. The lights over her bed are off, but the bathroom light is on, softly illuminating the room.

There in the bed is Harper, with her eyes closed. She has an IV hooked up to her arm, and the bag is about half empty. She's wearing one of those ugly looking hospital gowns that are usually itchy. Her hair is a tossed mess, splayed in many different directions on her pillow. There's a soft furrow on her brow as she tries to rest. Next to her hospital bed, there's a chair that I quickly make my way to so I can sit next to her.

I find myself hesitant to take her hand in mine because I don't want to wake her up if she's resting. The incessant need to touch her overrules my rational thoughts though, and I find myself lacing my fingers with hers.

She rustles a bit, turning her face toward me. A soft grumble leaves her lips, before her eyes open slowly. I see the moment her eyes come into focus and land on me. The moment they do, a small smile traces over her lips.

"Hey, you."

Chapter Thirty

Harper

W ELL, BEING HOSPITALIZED WASN'T on my bingo card for this trip, but here we are.

I don't entirely remember what happened, but I remember something running out in front of me. I remember trying to swerve so I could avoid it. Then, I remember tumbling before everything went black. I don't remember the ski patrol coming to me and assessing me before taking me to the hospital.

Everything became a bit more clear as I got set up in the hospital room and the neurologist came to check me out. After a bit of time, I was told that I had a mild concussion, and could benefit from some fluids before they would give me the okay to go home.

Once they set me up with the IV, I decided to rest my eyes for a couple minutes while I waited. It wasn't long after that that I felt something grabbing my hand. When I opened my eyes and looked over to the side of my hospital bed, I saw the concerned look on Xavier's face.

He refuses to let go of my hand while we wait to be discharged. I try to get Xavier to video call Evie so that she can see that I'm alright, but he refuses to do that. He told me I'm not supposed to be around screens with a mild concussion, and that my brain needs to rest. I try to eye roll at his behavior, but it just hurts my head, and I do my best to negotiate at least a phone call. He reluctantly agreed.

I'm discharged shortly after that, with a checklist of what my recovery is going to look like. The doctor tells me that a mild concussion should take anywhere from a week to two weeks to heal. I'm told to keep an eye out for worsening symptoms, and Xavier is very resistant to me going home at first.

"What if her symptoms worsen? Wouldn't it just be safer to keep her here for an additional twenty four hours to ensure it's just a concussion?" The doctor sighed, pinching the bridge of his nose. *This is probably not the first time he has dealt with Xavier like this tonight.*

"Like I have told you before Mr. Hawthorne. She is stable. She shows no signs of worsening symptoms, nor has she shown any indications that there is something more dire going on. As long as there is someone there monitoring her, she is perfectly able to go home and rest. At home."

Now, here I am, sitting in our bed at the ski lodge. Xavier has been in and out of the room getting everything I could possibly need to rest. He's taken away all of my electronics, despite my best efforts to get him to leave them. I almost got away with it too, until he came into the room and caught me trying to read something on my phone.

He's very neurotic and bossy.

Winnie is laying on the bed with his head on my lap as I look out the window across the room. I tried going to sleep for a bit, but my head is throbbing a bit. I asked Xavier for something for the pain, and he ran out of the room to retrieve it all.

There's a light knock on the door, before my best friend comes bursting through the room.

"I thought you could use some bestie time. I had to sneak past your bodyguard to get in here." She looks behind her, like she's expecting him to barge through the door and kick her out at any second. "He's a little...much."

I give her a tired smile that turns into a huge yawn. "Yeah, he's been hovering but if this is something that will make him feel better then, I'll let him do it."

Evie plops down on her back at the end of the bed, resting her hands on her stomach. Turning to face me, her green eyes bore into me. "You really scared the shit out of me today." There's a slight tremble in her voice when she says it.

"I'm sorry Evie. I really didn't mean to scare anyone. I was learning so much about skiing from Xavier, and truly having a good time with him. I felt confident to try something more. Maybe, I should have waited." I begin chewing on my thumb nail. I remember the concerned and haunted look on Xavier's face when I woke up.

"I know you didn't mean to, babes. It was scary nonetheless though. I'm just glad you're still here and not seriously hurt." She reaches for my hand, grabbing it and squeezing gently.

A moment later, Xavier comes into the room. Winnie quickly jumps off the bed to greet him, nudging his hand for pets. His stride falters slightly when he realizes Evie is in bed with me. He recovers quickly, continuing his long strides over to his side of the bed where he hands over some pain meds and a glass of water.

"You should be *resting*." His voice is firm, and I catch his eyes darting over to Evie pointedly before returning to mine.

"I *am* resting. Evie just came in to keep me company. We're going to have a bestie sleepover." I look up and give him my best puppy dog eyes. He stares at me for a minute before sighing. Xavier types quickly on his phone before putting it on the nightstand and crawling into his side of the bed.

I'm taken by surprise when he grips my hips, dragging my body down until he's able to lay down between my legs. A content sigh leaves him as he rests his head on my stomach, closing his eyes.

Evie stares at him, then up at me, with a raised eyebrow. I shrug my shoulders, a small smile breaking on my face as I play with his hair. His body relaxes more at my touch.

"I didn't know you were part of the bestie sleepover," Evie teases, when she realizes he's not leaving.

Xavier cracks open one eye. "Just pretend I'm not here."

Evie just stares at him blankly.

"Sure, it'll be completely easy to ignore the six foot tall, sexy vet who's currently wrapped around my best friend."

A snort leaves me as I witness the interaction. I didn't even get a chance to tell Evie that we've decided to end the fake dating and do this for real. Although, I'm sure that after this, she'll figure it out and drill me about it when we get a minute alone. *If* we get a minute alone.

Xavier's arm leaves me, but only to grab my hand, placing it back on his head before closing his eyes again. "And I plan to stay wrapped around her. But I promise that whatever is said in here, stays in here- because girl code or whatever."

"Well- okay, but don't say I didn't warn you..."

That's the only warning he gets before she proceeds to dive in and proceeds to tell me how hot she thought Josie and Monty were at the Christmas Eve party. Xavier snorts during the story, and it's probably because Evie still doesn't know that Josie and Monty might not be opposed to her joining in with them.

"What's going on with work? Is your temp job done now?"

A huge sigh leaves her as she slumps down in the bed, throwing an arm over her eyes. "Yeah, it's done. And there isn't anywhere hiring right now with it just being after Christmas. I've got some money saved, so I'm not going to be struggling per say, but it'll cover me while I try and find something else."

"I'll keep an eye out for you and send you anything I might come across."

"Thanks babes, I appreciate that. I'm not worrying about it just yet."

We spend the next couple hours talking. I eventually extract myself from Xavier's hold to lay down myself, but when I lay down Winnie crawls in between us and goes back to sleep with his head resting on my hip. Thank God for this California king bed, because I don't know how else we'd fit three adults, and a large dog, comfortably. Eventually Evie falls asleep on me, mumbling away about whatever adventure her subconscious is putting her through. I seriously need to behavior start recording our conversations to save. Xavier's alarm goes off once, and he checks on me to see how I'm feeling. I get out of bed to go to the washroom because all the water Xavier is making sure I drink is making me have to pee what feels like every ten minutes, I swear. I turn on the light and shut the door, quick to relieve my business and brush my teeth.

Once I return to the bedroom, Xavier is waiting on his side of the bed. He notices me as I start to walk toward him. His eyes don't stray from my movements. When I'm close enough, he grabs my hand and pulls me to stand in between his thighs and looks up at me.

"Are you sure you're good? You don't need anything?"

"I'm fine Xavier, I promise. It's just a mild concussion, I'll be back to my normal clumsy self in no time." My voice is laced with amusement as I gently shove at his shoulders.

His brows furrow, his hands that are placed on my hips tighten. "But it's not fine. I shouldn't have let you go on that hill. You would have been fine if we didn't go down." There's a tightness in his voice that brings concern to the surface. He can't seriously think that what happened is his fault.

"Xavier, this isn't anyone's fault. We couldn't have known a rabbit was going to run out in front of me and cause me to lose my balance."

Suddenly Xavier is up. He moves me backwards a few steps before he walks away from me, pacing with both hands running up and through his hair in frustration.

"But it is my fault!" He says loudly, before looking over to where Evie is sleeping and takes a breath before continuing. "I should've known better. I should've been closer behind. When I saw you lose your balance and tumble over, my whole world stopped, Harper. I couldn't get to you fast enough! And if you weren't wearing your helmet–" I watch as he spirals.

My heart squeezes as I remember him mentioning his past. Is this why he's reacting the way he is? Did he have a sibling that got hurt skiing? No, it couldn't be that. No one has mentioned a sibling that's no longer here. No, this is something else. I walk toward him with determination. Xavier's been carrying this weight for a long time.

When I'm close enough, I grab his arm to halt him in his tracks. He eyes zero in on where we connect before his eyes shoot up to mine. It's there in that moment, I see the despair and guilt written all over his face. He's beating himself up because of a fluke accident on a hill that I felt confident going down. It wasn't until that rabbit ran in my path that I had any concern of something going wrong.

"Hey." I move my hand up his arm slowly. I'm not sure how he is when he's in this state. Does he need to be touched? Held? Does he need space?

As my hand runs up his arm, I can see him begin to slightly relax. My touch is the confirmation that he needs that I'm alright. I don't second guess myself as I step into his space and wrap my arms around his neck, bringing him down slightly so I can hug him. He's still for a moment before his whole body melts into my touch. "What's going on Xavier? You can talk to me. Remember what I said before? I got you."

He tucks his face into my neck and takes a couple steady breaths before pulling back. He looks at the bed where Evie is out cold. Winnie is laying on the end of the bed, but he's alert and watching us. The dog's head tilts to the side as he assesses us. "Well, we might as well let him out for a pee." I say lightly, as I signal for him to come. Winnie immediately jumps off the bed and trots off to the door. I go to follow him, but grab Xavier's hand, dragging him with me. He follows with no arguments. We put on our coats and head downstairs to get our boots.

Winnie takes off down the deck to go find his perfect spot. Big white snowflakes are falling from the sky, coating everything we see with white fluff. The air is crisp and chilled, clouds puffing from our lips with each exhale. We stand there on the deck in silence, and watch. I'm anxious as I stand there. Should I start a conversation? Or should I keep it silent and let him open up to me. What if he doesn't open up at all though.

"Her name was Shelby. She was my girlfriend in high school."

My breath hitches as I look at him. He's looking down at his feet, one foot kicking at the loose snow that has accumulated on the deck from the sky. I don't say anything as I wait for him to continue.

"We had been dating for about a year, and it was the first time I was bringing her out here to celebrate Christmas with my family. Chloe was seven at the time, and she loved Shelby. Chloe was still spoiled, but she didn't act like the way she does now. Anyways, Shelby was a skier, and that's actually how we met—on the ski hill." A soft smile forms on his lips, and I know he's reliving a happy memory.

"We decided to go skiing one day. We had gone down the hill a couple times at this point, and were heading up to go one more time before we left back to the lodge. While we were going down the hill, her ski hit a hidden rock in the trail, and it sent her flying—similar to you, but she caught a bit more air. When she fell, she hit her head on hard snow. She wasn't wearing a helmet and had a cut at the back of her head, so we took her to the hospital for stitches." He pauses as he takes in a shaky breath. My heart is breaking as I think of everything that could go wrong in this story.

"She got stitched up and seemed fine otherwise. We got the okay to go home, and the doctor told us that she just had a mild concussion. We were instructed to look for any worsening conditions." He brings the heel of his hand to his eyes, rubbing at them. The silence is deafening as he tries to collect himself. I walk toward him and take one of his hands. He startles at the close contact, but he lets me continue. I lace our fingers together and place his hand over my heart. He looks at the connection, and then looks at me. There is a glassy look to his eyes, the unshed tears threatening to fall over.

"I got you." It's a gentle reminder to him that I'm not going anywhere. He gives me a curt nod, before exhaling a deep breath.

"So, we went home under strict instructions to rest. We were heading to her room and – sh-she started to slur her words for a moment." Xavier's breathes come sharper now. "I asked her if we needed to go back to the hospital. She told me no." His body is rigid as he tries to regain some semblance of control. His jaw is tight, and his breathing comes out in short bursts.

"She told me she was fine."

The suffocating silence makes it hard for me to breathe. The heaviness weighs down on the moment. I already know that the end of this story is tragic. Xavier shivers, and I'm positive it's not just from the cold.

"Come on, let's go inside and warm up." I use the leverage of our laced fingers to bring him back into the house. I call for Winnie, who races to the door and waits for us.

Making a path through the kitchen, I decide to lead him to the living room since Evie's still in our room. I know she'll be out cold, but I don't want to risk her waking up with him being so vulnerable. I feel the weight of him slowly follow behind me as we make our way through the halls. The house is quiet as we enter the room, and I bring him to the couch.

He plops down and rests his head on the back of the couch. His hands rub down his face before slumping onto his lap in defeat. I sit down next to him, and he immediately reaches over to grasps my hand.

"She was laughing." His red rimmed eyes meet mine for a brief moment. Sniffing he runs the back of his free hand under his nose. "Then she started complaining that her head hurts. She assured me it was just a headache."

I squeeze our joined hands, reassuring him that I'm listening. There isn't anything that I can say at this moment that will help make this story easier to tell.

"We were about to head upstairs, because she said that she was tired and..." His face is turned down in anguish. "She collapsed. I was right there to catch her. I-I thought she fainted." His words are barely a whisper. He releases his hand from mine as he leans forward, his elbows on his knees, hands woven through his hair.

"When I got her to the ground, I tried to wake her. I shook her. Called her name, but she wasn't responding." His head whips up, and he stares straight forward. "Then, I noticed her breathing wasn't normal."

His knee begins to bounce at a rapid pace, and his stare is far off into the distance. I watch as his eyes glaze over, like he's replaying the memories over in his head. "I called 911, and it was then that I realized her breathing had stopped completely."

I'm ringing my hands together as I watch a man I've grown to care about so deeply about fall apart while remembering something so heartbreaking. I wish I could take the pain away. I wish I could-

"The operator told me to start CPR on her while we waited for the ambulance. I don't remember what happened during that time– my brain shut off. I just wanted her to be okay. She *needed* to be okay."

What Xavier shares next is so soft, I don't think I would have heard it if I wasn't paying so close attention. "She was gone before the paramedics arrived."

A gasp left my lips. "Oh, Xavier." I reach out to place my hand on his shoulder, but before I can make contact, he shoots up out of his seat and begins pacing.

"I should have known better!" He says loudly, the anger taking over his grief. "I should have brought her back the minute she slurred her words. I believed her when she said she was fine. *I believed her.*" He collapses on the ground. A gut-wrenching sob leaves him as he finally lets everything go.

I don't think, I just move. In the blink of an eye, I'm by his side, rubbing a hand up and down his back as raw pain moves through him, and I wish I knew how to make it easier. Grief is never easy, and it doesn't go away.

"I'm so sorry, Xavier." My voice is tight with emotion as I try to soothe him. He looks up at me, tears flowing freely down his cheeks. I see the sad teenage boy who just lost his first love shining in his eyes, and I wish I could go back in time and change things.

"I wish the pain would stop." His voice is so quiet and vulnerable.

My eyes well with tears, and I pull him up toward me, wrapping him in a hug. I lower myself into a seating position, and his body slowly follows me as he gets comfortable in my embrace. His face burrows into the crook of my neck.

There isn't anything I can do to take his pain away, so I do the only thing I can do. I hold him.

"I've got you."

Chapter Thirty One

Harper

I'M WOKEN UP BY a blaring noise coming from my left. I don't know what time we made it back upstairs, but as soon as my face hit the pillow, I was out. At some point during the night, Winnie must have got up and moved, because now, he's wrapped around my back side, tucked between me and Evie. I scrub a hand over my face, noticing the corner of my mouth is wet. When I look down, I'm horrified to find a wet spot on Xavier's shirt.

"Oh my God, I'm so sorry." I grumble as I quickly wipe at my mouth, removing any leftover drool. He just chuckles as he reaches over to grab his phone, shutting off the alarm. I get a look at the time and see that it's two in the morning.

"Why do you have an alarm set for two a.m.?" I grumble.

He scrubs a hand over his face before looking over at me. He gently cups my cheek, his ocean blue eyes darting back and forth between my own before he leans down, kissing me sweetly. I lean into it.

When he retreats, I find myself following him. And when I open my eyes, I'm met with his blue eyes. The care layered deep within his gaze is a stark contrast to the concern furrowing in his brows. The warmth of his palm is still on my cheek, and he gives me a once over.

"How are you feeling? Are you nauseous? Do you need any more pain pills for your head?"

I take stock of my body at his question. I don't feel terrible. I have a slight pain in my ribs, but it's nothing like when I first woke up.

"I'm good. A little sore, but no worse for wear."

Xavier takes me in intently. Now that I understand the reasoning behind his hovering, I don't find it as overbearing. I place my hand over the one on my cheek and smile.

"I promise." I look sternly into his eyes, "I'm just a little sore, that's it. My head feels fine."

His eyes bounce back and forth between my own before he nods.

We fall back asleep, but Xavier makes sure to wake me periodically throughout the night to check on me. At one point, I take some more pain killers for the pain in my ribs, and Xavier pulls out a heating pad to use.

In the morning, Xavier brings in breakfast for both me and Evie. The smell of waffles floods the room, making me salivate. I crush the plate, inhaling them without conversation.

"I have never seen Harps so silent during a meal. I think the food broke her." Evie chortles.

A snort leaves me as I take another bite of the waffles and glare at my best friend. A cackle leaves her lips as she takes her own bite.

"But seriously. These are delicious." She adds, plopping another bite of waffle into her mouth.

Xavier just smiles at her before turning to me, "I'm just going to go hop in the shower, then I can run you a bath." He leans down, pecking me on my syrup covered lips. Licking his lips, he winks before turning toward the bathroom.

When the door clicks, Evie looks at me. "Okay, he looks hopelessly in love with you."

I roll my eyes. "Oh, please."

She raises an eyebrow at me expectantly. "So, you're going to tell me things *haven't* moved past fake dating at all?"

My cheeks heat as I think about everything that's happened up until now. Evie and I really haven't had a moment alone since she surprised me on Christmas Eve. I've been busting at the seams wanting to spill everything. I take a deep breath before I lean forward.

"Okay. So things have progressed." I mumble quietly, my hand moves to tuck a piece of my hair behind my ear. A sharp pain radiates on my left shoulder. Grasping it, I glare at my best friend. "Evie! What the fuck! I'm already hurting enough!"

"*Shit fuck.* Harps I'm so sorry– but how can you not tell me this?" Her brows are furrowed and guilt shines in her eyes.

I take a moment, milking the moment for a few more seconds. I rub my shoulder a few more times for added effect. "It's fine. You're just lucky Xavier isn't here, because I'm pretty sure he would have thrown you out of the room." Chuckling, I try imagining the scenario. He totally would with how protective he's been since I got home.

"I know you're trying to joke, but I wouldn't put it past him right now." Evie mumbles removing the hair tie from her hair, shaking her hair loose.

"Neither would I, honestly." A smirk forms on my lips at the thought. We spend the next bit talking about everything and anything, and I fill Evie in on anything I might not have shared yet. Evie is using every tactic she can to get the *good stuff* of my encounters with Xavier. My body hums at the memories of how Xavier took charge of our time together. I lean forward, ready to spill it all.

Then, the bathroom door opens, and a cloud of steam bellows before Xavier steps through in a pair of grey sweatpants and a white Henley shirt. This man truly looked at what a man should wear to make a girl drool, because saliva starts to form in my mouth as I take him in. I think about the other night and how he worshipped me on his knees. I want him to do it again. I press my thighs together, hoping that he doesn't catch on. When my eyes connect with him, I know I didn't get away with a single thing based on the cocky smirk he's sporting. He saunters his way over and offers his hand to me. When I place mine in his, he pulls me up and into his rock solid body. A breath leaves my mouth on the impact.

"On that note, I'm going to go for a swim. I'll see you later, babes." I don't look at her, but I hear her call for Winnie and take him with her. When the door clicks closed, Xavier erases the distance between us by sealing his lips on mine.

The kiss is soft and unrushed, and his hand cups my cheek gently. His thumb strokes my jaw. When he pulls back from the kiss, he rests his forehead on mine. "Come on, be a good girl, and get in this bath I got ready for you."

Biting my lip, I look up at him tilting my head to the side, feeling a little playful. "And what if I don-" My words are cut off as Xavier leans forward, grabbing me from behind the knees and hauling me up. A squeak leaves my body as I wrap my arms around his neck. "Put me down! I can walk!"

"Nope." he says, striding toward the open bathroom door. "You had your chance and you decided to be a brat instead."

When we reach the bathroom, he places me gently on the counter. His biceps flex as he crosses his arms across his chest, and he gives me a serious look. I think he's trying to be intimidating, but all it's doing is igniting a fire of arousal in my lower belly. It seeps down between my thighs, and I adjust myself on the counter to try to get some relief. It's been four days since we went skiing, and Xavier has been so focused on my concussion that he hasn't tried to touch me since Christmas Eve.

He catches my movements. The air between us thickens, the tension palpable as he takes in my sleep shorts that have ridden up my thighs from him carrying me in here. My legs are still slightly spread from when he placed me down on the countertop. His eyes are hooded with arousal, and I lean into the moment. My hands connect with the bottom of my sleep shirt. I pull it up and over my head, tossing it off to the side without breaking eye contact with Xavier.

"Touch me, please." I beg, as I bring my hands to my breasts and cup them. Xavier runs his hand through his hair. It is the only sign of distress he shows, but I can see how he's battling with himself. I slide off the counter and take a step toward him.

"I'm okay, Xavier. No headaches. No dizzy spells." I slip my thumbs in the waistband of my shorts before I push them down. "You want to take care of me?" The double meaning behind the questions makes Xavier pause.

His eyes bounce between mine before he nods quickly, "Yes." The answer is husky, and laced with a level of desperation that makes me want to climb him like a tree.

"Then, touch me." My answer is just as desperate as his own.

His hand hovers in the space between us, and I forget how to breathe while I wait for him to touch me. When his hand drops, my whole demeanor deflates. He's rejecting me. I quickly wrap an arm around my breasts as I look around looking for my clothes. *How could I be so stupid and desperate?*

But he quickly grips my chin, bringing my face to look at him. He leans forward. "I'm not saying no, babydoll. Just get in the tub before the water gets cold." My heart flutters at the pet name, doing exactly what I need it to do– reassure that he wants me.

He leads me to the tub and offers his hand to me. I take it, lifting my leg over before the other follows. The water is the perfect temperature, causing a groan to leave me as I slowly immerse myself. The hot water wraps around every curve, and my muscles instantly begin to relax. "Oh my God, this is *heaven.*"

Xavier settles himself on the ground beside the tub. When he's comfortable, he places his forearms on the side of the tub and rests his chin on his hands. "So, no headaches?"

I shake my head. "No headaches."

"No dizzy spells?"

I shake my head again.

He hums as if in thought as his eyes wander over my body. He shifts slightly, and one hand disappears beneath the water, resting on my knee. He begins tracing circles on my skin before he begins to trail up my inner thigh. My breath hitches as the movements of his fingers cause goosebumps to spread across my arms.

He pauses right before he reaches my sex, and moves his hands back down my thigh. I groan in frustration.

"Xavier!" I throw all my frustration into saying his name. "For fuck's sake, touch me already!"

My eyes widen at my outburst, my hand covering my mouth. Xavier lets out a hearty laugh, shaking his head.

"So demanding, babydoll," he says, words dripping with mirth.

Suddenly, he gets up on his knees and leans over the side of the tub, his fingers trailing back up my inner thigh. My lips part as Xavier's fingers finally connect with my clit. He begins slow circles around my bud, his lips finally connecting with my own. My hands shoot up and cling to his shoulders.

His fingers begin to glide between my folds and pause briefly in front of my opening. He pulls back, before ever so slowly pushing a finger into me. A groan leaves his lips. "Fuck, you're so tight, Harps."

He continues to finger me slowly before he adds a second, followed by a third finger. My thighs have fallen open, allowing him complete access to me.

He works me up effortlessly, my orgasm coming faster than it usually does. I pull his lips back to me and we are a tangle of tongues. I let him dominate our motions as he continues to drive me higher and higher. When he thrusts again, he moves his thumb over my clit, applying pressure. He thrusts in two more times, and that's all it takes, and my orgasm crashes over me. His mouth continues to work against mine as I ride the waves of my orgasm, claiming any noises that come from me.

My body slumps back in the tub, my chest heaving as I become aware of my surroundings again. Xavier has unplugged the tub and stands. I go to reach for his pants, but he just tsks.

"What about you?" My eyes fixated on the large tent he's sporting in the front of his grey sweats. My mouth waters slightly as I remember taking him into my mouth the other night. I want to do that again.

"Let's get you dried off first." He offers his hand to help me stand up. Taking his hand in mine, I stand up. Then I continue to move forward as the room becomes unbalanced, and Xavier's arms wrap around my naked body as he stops me from toppling forward.

"We *have* to stop connecting like this." I try to play off the fact that I just got dizzy.

He snorts. "Yeah, nice try there babydoll. Are you dizzy?"

"I'm fine, I just got up too fast is all–" I take the towel he offers me and begin drying off my arms. Xavier moves me to sit on the side of the tub to dry off the rest of my body.

"Yeah, I don't believe that for one minute. This is common though. If you overdo yourself, you can sometimes have some returning symptoms. You just need to rest." He brings over my pajamas, holding open the leg holes for me to feed my feet through.

Once I'm settled, he leads me back to the bed. He tosses back the blankets, and I crawl under. He leans over and kisses my lips softly. There's a softness to his features as he takes me in, and a wave of feeling content flows over me.

"Look, I know that you probably don't want to lay down right now. But you're still healing. I need you to rest and feel better."

I chew on my lip. This sucks, but at the same time, I understand what he's saying. I'm not *that* much of a difficult patient.

"Okay– but if I rest right now, then you have to promise me that I can attend the New Years Party your parents are hosting tomorrow. I'll go crazy if I have to stay in this room while everyone else socializes downstairs." I do the best puppy dog eyes I can muster, because now that I'm in bed feel the pull of sleep.

Shaking his head, a smirk forms on his face. "Fine. But you need to take it easy for the rest of the day, you hear me, babydoll?"

I squeal and wrap my hands around his neck bringing his lips to mine for another kiss. I pepper kisses all over his face until he starts chuckling.

"Okay, okay." He playfully pulls me off him, the most breathtaking smile on his lips. "Now, sleep. I'm going to go check on my parents. I'll be back later."

I nod, as I pull the blankets up to my chin and sigh with contentment. I try to follow Xavier out of the room, but my eyes close before he can shut the door behind him.

Chapter Thirty Two

Harper

I WAKE TO KNOCKING at the door. "Come in." I sit up slowly as I scrub my eyes.

I expect Penelope to come walking through the door, as she's the only person I expect to knock on the door. I'm shocked when I see Dalton standing there in the doorway of my room. He shifts back and forth at the door.

"Uh, hey." The confusion in my voice is obvious, but I wave him to come in. He hesitates for a minute before stepping forward. He leaves the door open, which I'm grateful for.

He grabs the chair that's by the window and pushes it closer to the bed. He sits down, and his body is stiff. I can see the tension vibrating through his body. He's nervous, and I don't entirely know why.

"I'm going to be honest. I didn't expect you to come visit." I readjust myself so I'm leaning up against the headboard. I see a water bottle on my nightstand and grab it. Uncapping it, I down almost half before I cap it again and set it in my lap.

Dalton has been sitting with his elbows on his knees, looking down at the ground. I'm just about to talk again, when he finally speaks.

"I owe you an apology."

A snort leaves me before I'm able to catch it. Dalton's head zips up, his eyes finally colliding with mine. As I look him over, I can see how exhausted he truly is. There are bags under his eyes, and his hair unkempt, like he hasn't tried to properly take care of himself. It is an odd thing to see, because Dalton has always taken care of himself. I used to joke sometimes that he spent more time getting ready than myself when we would go out.

"I would say that you're quite late for that, Dalton. But color me curious, what are you apologizing for?"

A sardonic laugh leaves him as he leans back, running a hand over his face. "I have thought about what to say to you for the last two months. Now that I'm here, I don't even know where to start."

I sit there in silence and wait. I'm not going to direct this conversation. If he is truly sorry, and wants to apologize and explain himself, he's going to have to start talking.

"Over those two months, I've realized that my biggest regret is cheating on you."

My eyebrows shoot up to my hairline, but I stay silent.

"I don't even know what happened. I know we were drifting apart, and I'm not going to play it off like I wasn't the problem, because I was part of it, for sure. I was so focused on working as a junior associate, trying to prove myself. I worked myself to the bone. I needed to earn my place and show my worth. Once I became a senior associate, I started taking on more complex cases. I had great mentors I worked under, so I was feeling so confident about it all." He pauses for a minute, taking off his glasses. He begins to clean them off with his shirt.

"Chloe started shortly after I became a senior. She really was clueless at the beginning. She got her job through Theo, who's a partner at another law firm, but good friends with one of the partners at our place. Anyway, I felt sorry for her, she kind of got thrown in the trenches. I helped her out a bit, a few things here and there. I didn't answer the phone for her or anything like that, but I helped her with the scheduling software on the computer. I sometimes did some filing for her if I was already heading that way. Small things until she started to get a better handle of things."

"Well, that's convenient now, isn't it." I tried. I really tried to stay quiet, but I never said I was perfect.

He stays quiet for a minute. "Okay, that's fair. I truly was just trying to help her, though."

Another stretch of silence, and when Dalton realizes I'm not going to say anything else, he continues, "One day back at the end of June, my mom stopped by to go out for lunch. You know how she did that every couple months." I make a noise of acknowledgement, because she did, and I think she used it as an opportunity to brainwash him. I don't say it out loud, because it's pointless now.

"She arrived at the office, and I was at the front helping Chloe with the scheduling program again. She introduced herself and then invited Chloe to join us for lunch. The lunch was awkward, and weird, to be honest. But my mom just loved Chloe, they talked the whole lunch, and I barely got a word in. They exchanged numbers and I didn't think much of it. My mom called me later that day, and she just kept boasting about Chloe. She said she was such a lovely girl. I dismissed her and explained that she was just the receptionist that I was helping out while she was getting her role figured out. She dropped it, or so I thought."

He stands up and begins pacing a bit. I'm not sure where he's going with this story, because it just feels like the narrative of how he ended up cheating on me.

"A month goes by, and Chloe seemed to be finding whatever excuse she could to get my help. When she realized that asking for help wasn't working, she started making sure my days were always set up for me. It's not something I expected, I was fine with getting my stuff organized for the day, but it was – nice. Then I don't know what happened, but my mom convinced me that it would be fine to go out to dinner with her one time. Told me to say it's with colleagues, and see what happens. It was only supposed to be one time, I swear, Harper. Just dinner."

"Well, we all know where that led us." My arms are crossed over my chest. "I really don't understand why this is important. I don't need the backstory to how you started fucking Chloe behind my back and getting her pregnant."

"That's the thing, though." He returns to the chair and sits down. "I used a condom, she said she was on birth control. She shouldn't have gotten pregnant!"

"You know another way to avoid getting someone pregnant, Dalton? You don't fucking sleep with them, especially when they aren't your partner!" I'm just annoyed at this point. "Is there a point to this?"

Dalton runs his hands through his hair. "There is. I'm getting to it now. I just– I was under so much pressure at work. I'm on the fast track to making partner if I play my cards right. I was never ashamed of you, the other partners actually loved you. I let my mom get in my head. I let her make me believe that having Chloe by my side would make everything happen. I was going to end it, but then she told me she was pregnant. I was still going to leave her, and just– figure that out when the news broke out."

His eyes are shining with unshed tears. "Then I heard the heartbeat." He sniffs loudly, running the back of his hand under his nose.

"And you knew you had to stay. Not for Chloe, but the baby." It makes sense now. Out of all the years I knew Dalton, I knew being a parent was something he was excited about. To find out you made a life, I knew in this moment, that he wouldn't have walked away, even if it meant hurting me in the process.

"Yes. I'm having a little girl you know." A soft smile forms on his face. "I have no idea what I'm going to do, but I'm excited for that little girl."

A single tear runs down his face, and he wipes it away quickly before clearing his throat. "Anyways, I owe you an apology for how I treated you. I hurt you. I threw away one of my best relationships, and lost my best friend in the process. I miss my friend."

There's a heavy silence, the weight of everything he said lingers between us. Sitting there, I soak it all in. I've known him since I was a teenager, and I can see how much this is hanging on him. Deep down, I know this was all Judith's work. She never liked me, and maybe it was because I didn't fit what the *perfect woman* for Dalton was in her eyes. I'll never know, but I know one thing for sure. We were never meant to last.

"I miss my friend too." A sad smile pulls at my mouth. "I don't think I can fully forgive you." I watch the way Dalton's face drops.

"Oh, yeah, that's fair." He tries to stand, and I stop him.

"Wait." I sit up straighter, criss crossing my legs in front of me. "You didn't let me finish, Dalton. I don't think I can fully forgive you, at least not right now. It doesn't mean it's going to stay like that. You were the biggest part of my life, aside from Evie. You did hurt me, and I'm still healing from that. We're going to continue to be in each other's lives if we're going to be staying with our respective partners." My phone dings at that moment. I look and see it's a text from Xavier.

> **Xavier:** Let me know when you're up, and I'll make you tea.

> **Harper**: I've been up for a little bit. Dalton is here– apologizing.

> **Xavier:** Are you okay? Do I need to come up there and kick him out?

A smile pulls at my lips as I read the protectiveness in his response. If you would have asked me at the beginning of this whole thing when he asked me to be his fake girlfriend, I could have given you a million and one scenarios with how it would play out. Not one of those scenarios would end with where I'm at right now.

> **Harper:** I'm good, come up once you're done making tea.

> **Xavier:** You got it, babydoll.

I look up, my eyes meeting Dalton's. "I think that one day– we can become friends again."

He nods his head. "I want to earn your friendship back, even if Evie is plotting my death."

"I don't think you're wrong."

I see the moment the tension in his body relaxes, and he stands, a soft smile forming on his lips. "Thank you, Harper. I don't deserve anything nice from you after what I did, and I didn't stand up for you when I should have- but thank you for doing it anyway." He turns, heading to the open door.

I don't know what comes over me. "Harps." I correct him.

He looks over his shoulder, eyes widened at the importance of what I just said. "Harps."

I'm not alone for more than a minute before Xavier comes sauntering into the bedroom with two mugs in his hands. The steam billows over the rim of the cup, and when he's within reaching distance, he hands me the mug. Grasping it with both hands, I bring it to my lips and take a sip. The warmth of the liquid spreads across my chest and through my body. I look up and smile my thanks to Xavier. He leans down and presses his lips to mine.

The sound of thunderous paw prints starts from down the hall, causing my head to whip in the direction of the door as Winnie comes barreling into the room. He stops a couple feet before us, jumping on his back legs. When his two front paws thunk on the floor, a deep woof comes from deep in the furry creature's chest. He stands stern, with a rather grumpy look on his face.

"What's up, buddy?"

When those brown eyes connect with mine, his back end moves back and forth with happiness.

Xavier laughs, pulling my attention back to him. His ocean eyes look at me with such a deep force of affection that it takes my breath away. He reaches for my hand, pulling it away from my mug to kiss my inner wrist.

"I love you." The words spill from my lips like a sigh. I wait for the panic to set in at the confession, but nothing comes.

His glossy eyes connect with mine, "I-" He inhales deeply, leaning forward and pressing his forehead to my own. "I love you too."

"Come on," Xavier holds his hand out to me. "Let's take this boy for a bit of a walk, and we can talk about the New Years Eve party."

I couldn't hold back the huge smile even if I tried. "Really?"

"Really." With my hand intertwined in his, we head toward the door. "I may not have known it back then, but you've had me from the moment you fell into my lap."

Epilogue

xavier

"T EN...NINE...EIGHT...SEVEN..."

"Shit!" Our countdown is interrupted when I hear Josie groaning loudly to my left. Looking over, Monty has an arm wrapped around her, and Josie is keeled over with a tight grip on his other arm. It's then that I notice the puddle that's surrounding her feet.

"Oh shit," I mutter. My hands are already in my pocket, feeling around for my phone. Harper left my side as soon as she noticed the liquid on the floor. She's only gone a minute before she reappears with towels.

"This is all I could find! What do you need?" Kneeling on the floor, she uses the towels to clean up the floor.

A snort comes from Josie. "Don't worry about that mess, there's going to be more." Turning her head, she directs Monty. "Babe, call my parents and let them know what's happening."

Monty's brows furrow, his skin paler than it normally is. "But, you need me."

"I've got her!" Evie appears out of nowhere, offering her hand to Josie, who takes it with a painful smile.

"911. What's your emergency?" The unfamiliar voice of the operator reminds me what I'm doing.

"Hi there. My best friend's water just broke, and we're going to need an ambulance."

I spend the next couple minutes telling the operator the address and all the information I can. When I get off the phone, Monty has returned with a bag.

"I called for an ambulance, and they'll be here shortly." My friend looks over to me and a huge smile spreads across his face.

"We're having another baby."

I slap my hand on his back, my own smile matching his. "Fuck yeah you are!"

Evie and Monty help Josie walk to the front door with Harper following behind, holding their hospital bag.

⁘⁘⁘⁘⁘

They've been back there for too long. Every time I'm in this fucking hospital, something goes wrong. My best friends are behind those doors, and something doesn't feel right.

A soft hand catches my elbow, stopping me in my tracks. Turning around, I come face to face with Harper.

"They've been back there too long. Something's not right." My pulse thundering in my veins, my dress shirt feeling too tight. My fingers hastily undo the buttons of my shirt, and suddenly, I can breathe a little better.

Harper's hands frame my face, the warmth a comfort that stills my racing thoughts. She holds a quiet command, while her thumbs trace my cheeks, grounding me to the present.

"It's going to be okay. Babies take time, and sometimes it takes a little longer than we expect."

Her hands fall from my face, but she quickly grabs my hand to lead me to a seat. When I sit down, I expect her to sit down next to me.

She surprises me instead when she sits on my lap.

My arms wrap around her, pulling her in closer, tucking my face in her neck. Her fingers graze through my hair, scratching at my scalp. The movement has a calming effect on my soul. This feeling I have with Harper isn't like what I had with Shelby.

Yes, I loved Shelby. We were young and in love, and I saw a future with her. We never got to live that future though, so I didn't get to feel this contentment that I feel right now. This rightfulness. This feeling of home. *Home.*

"Move in with me." The words leave my mouth like it's the most natural thing in the world.

Her fingers stall on my head, before she grips my hair, pulling my head back so we are face to face. Those deep green gems swirl with a mixture of emotions.

"What did you just say?" Her whisper is so soft, if I wasn't right in front of her, I don't think I would hear it.

"You heard me, babydoll." My arms tighten around her. "Move in with me. I don't care if anyone thinks it's too soon. You belong there, in my home, in my bed. I won't take no for an answer."

Her eyes begin to shine with unshed tears as she stares down at me. "I love you." She breathes before pressing her lips onto mine. "Yes. I'll move in!" She begins peppering kisses along my face, causing a laugh to leave my chest.

"Okay, okay." A smile spreads across her face, so carefree and natural, I find my own lips tipping up. "I love you too."

The sound of doors opening breaks me from my concentration as I look over Harper's shoulder and see Monty walk toward us with a huge smile on his face.

"It's a boy!"

ONE AND A HALF *years later*

"Come on, where are they?" I grumble, shuffling through the kitchen. This is what I get for feeling inspired to rearrange the kitchen. Now, I can't find the damn napkins. Resting my hand on the cupboard door, I'm startled when a voice comes from behind me.

"Auntie Harps! Uncle Xavy told me to tell you that the napkins are outside already," Shiloh says.

"Oh Shiloh, you scared me." Closing the cupboard door, I turn to him. "Thanks for letting me know, sweetie. How about we grab a popsicle while we're here?"

His eyes light up, and he nods his head with enthusiasm. Opening the freezer, I grab the Bomb Pops, and quickly remove the wrapper before handing it over.

"Thanks, Auntie!" He yells behind him as he takes off to the backyard.

Suddenly, a hot flash washes over me, and sweat begins to form on my forehead. Fanning my face, I turn to face the freezer again. The cool air fans over my heated face, giving some relief.

I love the summer, but I'm overheated. The feeling of sweat on my skin makes my skin crawl, and my shirt all of a sudden feeling too tight. Closing the freezer door, I head toward our bedroom. The need to get out of this shirt is overwhelming.

In the room, I strip out of my clothes and toss them into the laundry hamper. Grabbing my favorite olive colored sundress from the closet, I slip it over my head. The soft fabric slides down my curves; the cinch around my bust frames my shape, while the skirt flows down and ends at my knees.

Instantly, I'm more comfortable than I have all day. Checking my reflection in the mirror one last time, I turn and head back to our guests. As I reach the bottom of the stairs, Dalton walks through the door, his hair is a mess, glasses tilted at an angle. He looks flustered, especially with the crying toddler attached to his hips. Making my way over to him, I take the screaming toddler and console her.

"Oh come here, my sweet girl, let's give your dad a bit of a break." Placing her on my hip, I begin rocking back and forth, humming *You Are My Sunshine*. Like all the other times, she begins to calm down, resting her head on my shoulder as soft snuffles come from her.

"I don't know how you can calm her down so easily," Dalton says, straightening himself out. When he looks up a soft smile forms on his lips, as he takes his daughter in.

"What can I say? Auntie Harper is the baby whisperer." Placing a kiss on her forehead, I motion toward the back. "Come on, everyone is out this way. I think Xavier is almost done with everything on the barbecue."

The backyard is busy with laughter and tiny humans. Xavier is at the barbecue, plating the last of the burgers onto a plate, Winnie sitting faithfully at his side, watching the plate of food with longing. He speaks with Monty, whose arms are moving around dramatically as he tells a story. Dalton has taken off with Elodie over to the guys to join in on the conversation.

Dalton has turned everything around since Elodie was born. He's still working hard at work, but he makes sure he comes home every night to put her to bed. He really flourished in his role as a dad, although he didn't really have a choice, since Chloe didn't take to the mothering role like everyone hoped she would.

Over at the picnic table, Josie has Hayes in her arms. While she talks to Evie, she feeds him pieces of watermelon. The juices of the fruit fall all over the little guy's face as he aimlessly eats, watching his surroundings. Shiloh's stained face of blue and red is concentrated as he colors adamantly beside her.

When Evie catches me standing there, she makes her way over to me, a huge smile spread across her face. Her blonde locks are up in two french braids, and she's wearing a tank cropped top with a flowing lace skirt. She embraces me fully.

After a moment of time wrapped up in each other, Evie pulls away. "Damn girl, you look so good!" She praises, taking in my hot-mess glory. She lets her arms fall from my shoulder, but not before she places one hand on her swollen stomach, rubbing circular motions along her stretched skin.

I find myself copying her motion, my hand instinctively going over my own stomach. "You should speak for yourself. I don't know how you can look so good pregnant. I just feel like a house."

Just then, strong hands wrap around me from behind. I know exactly who it is before he speaks low in my ear. "You look delectable, Mama. I can't wait for everyone to go home so I can spend the rest of the night between your thighs." An obnoxious giggle leaves me as I try to wiggle out of his grasp, but it only causes him to hold me tighter.

"You guys are grossly adorable," Evie interrupts us from our own personal bubble. "But I'm starving, is it time to eat?"

Xavier laughs, placing a quick kiss below my ear before pulling me toward the table. Monty arrives beside us with the food from the barbeque, and Josie passes the plates.

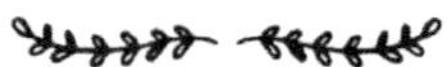

My heart is full as we sit around the bonfire with the family we've created. It's not blood, but it's the people we hold close to our hearts, that are family.

"Do you want another apple cider, babydoll?"

Turning my head, I look up to the man who has become someone so important to me. Over the last year, we have accomplished so much. I moved in with him as soon as we got back from the lodge. Xavier was busy with getting the spay and neuter clinic open, so he worked long hours. I think I fell more in love with him as I watched him put so much blood and sweat into making sure everything was perfect.

Xavier surprised me in the spring with a she-shed home office. I sobbed when he showed me. The thoughtfulness that was put into every detail was so touching. He even included one wall that was just a book-shelf with a ladder on wheels. A *girl's dream.*

Winnie adjusted to the move fairly quickly, and he loved the extra room to run. He is mischievous, and still loves to harass the ducks. Karma, if you ask me.

I snap myself out of my happy haze. "Yes, please." Xavier lifts from where he's seated, and I take the moment to adjust my body to be in a more comfortable position. When I'm finally comfortable, I take in the conversations happening around me.

Low chatter filters through the night. Dalton has a sleeping Elodie on his chest as he gently sways back and forth. Shiloh has a marshmallow stick over the fire. Monty tells him to pull it back, and in the next moment, the marshmallow catches on fire, causing Monty to grab the stick pulling it toward his face to extinguish the flames.

Admiring how Monty is with Shiloh, I envision what it would be like when our own little one enters this world. I already know that Xavier is going to be the best father.

A cold wet nose nudges my hand, and I glance down to see that Winnie has a...bow on??

"What do you have on your collar, Winnie baby?" I lean forward to take a closer look at his bow, and then I see a piece of paper hanging from it. My brows furrow, fingers gripping around the note. Unravelling it, I notice Xavier's handwriting

Turn around.

Looking up, I see everyone around me staring at me with a smile on their face. "You all look like serial killers right now. Why are you all smiling like that?"

Evie snorts loudly. "Do what the note says, babes. *Turn around.*"

My body starts to move before my brain catches up. The air in my lungs ceases to exist as I witness Xavier getting down on one knee. "What is happening?"

The side of his lips tilt up in a smirk. "I think you know what's happening, babydoll."

Shaking my head, I get out of my seat, moving until I'm right before him. Tears begin to flow down my cheeks as the reality finally sets in. Xavier pulls out a little black box.

"I never thought I would find someone to make my heart beat again. I was content living my life the way it was, working in the clinic and taking care of animals. I thought that was it for me. Then you came falling into my life, and you were the greatest thing I could have ever caught." Those ocean blue eyes shine at me with unshed tears as he takes a deep breath.

A sob leaves me, and throwing a hand over my mouth, I nod, encouraging him to go on.

"What started off as a ruse turned into something so much more. Harper, you are my home. You are my heart. The mother to our child, I can't imagine doing this with anyone else." He opens the box, revealing a stunning white gold, pear shaped emerald ring, with three diamond leaves on each side.

I am full on ugly crying at this point. I think I hear Evie joining behind me, but I don't pay her any attention. My sole focus is the man in front of me, on bended knee.

"Harper Amelia Beckett, will you please do me the honors of becoming my wife?"

I'm on him just as he finishes his last word, and he has just enough time to catch me to avoid us crashing to the ground. My lips crash to his in a deep passionate kiss. "Yes. Yes of course I will!"

The boom of cheers comes from behind us, as Xavier pulls the ring from its box, placing it on my left finger.

"What do you think?" he asks, holding my hand up so it is lit by the bonfire's glow.

"It's perfect." I sigh. "You're perfect. I love you, Xavier."

"I love you more, babydoll."

About the author

Hi all! I am a Canadian author from Northern Ontario. I live with my fiancé Mike, with our daughter, two cats and reptiles.

I have always enjoyed reading from a young age. While there have been times where reading went to the way side, I always circled back to it. As a child, I was always intrigued by writing my own story. It started off with sharing a notebook with a childhood friend. We would take turns writing our story of our fantasy world. Now here I am, many years later, using my creativity and love for books to create my own stories for others to read.

When I am not writing or spending time with my family and/or friends, I am working my full-time job as a Mental Health Wellness Worker. Mental Health has always been an important part of my life, and I love my job. Other things I enjoy are card games, playing on my switch and I've recently taken up crocheting.

Acknowledgements

Holy crap guys! Maybe, Probably is out in the world! I put some a lot of sweat and many tears into getting this story out there and I couldn't have done it without all the supportive people in my life.

First and foremost, I'd like to thank my fiancé Mike, who has always had my back, and been one of my cheerleaders. He has supported me through all my late nights writing until midnight to get this story completed. He has celebrated my wins, and hugged me when things have not gone the way I would have likes. I'm truly grateful to have such an amazing partner in my corner.

To the friends and family who have supported me through this journey. You guys have stuck by me through this whole process, and cheered me on every step of the way. The friends who stayed through it all, I appreciate your support more than you know.

To my alpha readers, I adore you. You guys dealt with the raw version of Maybe, Probably. Jessie, you were amazing, and still forgave me when I called you by the wrong name. I still have second hand embarrassment about this subject matter. Kris, one of my loudest cheerleaders. You two helped me in more way than I can count! Love you!

Katelyn, I honestly wouldn't be here publishing if it wasn't for you. Your inspiration with publishing your own book gave me the motivation and the kick in the ass to do it myself. I'm so thankful for you being apart of this story from day one. For listening to every single one of my eight minute voice memos of me talking through so many things in the developmental stages. For reading every version that came out before the final copy, and being one of my biggest supports. I don't think I can say thank you enough, or put into words how much I love and appreciate you.

Nova, when I came to you as a baby author and asked if you had the time to go over my book, you agreed with no hesitations. You were thorough and helped me talk through a few areas I still wasn't sure about.

Another shout out to Daisy, my friend and an author I love. Thank you for offering all your help and support. From answering all my author questions, and I know I had quite a few! The help and tips with creating my blurb. You are someone I look up to as an author. I'm eternally grateful for you.

Paige, my PA, thank you so much for wanting to work with me while I navigate publishing my first book. I'm so appreciative of everything that you've done. From helping me plan, to doing graphics and helping organize ARC management. I'm so happy to have you in my life, and by my side while I go on this journey of becoming an indie author!

And of course to all the readers who have read my story. I hope you enjoyed it as much as I did writing it. I hope you continue to join me on my journey as I write more stories.

What's next?

Did you love Harper and Xavier's story? Are you wondering what's next?

Have no fear! Maybe, Probably was only book one of the Love Me, Maybe series!

Book two coming early 2026!

Make sure you follow me to get the most up to date news on what's next!
Instagram: @authordeejordan
Tiktok: @authordeejordan
Threads: @authordeejordan